THE GHOST
AND CHRISTMAS MAGIC

HAUNTING DANIELLE

THE GHOST OF MARLOW HOUSE

THE GHOST WHO LOVED DIAMONDS

THE GHOST WHO WASN'T

THE GHOST WHO WANTED REVENGE

THE GHOST OF HALLOWEEN PAST

THE GHOST WHO CAME FOR CHRISTMAS

THE GHOST OF VALENTINE PAST

THE GHOST FROM THE SEA

THE GHOST AND THE MYSTERY WRITER

THE GHOST AND THE MUSE

THE GHOST WHO STAYED HOME

THE GHOST AND THE LEPRECHAUN

THE GHOST WHO LIED

THE GHOST AND THE BRIDE

THE GHOST AND LITTLE MARIE

THE GHOST AND THE DOPPELGANGER

THE GHOST OF SECOND CHANCES

THE GHOST WHO DREAM HOPPED

THE GHOST OF CHRISTMAS SECRETS

THE GHOST WHO WAS SAY I DO

THE GHOST AND THE BABY

THE GHOST AND THE HALLOWEEN HAUNT

THE GHOST AND THE CHRISTMAS SPIRIT

THE GHOST AND THE SILVER SCREAM

THE GHOST OF A MEMORY

THE GHOST AND THE WITCHES' COVEN

THE GHOST AND THE MOUNTAIN MAN

THE GHOST AND THE BIRTHDAY BOY

THE GHOST AND THE CHURCH LADY

THE GHOST AND THE MEDIUM

THE GHOST AND THE NEW NEIGHBOR

THE GHOST AND THE WEDDING CRASHER

THE GHOST AND THE TWINS

THE GHOST AND THE POLTERGEIST

THE GHOST WHO SOUGHT REDEMPTION

THE GHOST AND WEDNESDAY'S CHILD

THE GHOST AND CHRISTMAS MAGIC

THE GHOST AND FAMILY SECRETS

HAUNTING DANIELLE - BOOK 37

THE GHOST
AND CHRISTMAS MAGIC

USA TODAY BESTSELLING AUTHOR

BOBBI HOLMES

The Ghost and Christmas Magic
(Haunting Danielle, Book 37)
A Novel
By Bobbi Holmes
USA TODAY BESTSELLING AUTHOR
Cover Design: Elizabeth Mackey

Copyright © 2025 Bobbi Holmes
Robeth Publishing, LLC
All Rights Reserved.
Robeth.net

ISBN: 978-1-968738-20-4

ONE

Walt and Danielle Marlow sat across from Adam and Melony Nichols at Pier Café. Two pieces of carry-on luggage sat at the end of their booth, each partially wheeled under the table. The two couples had sat down moments earlier, and Adam had just finished grabbing menus from the end of the table and handing them to his wife and friends when Carla appeared, coffeepot in hand, her hair now pastel green and recently cut and styled shoulder length.

"Where's my little buddies?" Carla meant the twins. She began flipping coffee cups right side up and filling them without asking if anyone wanted coffee.

"They're having a playdate with Heather and Brian," Danielle said with a chuckle. She slid the cup of coffee Carla had filled closer to her.

Carla paused a moment and looked at Danielle, arching her brow slightly. "Brian too?"

Danielle grinned up at Carla. "Heather announced this weekend that she was giving Walt and me our Christmas gift early. She said since we can buy ourselves whatever we want, her gift to us

"

is eating out once a week for the next year. Oh, she's not paying for our food, but she's providing childcare."

"And she dragged Brian along this morning," Walt finished for his wife, without adding that Marie was also helping with the twins. That wouldn't be something Carla, Adam, and Melony would understand, considering Marie, Adam's grandmother, had passed away four years earlier.

Carla bumped into the protruding luggage at the end of the table and glanced down, her right hand still clutching the coffeepot. "I was going to ask about the luggage. Does Heather know you two are running away?"

Adam laughed and said, "The luggage is ours."

Setting the pot on the table, and placing one hand on a hip, Carla looked to Adam. "Yeah, I know. I saw you guys bringing them in. Where you two going? And why didn't you leave them in the car? Cars rarely get broken into in this neighborhood." *Just people getting murdered*, Carla added silently.

"Adam and I are flying to San Francisco for a couple of days, and our Uber is picking us up here and driving us to the airport. Walt was kind enough to pick us up this morning, so we can all have breakfast first," Melony explained.

Carla's eyes widened. "Oh, nice. San Francisco. A little fun getaway?"

Melony shrugged. "Not exactly; it's a legal conference."

"I'm tagging along because my brilliant wife is the keynote speaker. And I want to be there to show her off," Adam bragged.

They chatted for a few more minutes before Carla took their order and left their table. When she walked away, Danielle noticed Joe Morelli sitting on the other side of the diner with a man wearing a police uniform like Joe's.

Danielle nodded toward Joe's table. "The guy with Joe must be the new officer the chief recently hired." Everyone else at the table turned to look briefly at where Danielle had nodded.

"Brian mentioned he was starting today," Walt added before taking a sip of his coffee.

"Mark Summers," Adam said. "I rented him a house."

A few minutes later, the subjects of their conversation left their table and started toward the exit yet stopped abruptly at their booth when Joe noticed them.

"Morning." Joe glanced briefly at the suitcases, then looked back at his friends. "Someone taking a trip?"

Melony quickly explained where she and Adam were going.

After she finished, Joe said, "I'd like you all to meet Mark Summers. This is his first day. Mark, this is Adam and Melony Nichols." Joe motioned briefly to the couple.

Sipping his coffee, Adam gave the new officer a nod and then said, "I've already met Mark." Adam explained how he had met Mark before Joe finished the introductions.

As they all exchanged brief greetings, Danielle studied Mark Summers. She guessed he was in his mid-twenties, just under six feet, with short-cropped sandy-colored hair and boyish features. He didn't look as intimidating as the police department's last hire, Clay Bowman, who turned out to be a murderer.

Still standing by the table with Mark, Joe looked at Danielle. "I'd ask you where the twins are, but Brian mentioned he was going over to your house with Heather this morning to babysit."

"Not sure if that's how he wanted to spend his morning off," Walt said with a chuckle, "but he's a good sport."

Joe glanced briefly at Mark. "Walt and Danielle have twins. Brian, I mentioned him to you, he helped deliver the babies."

Mark cringed. "You guys deliver babies?"

Melony laughed. "I think you're scaring him. I suspect the idea of helping deliver a baby might be more intimidating than dealing with criminals."

Mark visibly blushed. Joe looked back at Walt and Danielle and asked, "How old are they now?"

"They'll be eight months right after Christmas," Danielle said. "We put the Christmas tree up on Saturday. So that has been fun, keeping them from pulling down the ornaments and toppling the tree."

They chatted a few more minutes before Walt asked, "Mark, do you have family in Frederickport?" Brian had already told Walt and

Danielle that morning that the new hire was from Portland and had moved to town that weekend so he could start his new job on Monday. But Walt wondered if he chose Frederickport because he had family here.

Mark shook his head. "I'm not from the area."

"Welcome to Frederickport," Danielle said.

They exchanged a few more words before Carla brought food to the table. Joe and Mark said their goodbyes, Carla finished delivering all the food, and a few minutes later the four prepared to eat their breakfast.

About to take a bite of her waffle, Danielle glanced across the table and noticed Adam staring at his food, making no attempt to pick up his silverware, his complexion noticeably paler than minutes earlier. "Adam, are you okay?" Everyone stopped eating and looked at Adam.

Instead of answering Danielle's question, Adam stood abruptly and bolted from the table, his hand now covering his mouth as he ran towards the restrooms. Melony dropped her fork on the table and started to stand up, but Walt stopped her.

"He went into the men's room. Let me go."

Ten minutes later, Walt returned to the table with Adam, who looked worse than he had when Danielle had asked her question.

"What's wrong?" Melony asked as Adam silently slumped back in his seat.

"I think we need to take Adam home," Walt said. "It's food poisoning, or he's coming down with the flu."

Melony placed her palm on Adam's forehead. "It's cool. Did you throw up?"

Adam nodded. "I'm sorry. But Walt's right. It just hit me." Adam pushed his plate of food to the center of the table. "I smelled the…" Adam was about to say sausage, but even saying the word turned his stomach.

"I'm sorry. I'll call the Uber and cancel," Melony said, "if Walt and Danielle don't mind driving us back to the house."

Adam shook his head and looked at his wife. "No, Mel. You need to go. You have friends there you've been looking forward to seeing. And you're giving the keynote speech. I'll be okay. I just want to lie down…and barf some more." Adam's right hand flew to his mouth, and once again he stood up.

Melony, Walt, and Danielle watched Adam rush toward the bathroom again. Danielle looked back at Melony. "He's right. You need to go. We'll make sure he gets home okay. We'll check on him while you're gone. And if he needs to see the doctor, we'll make sure he gets there."

Melony let out a sigh. "I'm pretty sure it's food poisoning. Last night when we were watching a movie, Adam decided he was hungry and started scavenging through the refrigerator. There were some leftovers I meant to throw out, and Adam got to them before I could stop him. He insisted they tasted okay, and he seemed fine after he ate them."

"It can take six hours or more before food poisoning kicks in," Danielle said.

"This sort of killed my appetite." Melony pushed her plate away from her.

Danielle nodded. "Yeah, I know what you mean."

"If you guys want to take Adam home, I'll pay for the breakfast and wait for the Uber."

Taking the napkin from her lap, Danielle nodded and tossed it onto the table. She and Walt stood.

Danielle glanced down at the suitcases. "Which one is Adam's?"

"The black one. I'll walk you to the door. I want to say goodbye to Adam." Melony paused and then looked back at the table and then at Walt and Danielle. "You guys want to take your food home? You didn't even touch it."

"No, we're okay. I'll go tell Adam we're taking him home," Walt said before heading to the restrooms.

Danielle grabbed hold of Adam's suitcase while Melony took her own.

DANIELLE HAD INSISTED Adam sit in the front passenger seat while she sat in the back seat of the Flex, and Walt drove them back over to Adam and Melony's house. When Walt pulled up in front of the house, he didn't turn off the engine but left it running while Adam got out of the car and thanked them again. Danielle quickly got out of the back seat, walked to the rear of the vehicle, and opened the hatch before removing Adam's suitcase.

"You call us if you need anything." Danielle handed Adam his suitcase. "And if you decide you need to go to the doctor, one of us can drive you."

Adam grabbed hold of the handle of his suitcase. "Thanks. But I'm pretty sure it's food poisoning. It's my fault; I shouldn't have eaten those leftovers last night. Just glad Mel didn't eat them."

ADAM STOOD BRIEFLY on the porch, his hand holding the handle on his suitcase as he watched Walt and Danielle drive away. He gave them a final wave before turning back to the front door, unlocking it, and walking inside, pulling his suitcase in behind him.

After shutting the door, he left the suitcase by the front door and walked down the hall but stopped abruptly when he came face-to-face with two men he had never seen before. One held a gun, and the next minute, said gun pointed in his direction.

"Where is your wife?" the armed man demanded.

Adam stared at the gun's muzzle, momentarily paralyzed. The man repeated the question, this time shaking the gun at Adam.

"She's on her way to the Portland airport."

"Why aren't you with her?" the other man demanded.

Instead of answering, Adam vomited in the hallway.

ADAM SAT in one of the dining room armchairs, his wrists bound with rope to the armrests and his ankles secured to the front two legs of the chair with the same long piece of rope. After being brought to the dining room, the armed man had told him to sit down in the chair while his partner rummaged through their cabinets, searching for rope. He found one in the broom closet.

"What are we going to do now?" the man asked his partner after tying Adam to the chair.

The man with the gun considered the question as he glared at Adam, his shaking hand still holding the gun pointing in Adam's direction.

"I think we wasted some good rope."

His partner frowned. "What are you talking about?"

"He's seen us. His wife is on her way to the airport. We have time to do what we need. I don't want to risk him getting away while we look. We're going to kill him anyway."

Adam's eyes widened as the man who had tied him to the chair yelled, "What do you mean? Killing someone wasn't part of the plan."

"It is now." The man raised the gun slightly, aiming it at Adam's forehead as he prepared to fire.

TWO

Marie Nichols had been murdered days before Thanksgiving, four years earlier, in a nursing home where she had gone to recover from hip surgery. Her spirit had stuck around after discovering some of her living friends were mediums. Plus, she wanted to keep an eye on her favorite grandson, Adam.

The image she showed to her medium friends was that of a woman in her eighties, when in truth, she had passed in her nineties. Instead of one of the sundresses she normally wore today, she wore a green jogging suit and had substituted her favorite straw gardening hat for a red Santa hat. The twins enjoyed grabbing the fluffy pompom at the hat's pointy tip. Of course, if they caught it, their tiny fingers slipped through it like air.

When Walt and Danielle arrived back at Marlow House, they found her with Heather, Brian, and the twins in the living room. Heather was surprised to see Walt and Danielle back so soon, and after they explained what had happened with Adam, Marie said a hasty goodbye and left to go check on her grandson.

Marie arrived at Adam's just as a man she had never seen before said, "We're going to kill him anyway," while pointing a gun at her grandson. A second man argued with him, yet Marie wasn't about to wait around to see if he could convince his partner in crime to put down the gun.

WHEN ADAM HAD WALKED in on the two men, he initially assumed he had interrupted a robbery. After the gun-wielding man told his accomplice to tie him up, Adam experienced a pang of relief. The man could have killed him in the hallway, but instead he wanted to tie him up. Adam assumed they intended to rob him and then leave him bound to the chair. Had he thought for a moment they planned to kill him after securing him to the chair, he would not have been so passive while the man tied his wrists and ankles with rope.

Adam's heart raced, and sweat formed on his brow. So focused on his urgent situation, he didn't question whether it was a symptom of food poisoning or imminent death. It was probably both. As the two men argued over his fate, Adam glanced around the room and spied his cellphone sitting on the nearby dining room table. The men had taken it from him before tying him to the chair.

Looking back to the arguing men, Adam stiffened his body, preparing to flip himself and the chair onto the floor should the man arguing for his life give up. He wasn't sure what he intended to do once he fell onto the floor, but he refused to sit passively while being gunned down.

Before Adam did anything, the gun flew from the man's hand, flying up and across the room, landing in the Tiffany light fixture hanging over the dining room table.

Both men froze and stared at the light fixture. It all happened so fast that Adam wasn't sure what he had witnessed. Had the gunman been shaking the gun in anger over the other man's reluctance to kill him, and then the weapon slipped from his grip, sending it flying? But how did it go so far, and so high, landing in the inverted glass cone of the Tiffany fixture? He didn't have long to think about it because just as he looked from the stunned men back to the light fixture, one of the men cried out.

Adam looked back at the two men. The man who had been holding the gun was now on the floor while his accomplice sprawled atop him. The two men looked into each other's faces as the man on the bottom shouted for the other man to get off him. Instead of moving off his partner, the man on top started flopping around like a fish that had jumped out of the ocean and was now stuck on the sand. The man on top continued to flop around helplessly while screaming, "Make it stop!"

Adam couldn't process what was happening, but this was his chance to get free. He struggled with the rope bindings, and to his surprise, they slipped off with remarkable ease, landing in a pile on his shoes. Adam kicked at the rope while standing up, and to his shock, the rope flew across the room, as had the gun earlier. It landed atop the two men.

Momentarily paralyzed by the bizarre sight, Adam watched as the rope wove around the men like a snake preparing to subdue its prey. Confused by the sight, Adam stepped back, knocking into the chair he had just been sitting in. Stumbling slightly, his eyes never leaving the two men, he fumbled around the chair and moved closer to the table.

Hands shaking, Adam reached for his cellphone the men had set on the table, and dialed nine-one-one.

OFFICER CARPENTER and her partner had been close to Adam's house when his call came in, so they were already turning down his street by the time he made it out of the house. Adam had run outside after making the call, clutching his cellphone and leaving the gun in the light fixture while the two men continued to squirm together on the floor, the rope still moving around them.

Adam reached the end of his driveway when the police car pulled up. It parked, and Adam ran to the officers. As they stepped out of the vehicle, Adam frantically explained what had happened, yet much of what he said made little sense. Officer Carpenter immediately called for backup.

After backup arrived, the police entered first yet found the two men not in the dining room, as Adam had told them, but in the middle of the hallway, sitting on the floor a few feet from where Adam had vomited. They sat back to back, securely tied by a rope.

The police yelled to Adam that it was okay to come in. Reluctantly, Adam reentered the house as several police officers pulled the two men to their feet, removing the ropes and putting them in handcuffs.

Backup included Joe Morelli and Mark Summers. Joe was initially confused about why Adam was at his house, considering they had seen him that morning, and he understood Adam had been on his way to the airport.

"You said something about a gun?" Officer Carpenter asked Adam while three other officers secured the prisoners.

"Yes, in there." Adam walked to the dining room doorway and was about to point to the light fixture, but when he looked into the room, he spied the gun sitting on the table.

Confused, Adam walked to the table and absently set his cellphone down as he looked at the gun and then up at the ceiling. There was obviously no longer a gun in the stained-glass fixture. But how did it not break the glass when the gun landed in it? And how had the gun moved from the fixture to the table?

Dazed, Adam turned back toward the hallway and frowned. How had the men moved into the hallway? How did they get tied up?

Voices filled the space around him. Questions swirled in his head, and in that moment, he didn't know if the questions came from the people around him or from inside his head. But he had no answers. The voices continued to buzz around him like annoying and persistent bees.

Feeling his world spinning, Adam made his way to the armchair that was pulled out from the end of the dining room table. The same chair that he had been tied to. Ignoring the persistent voices and endless questions, Adam stumbled to the chair, reached out to one of its armrests to steady himself, and then sat down. Adam stared ahead, saying nothing.

MARIE HAD LEFT Adam's house after the police pulled the men from the floor. She returned to Marlow House and found Heather and Brian still there. After explaining what was happening at Adam's, Heather repeated Marie's encounter to Brian, who wasn't a medium. While he couldn't see or hear Marie, he understood she was there.

When Heather finished the retelling, Brian immediately picked up his cellphone and called the chief. Walt, Heather, Danielle, and Marie silently listened to Brian's side of the conversation with Chief MacDonald, while the twins played with random toys on the quilt spread over the floor next to the sofa.

"What did he say?" Danielle asked when Brian ended the call.

"He's talked to Joe. Joe and the new guy are bringing in the two men."

"Who are they?" Heather asked.

"According to the chief, they didn't have identification on them. No cellphones or car keys. And they aren't talking. If they have a car, they didn't park it in Adam's neighborhood."

"Does Adam know who they are?" Walt asked.

Brian shook his head. "No. We're assuming it was a robbery attempt. Someone who found out they were leaving town for a few days."

"What does Adam say?" Danielle asked.

"Adam's not saying much. It sounds like he's in shock." Brian glanced around and then looked at Heather. "Where is Marie?"

Heather pointed to Marie. "Right there. Why?"

Brian looked to where Heather pointed. "Marie, you said you tied up the men. I assume Adam saw you?"

The mediums all looked to Marie.

Heather frowned and looked back at Brian. "What's going on?"

"Well…he didn't see me exactly," Marie muttered.

"Oh, I think I understand where this is going." Danielle groaned.

"Yes, I suppose he saw what I did. But what was I supposed to do? Let them shoot my grandson, and then when Adam came over to my side, I have to explain why I didn't save his life when I had the chance?"

Heather repeated Marie's words to Brian.

Brian nodded. "That's what I thought."

"What did the chief say?" Danielle asked.

"From what Joe told the chief, it sounds like Adam is in shock. When the police first arrived, he was understandably shaken, but he was able to tell them that the men were inside. He also mentioned a gun. When they got inside, they found the men tied up in the hallway. Outside, Adam had mentioned one of the men had thrown the gun into a light fixture in the dining room."

"Why do ghosts always put guns in light fixtures?" Danielle asked.

"To get them out of reach," Walt said before Marie could make a similar response.

"But when they walked into the dining room, the gun was sitting on the dining table, not in the light fixture."

They all looked back at Marie, who shrugged and said sheepishly, "I was just trying to be helpful. I figured it would make more sense for the police to find the gun on the table instead of up in the light fixture. That's a glass Tiffany shade; I was very careful when I put it up there. If someone had actually thrown it, it would have shattered the glass. I was trying to make it more believable for Joe."

Heather told Brian what Marie had just said.

"At least the chief now understands what's going on with Adam —that Marie saved his life," Brian said. "But it was after Adam saw that gun sitting on the table that he shut down."

"What do you mean he shut down?" Danielle asked.

"He sat on one of the chairs, stared off into space, and hasn't said a word. They keep asking him questions, but he's not responding."

"Oh my," Marie muttered.

"What are they going to do?" Walt asked.

"Now that the chief knows why Adam isn't willing—or able—to answer their questions right now, he's going to have Joe and the new guy bring the men in for questioning. He wants me to go over to Adam's. Until I get there, Carpenter will stay with him." Brian looked at Danielle. "The chief was wondering if you would go with me."

"Sure, but why me in particular?"

Brian shrugged. "You have a knack for making people think what they saw was something else."

"I'm not sure how I'm going to convince Adam he tied up his attackers, or that there was a third person there he couldn't see."

"Well, there was someone else there he couldn't see," Heather reminded her.

THREE

Brian Henderson, a police officer for the Frederickport Police Department, and Heather Donovan, a quirky medium who had once been accused of being a witch, had been a couple for around sixteen months. Theirs was an unlikely pairing, and it wasn't just their age gap.

The stocky man with gray hair had always seemed far too conservative to be dating someone like Heather. Their unlikely relationship began after the two had been kidnapped and escaped. It was during that incident that Brian learned the truth about Walt and the reality of the local mediums.

It wasn't Heather's youth that attracted Brian; it was her uniquely generous spirit and rigid code of honor. Age didn't prove an obstacle because neither wanted marriage nor children, and no one could accuse Brian of pursuing Heather out of a desire to groom and control a much younger woman, because even a ridiculously handsome man like Heather's boss, Chris Glandon, aka Chris Johnson, with an even more ridiculous amount of money, couldn't control Heather. And if Chris couldn't, Brian would be a fool to think he could.

Not long after Brian asked Danielle to go with him to see Adam,

Marie said her goodbyes and returned to her grandson. While she couldn't help him now, she felt compelled to go. After Marie's departure, Heather offered to stay with Walt and help with the twins while Danielle drove over to Adam's with Brian.

"I think you should go with them," Walt suggested. "I can handle these two on my own, and they're about due for their nap, anyway. Danielle might need your help with Adam."

Less than fifteen minutes later, Danielle and Heather sat in the car with Brian, with Danielle in the back seat. Sitting in the front passenger seat, Heather turned around. Wanting to face Danielle, she stretched out her seatbelt as far as possible before hooking it.

"Does it feel weird not breastfeeding anymore?" Heather asked.

"My blouses fit better now. My boobs aren't as big, which surprisingly is kind of nice."

"Hey, I can hear what you're saying," Brian said uncomfortably.

Both women laughed. "You delivered the babies," Heather reminded him.

"I still don't want to discuss Danielle's…" He didn't finish the sentence but steered the car into the street.

Danielle giggled and then grew serious. "I wanted to breastfeed until they were a year old, but it just didn't work out. And I read it's most important during the first six months, which I could do."

"Well, I thought that was amazing you breastfed them for that long without using formula. And I guess it's more convenient now."

"It's easier to leave at a moment's notice, that's for sure."

Heather and Danielle continued to chat while Brian drove until, suddenly, Brian put his foot on the brakes and said, "What the hell?"

Heather turned around in her seat, and Danielle leaned forward. They both peered out the front windshield, looking for what had caught Brian's attention. It was raining outside—a gentle sprinkling. Down the street they saw a parked police car pulled over to the side of the road. It appeared to be empty.

"What is it?" Heather asked.

"That's the squad car Joe and I drive."

"Didn't the chief say he and that new guy took the men they

arrested to the police station? This isn't the way to the station from Adam's house," Heather said.

"Exactly." Brian pulled over to the side of the road and turned off the engine, keeping some distance between his car and the squad car. Brian removed the car keys from the ignition and handed them to Heather. "Danielle, call the chief and tell him what I found. And Heather, be prepared to drive away if I yell at you."

"What is that supposed to mean?" Heather squeaked.

"Just do what I ask." Brian reached into the center console and pulled out his handgun and got out of the car, ignoring the rain. Reluctantly, Heather unbuckled her seatbelt and awkwardly slid over to the driver's seat while keeping her eyes on Brian. In the backseat, Danielle took out her cellphone and called the chief.

BRIAN CAUTIOUSLY APPROACHED the police car, gun in hand, while surveying the area. It was a quiet residential street, and no one appeared to be outside, which wasn't surprising.

He was about ten feet from the rear of the police car when he noticed something lying on the ground near the vehicle, between the car and the side of the road, partially hidden from the traffic. Shoes —with a body attached. Brian rushed to the body, gun in hand.

Once he reached the car, he quickly glanced inside, saw it was empty, and knelt next to the body. The person wore a familiar police uniform, his back facing Brian, with the head turned to one side, the face partially concealed by leaves; perhaps they had settled there after a scuffle or gust of wind. Holding his breath, Brian brushed away the leaves, revealing the face. As he suspected, the downed man was Joe.

Brian's fingers gently pressed against Joe's carotid artery, and he detected a strong pulse. A surge of relief swept through Brian.

DANIELLE AND HEATHER stood in the drizzling rain on the side of the road, leaning against Brian's car, watching the commotion. They could have remained inside the car and stayed dry, but they wanted to get a better view. Each wore a lightweight rain jacket and had pulled their hoods up, covering their hair. They stood with their arms crossed, staying out of the way of the responders who had just arrived. Joe had regained consciousness just as the paramedics pulled up, and they were preparing to load him into the ambulance. Some of the local residents had stepped out of their houses to see what was going on.

Police Chief Edward MacDonald walked from the ambulance to Danielle and Heather.

"How is Joe?" Danielle asked.

"He's got a nasty bump on his head. It looks like they have his gun. Brian told me Heather has his car key. I think it would be best if you two took his car, go back to Marlow House, and stay there with Walt. It's entirely possible our escaped prisoners are hiding out in one of these houses, and I don't need to worry about you two."

Before either woman could respond, a resident called out to the chief.

The chief turned to the man and greeted him, "Bob." He stepped away from Heather and Danielle and shook Bob's hand.

"What's going on? I saw all the police cars pulling up and the ambulance. What happened?"

"We have prisoners who've escaped, and I'm concerned they might be holed up somewhere in your neighborhood. Have you seen anything suspicious today?"

Bob considered the question for a moment and frowned. "I'm not sure I would call it suspicious. But this morning I noticed two guys I've never seen before parking their car in front of my house. They got out. Figured they were visiting one of my neighbors. I looked out the window, watched them walk down the street, and didn't see them go into any house."

"Which car?"

"Thing is, not even half an hour ago, I heard what sounded like a gunshot, looked out my window, saw the car drive away. I figured it was their car backfiring."

"Did you see the same two men getting into the car?"

Bob shrugged. "I didn't really see who was in the car when it drove off. Assumed it was the same guys who parked it there."

"Just a second," the chief said before calling out to an officer who had been at Adam's house during the arrest. Once the officer was by their side, the chief looked back to Bob. "Can you describe the two men?"

Bob described the men, including what they were wearing.

"Sounds like our guys," the officer told the chief. The chief seemed to forget Heather and Danielle as he and the other officer continued to interview Bob, now getting details on the vehicle.

Danielle and Heather had only overheard snippets of MacDonald and Bob's conversation and now assumed the escaped prisoners had taken off in the car, so they didn't take the chief's suggestion to drive back to Marlow House. Instead, they remained by Brian's car, watching.

A few minutes later, MacDonald and Brian moved to stand by the open back door of the ambulance. They were talking to Joe, but Danielle and Heather couldn't hear what they were saying. A few more residents had come outside, trying to see what was going on.

Danielle glanced around the scene. She started to say something to Heather but stopped mid-sentence and grabbed hold of Heather's wrist. Heather glanced down at her wrist, now in Danielle's grip, and looked up at Danielle with a frown. Danielle stared ahead. "What is it?" Heather asked.

"Look at that guy." Danielle released hold of Heather's wrist and pointed to a man standing near the squad car where they had found Joe. He wore a hoodie, its hood down, not covering his hair, his hands buried in its pockets, causing the front of the hoodie to come together as if zipped.

Heather looked to where Danielle pointed. She frowned. It was a young man she didn't recognize. "Who is he?"

The man glanced around and noticed Heather and Danielle staring at him. He stared back.

"He's looking at us now," Heather whispered.

"Yes, he is," Danielle said evenly, her eyes staring back at the man, meeting his gaze.

"He's coming over here," Heather hissed. "Why are you staring at him?"

"It's interesting how his hair doesn't look wet," Danielle said calmly, her head tilting slightly to one side.

Heather frowned at Danielle and looked back at the man; he came closer.

The man stopped abruptly, about five feet from Heather and Danielle, and said, "You can see me, can't you?"

Heather's eyes widened. She looked from the man to Danielle, back to the man. "How did you know?" she asked Danielle. "No way could you tell his hair was dry when he was standing by the squad car."

"It was the fact he walked through the squad car that tipped me off," Danielle said with a shrug.

The man, or more accurately ghost, removed his hands from his pockets and let the jacket—or image of a jacket—open naturally. It revealed something Danielle and Heather hadn't noticed before, a gunshot wound through his chest. He repeated his question.

"Yes, we can see you. But no one else can. I was going to ask what had happened. But…" Danielle nodded toward his now exposed chest. The T-shirt under the jacket was stained with blood.

The man glanced down. "They shot me."

"Who shot you?" Danielle asked.

"No one was supposed to get killed," he said.

"Where did you come from?" Heather asked.

The ghost turned around and pointed down the road, past the squad car, to the row of thick bushes in front of Bob's house. "Over there." He vanished.

Heather and Danielle exchanged glances and started toward the chief and Brian. When they reached the ambulance, Danielle said, "Chief, when you have a moment, we need to talk to you."

The chief understood whatever Heather and Danielle needed to tell him might be something they couldn't say in front of Joe or the paramedics, so he gave the women a nod and said a few final words to the paramedics and Joe before he and Brian stepped away from the ambulance.

They watched as the ambulance doors closed, and it left to take Joe to the hospital.

Before Danielle could tell the chief about the spirit, a shout came from one responder down the road, by the bushes in front of Bob's house. Moments later, they knew what the responders had found—another body. This one was dead.

"I want to see it," Danielle told the chief.

"Instead of going back to Marlow House, I'd like you both to go to Adam's. Brian said Marie is with him, and I need you to tell her what's going on. Those men might go back over to Adam's house. We don't know why they were there. But they have kidnapped one of my officers, killed someone, and could have killed Joe. Carpenter is also with Adam, but I would feel better if Marie understood what was going on."

Danielle nodded. "Okay. But before we go over, I'd like to see that body. Heather and I saw a ghost, and I suspect it belongs to your guy."

Heather and Danielle walked with Brian and the chief to where the responders now stood blocking off the fresh crime scene. Just as they were within earshot, the officer who had listened to Bob's description told the chief, "It's one of the escaped prisoners."

The chief frowned and walked closer to the scene. He looked down at the body still partially shoved under the bushes. "We haven't found the gun," the officer added.

"So who killed him?" the chief muttered. "We just talked to Joe, and he can't remember what happened. He doesn't even remember leaving Adam's house. Did Mark shoot him while trying to apprehend him after they escaped? Something happened, and he was taken hostage?"

Danielle stepped closer to the chief and looked down at the body. "Well, if Heather and I run into him again, we'll be sure to ask him," she said in a whisper just loud enough for the chief.

FOUR

When Heather and Danielle arrived at Adam's house, Officer Arleen Carpenter greeted them. The chief had called Arleen minutes earlier and told her to expect Heather and Danielle. She was already opening the door as the two women walked up to the front porch.

"How is he?" Danielle asked as she reached the open doorway.

Arleen, her hand still on the doorknob, stepped aside and opened the door wider while Heather and Danielle walked into the house. "He's still sitting in the dining room. I don't know if the chief told you, but he hasn't said a word since he walked into the house after we arrested the intruders."

"Yeah, that's why the chief wanted us to come over and talk to him." Danielle glanced around the entry while Arleen shut the door. She noticed Adam's carry-on suitcase, the one he had at the diner that morning, sitting in the corner.

"Oh, you're here!" Marie chirped when she appeared in the entry hall a moment later. "Dear Adam is in shock. I wish I had handled it differently."

Arleen, who couldn't see or hear Marie, was about to say something when Heather announced abruptly, "I need to use the bathroom." She gave Marie a facial gesture and head nod, signaling for Marie to follow her.

When the two stepped into the bathroom and Heather closed the door, Marie said, "Not sure what you need to tell me, but don't be surprised if Arleen goes back to the station thinking Brian's girlfriend has a severe tic."

Heather frowned at Marie. "What is that supposed to mean?"

"That thing you did with your head and face out there to get my attention."

"I couldn't very well say, Marie, I need to talk to you."

Marie let out a sigh. "Sorry, dear. What is it?"

Heather told Marie what had happened since she had returned to Adam's house.

"Is Joe alright?"

"They took him to the hospital to be checked out, and from what I understand, he has some memory loss. I'm not saying he doesn't know who he is, but he can't remember anything after he left here this morning. For now, they don't know why they turned down a street that didn't lead to the station or how he got knocked out. The chief wonders if those men might come back here."

"Oh, my…" Marie thought about what she had just been told. After a moment, she looked at Heather. "And that other young officer who started today—he was kidnapped?"

AFTER HEATHER HEADED to the bathroom, Arleen looked at Danielle and said in a serious tone, "I don't want to question the chief, but I don't understand why they didn't take Adam to the hospital to be checked out."

"From what the chief told me, Adam hadn't been physically attacked." As Danielle said the words, she knew Arleen wasn't talking about Adam's physical health. Yet she also understood why the chief didn't want Adam sent to the hospital, where he might be seen by a psychiatrist or psychiatric nurse. At the moment, Danielle understood Adam thought he was going insane, and if he saw a psychiatrist right now, they might agree with him.

"I'm not talking about his physical health."

Danielle smiled kindly. "I understand. But I'm close to Adam, which the chief knows. I suspect he feels I might have better luck with him. You might say we're family, considering how close I was to his grandmother, and his wife, Melony, is my cousin."

Arleen arched her brows. "She is?"

"Yes. And Mel is on her way to San Francisco. I haven't had a chance to tell her what's happened. Heather is also close to Mel and Adam. After we talk to him, we can tell Melony what's going on, and she can decide what to do. And on a side note, the chief and Mel go way back; she was his late wife's best friend. So I think he's trying to do what the family would want."

Arleen considered Danielle's words for a moment. Finally, she let out a sigh and nodded. "Okay. I guess I can understand."

When Heather stepped out of the bathroom, she found Danielle and Arleen where she had left them. A few moments later, the three women started down the hallway. Before they reached the doorway leading to the dining room, Heather stopped abruptly and looked down at the dried vomit on the carpet runner. "What happened?"

"When we first arrived, we found our suspects sitting on the floor, tied up in the middle of the hallway. They were sitting just a few inches from that. Since neither of them would say a word, and Adam stopped talking not long after we arrived, we aren't sure what happened there."

"Adam got sick this morning at Pier Café. That's why he came home. He obviously threw up again." Danielle looked at Arleen. "Has he had anything to drink since you've been here?"

Arleen shook her head.

"Well, we need to get him to drink some water," Danielle said.

ARLEEN WALKED Heather and Danielle to the dining room, where they found Adam still sitting on the chair, staring ahead blankly. Soon thereafter, Arleen said her goodbyes and left, locking the door behind her.

Heather and Danielle stood across the room and studied Adam, neither one approaching him.

"How are we going to handle this?" Heather whispered.

"Let me try first. I'll get him a glass of water. He needs to drink something. Not sure if he's ignoring us or if he has checked out somewhere."

Marie joined them. "I hope I didn't push that dear boy over the edge."

"Well, look what happened to that guy after you and I convinced him I was a witch," Heather reminded her.

Marie's eyes widened in fear as she looked across the room at Adam.

"Adam's going to be okay. Stop freaking Marie out." Danielle headed for the kitchen to get Adam a glass of water.

Heather looked at Marie. "While Danielle talks to Adam, why don't we clean up that mess in the hallway? I'll go see if they have any paper plates in the kitchen, and maybe you can find a bucket and fill it up with hot water."

"Why do you need a paper plate?" Marie asked.

"Paper plates work great for cleaning up these kinds of messes. Like the time the door to the room with the litter box got closed and Bella went on my carpet." Heather grimaced at the memory and continued, "I didn't want to pick it up with a paper towel and smear it around on the floor or get it on my hands. So I took a paper plate, tore it in half, set each half on either side of the mess, torn edges facing each other, and moved the sides together like I was putting the plate back together and scooped up the mess. After that, I simply carried the mess to the trash and threw it and the plate away. Easy peasy."

"Or I could simply harness my energy and pick it up and let it float to the trash," Marie said.

Heather stared at Marie a moment and grumbled, "Show-off."

WHEN DANIELLE RETURNED to the dining room, she knelt before Adam, glass in one hand and a paper towel in the other, and said gently, "Hey, Adam, it's Danielle."

Something flickered in Adam's eyes, but he said nothing.

"I need you to drink some water." Danielle lifted the glass to Adam's mouth, gently pressing it to his lips. Adam didn't move. Danielle pressed it a little firmer against his mouth, tilting it slightly, water slipping out. At first, he did nothing, but when water started dribbling down his chin, he drank the water, a little at first and then more until he started gulping.

"That's enough for now," Danielle said, removing the cup and wiping his chin with the paper towel. She didn't want him to get sick again. From behind Adam, a phone rang. Danielle stood and looked at the dining room table. She saw a cellphone.

Danielle walked over to the table while Adam remained sitting quietly in the chair. Setting the glass and paper towel on the table, she picked up the cellphone and looked at it. It was Melony calling. Danielle glanced at Adam, his back to her. Deciding to take the call, she moved away from Adam, toward the doorway leading into the kitchen. She answered the phone, keeping her voice low.

After Melony realized who was on the phone, she asked, "Danielle? Did you stop by to check on Adam, or did he call you to take him to the doctor? Is he okay? Did he get worse?"

"Some things have happened," Danielle began, keeping her voice low so Adam wouldn't overhear. She told Melony about the break-in, omitting significant details, such as how Marie saved his life.

"Oh, my gawd, but is he okay? They didn't hurt him?"

"No, they tied him up, but he escaped and got to his phone and called the police, but I don't know exactly what happened. He really can't talk right now, he, well, is sorta in shock. I think the guy intended to kill him, and well, he is understandably freaked."

"This is crazy. I was calling Adam to tell him my flight was a little delayed, but now I'll cancel and come home."

"Are you sure you want to cancel your trip? Adam is more than welcome to stay at Marlow House with Walt and me."

"No. There is no way I can go now. They'll understand."

Heather, who had stopped looking for cleaning supplies and had wandered over to Danielle, had been eavesdropping on the call. "Is that Mel? Her flight hasn't left? She wants to come back tonight?"

Still holding the cellphone to her ear, Danielle looked up to Heather and nodded and then said into the phone, "Are you going to get another Uber?"

"No," Heather said, practically grabbing the phone from Danielle's hand. "Mel, this is Heather. You're cancelling your trip and want to come home?"

"Heather, hi. Danielle didn't mention you were there too. But yeah. Glad I have a carry-on and didn't check any luggage. Not thrilled about another Uber, but whatever."

"I don't think you need to Uber. Chris is in Portland on business this morning, which is why I have the day off. Let me call him. I know he would love having your company on the ride home."

"Oh, Heather, that would be wonderful! Thank you."

TWENTY MINUTES LATER, Heather had already arranged for Chris to pick up Melony at the airport, she and Marie had cleaned up the carpet in the hallway, Marie had gone outside to patrol the exterior of the property, and Danielle sat in a chair facing Adam, trying unsuccessfully to engage him in conversation.

Now standing over Danielle, her hands on her hips, looking from Danielle to Adam, Heather asked, "Is he pulling an Olivia and is on some astral-projection trip out in la-la land?" Heather asked impatiently.

Danielle shrugged. "He had some water, but he refuses to talk."

Heather gave Danielle's shoulder a nudge. "Move. Let me try."

Danielle reluctantly moved off the chair. Heather sat down, now facing Adam. She scooted the chair a little closer to him, their knees now touching. She leaned forward. "Adam, it's Heather. Talk to me."

Eyes narrowing, Heather studied Adam for a moment, and, to

Danielle's surprise, Heather raised her right hand and gave Adam a firm slap across his face.

Danielle was not the only one surprised by the slap. Adam's left hand flew to his face, covering his now red cheek with his palm. He looked up at Heather, his eyes wide. "Damn, Heather, why did you hit me?"

Heather smiled with satisfaction. "I knew you were in there."

"You hit him," Danielle sputtered. "I thought you swore to stop smacking people."

Heather shrugged. "It was for a good cause."

FIVE

Still rubbing his injured cheek, Adam eyed Heather with caution. "I can't believe you did that."

Danielle knelt beside Adam and said gently, "You have been sitting there for over an hour, refusing to talk to anyone. We are concerned about you. It was Heather's way of jolting you back to reality."

"It was a jolt alright," Adam grumbled. He glanced around the room and then looked back at Danielle. "Did she leave?"

Danielle frowned. "Who?"

"That woman cop. I don't remember her name."

"Arleen Carpenter. Yes, she left. I understand you're trying to process everything that happened to you this morning. But you need to talk to someone, and Heather and I are here for you."

"I...I talked to Carpenter when she first got here...they just..." Adam looked down at his hands and then clasped them together and set them on his lap. Silently, he shook his head, muttering words no one could hear.

"They just what?" Danielle prodded. Adam grew still for a moment, no longer muttering silent words. Danielle repeated her question. When he didn't answer, she asked again, this time louder.

"They kept asking me questions. Some of it just made no sense, and I was trying to figure it out. But couldn't." Adam shook his head, unclasped his hands, and anxiously ran his fingers through his hair. He stood suddenly, announced he was going to the bathroom, and left the room.

"At least he's talking," Heather said after Adam was out of earshot.

"I hope he doesn't leave the house to avoid talking about what happened."

"Well, if he does, Marie is outside, and she would probably bring him back."

Danielle groaned. "Further compromising Adam's mental state."

Heather stood. "I don't think he will try running away. Where would he go? But he might have locked himself in the bathroom to avoid talking to us. Or maybe he's getting sick again. His color doesn't look great."

"You're probably right. I'll wait for him in the hallway. When he comes out, let's go in the living room; it's more comfortable there."

Heather grabbed the almost empty water glass sitting on the table. "I'll get him more water. He might need it."

Danielle was waiting for Adam when he finally got out of the bathroom. He passively allowed her to lead him to the living room, where he found Heather sitting on the sofa.

Heather pointed to a large glass of iced water sitting on the sofa's end table. "I fixed you a fresh glass of water. I thought you might be thirsty."

Adam gave Heather a quick nod of thanks and sat at the end of the couch. "I understand you guys are trying to help." He paused a moment and looked to Heather and added, "Well, Danielle at least."

"Hey, I brought you iced water," Heather countered.

Adam leaned back on the sofa. "I just need to figure this out, and talking is not going to help."

"Trust us, we can help you," Danielle said. "I understand you had a terrifying experience. Your home was violated. But Heather and I understand."

Adam lifted his head from the back cushion of the sofa and studied Danielle for a moment and then looked at Heather. He let out a harsh laugh. "How many people can say they've been attacked in their home and their lives threatened? Everyone in this room. What are the odds of that?"

Danielle smiled. "You have a point."

"But… but this is something else. I'm not talking about the threats each of us have experienced; this is about my brain's reaction. Nothing makes sense. Talking about it is going to make me seem crazier."

"Adam, people are always thinking I'm crazy. But I've survived. So will you," Heather half teased.

Adam glanced at Heather and smiled. "Yeah, well, even you would think I'm crazy."

"How about this?" Danielle interrupted. "Let's just start with you telling us what happened—before—before it went crazy, as you said."

Adam frowned at Danielle. "Why?"

"For one thing, the police wonder why those men targeted your home. If it was just a random robbery or something else. It's not important for them to understand how you escaped," Danielle said.

Adam narrowed his eyes at Danielle. "How do you know that's when everything seemed to go crazy?"

"Because…well, as you mentioned, both Heather and I have gone through similar experiences. I remember what it feels like to be so terrified that it's difficult to think straight, and everything moves so fast you can't keep track of what's happening. And then, when you look back, there are things you can't remember or wouldn't be able to explain if someone asked you. That's why you need to tell us what you remember now. Because trust me, the more you obsess over it, the more convoluted your memories of the event will become."

Adam considered Danielle's words for a moment. Finally, he

took a deep breath, exhaled, and gave a nod. "I sort of understand what you're saying."

"Then go on, tell us what you remember," Danielle urged.

Adam sat up straighter on the sofa, then leaned over, placing his elbows on his knees while propping his chin on his balled fists. He stared ahead, trying to remember the events as best he could. After a few moments of silence, he said, "When I came home after you and Walt dropped me off, I walked in. I noticed nothing unusual. But when I walked down the hall, there were these two men standing in our house. One was pointing a gun at me."

"Did you recognize them?" Danielle asked.

Adam shook his head. "I don't think I've ever seen them before. One asked where my wife was, so they obviously knew I was married."

"Or they had already gone through the house and figured there was a wife by what they saw," Heather suggested.

Adam leaned back on the sofa again. "Yeah, that could have been it too. But I got the feeling they expected the house to be empty. Almost like they knew Mel and I were going out of town." Adam stopped abruptly and looked around. "Where is my phone? Mel has probably tried calling me. She's going to wonder why I'm not answering the phone."

"I already spoke to Mel," Danielle explained. "Her flight was delayed, and after I told her what happened, she canceled her trip. Chris is bringing her back; he was in Portland on business anyway."

Adam slumped back into the sofa cushion again. "I'm sorry I screwed up Mel's trip. First with me getting sick, then this."

"I think Mel is more relieved you're okay," Danielle said. "And what happened this morning was certainly not your fault."

"Adam, do you think this was a random robbery, or could the guys have been looking for something in particular?" Heather asked.

"I don't know. I'm assuming Joe will find out more when he interrogates them."

Heather and Danielle exchanged glances, and then Danielle asked, "Tell us what happened after you found them in the hallway. Did they say anything?"

"They asked where my wife was. I told them she was on her way to the airport, and they asked why I wasn't with her. Now that I think about it, I think they expected me to be with her."

"What did you tell them?" Heather asked.

Adam let out a snort. "That's when I got sick again. In the hall. After that, they took me into the dining room and made me sit down in the chair to tie me up. One of them said something about needing time to look. I don't know if they meant just to look for stuff to take or to look for something in particular. But if it's the latter, I can't imagine what that would be."

"The police know the car they were driving was parked a couple of blocks from here, which means your attackers had to walk from their car to here," Danielle said.

"If you're going to rob a house, do you want to carry your loot a couple of blocks? Sounds like they were looking for something small, something they could carry," Heather observed.

"Did they say anything else?" Danielle asked.

"It's all a blur. I thought they were just tying me up to rob me, but then I had a gun pointed at me and some guy saying he's going to kill me. His partner wasn't on board, and they started arguing." Adam shook his head. "I don't want to talk about it anymore."

Danielle reached out and touched Adam's arm. "It's okay. It's traumatizing to be that vulnerable and think you're about to die. Don't dwell on it. Just be glad it all worked out."

Adam turned to Danielle and stared at her for a moment before saying, "Don't dwell on it? The gun flew out of the man's hand and landed in the lamp over the dining room table. After the police arrived, the men were tied up in the hallway, and the gun was no longer in the lamp, but on the table. Who put the gun on the table? Who tied up the men? None of it makes sense. At first, I thought the guy who didn't want me shot attacked his partner, but then..." Adam didn't finish his sentence but shook his head.

"Adam, sometimes in situations like this, our brain makes us forget things because it's just too traumatic to remember. It's a way that we protect ourselves. It's obvious to me what happened."

"Then explain it to me; I'd like to know."

"Well, like you said, you remember the two men arguing, and then they started fighting."

"That's what I thought at first, but it looked…" Adam shivered at the memory.

"What probably happened, as the men were fighting, you managed to free yourself from the rope. While they were fighting, you got your hands on the gun, you walked them into the hallway and tied them up. But you were so terrified knowing the two men could overcome you and kill you that tying them up and holding them at gunpoint was the most frightening thing you've ever done. You're the one who set the gun on the table while you called the police. You imagined you threw it into the lamp, and you ran out of the house. And later, after the police came, your brain refused to remember that part; it was too terrifying."

"I suppose I could tell the police that," Adam said dully before standing up and announcing he was going to the bathroom again.

"Dang, Danielle, you did some major gaslighting on Adam," Heather said, sounding impressed.

Danielle, who had been staring at the doorway leading to the hall since Adam left the room, said quietly, "Maybe, but he didn't buy a word of it."

"What do you mean?"

"He knows that's not what happened. But that's what he'll tell the police."

SIX

Kelly Morelli and her mother, June Bartley, had planned to go Christmas shopping that morning. Kelly was getting into the Christmas spirit, especially looking forward to spending time with her nephew, Connor. While her niece, Emily Ann, was too young to appreciate Christmas, Connor had turned two in September, and Kelly believed he was the perfect age to experience the magic of Christmas.

Before hitting the stores, the two had stopped at Lucy's Diner for breakfast. The server had just filled their coffee mugs, taken their order, and walked away from the table when June said, "I wish we were all spending Christmas together."

"Mom, we're all going to be together on Christmas Eve at Ian's. And I told you Joe and I would stop by Christmas morning before going to his parents' house. We spent Thanksgiving together. It's Joe's family's turn this year."

"I know. But I still wish you could be with us."

"Mom, I'll be honest—between you and me—I'm kinda bummed that I can't go to Marlow House with all of you for Christmas. But like I said, it's Joe's parents' turn to host Christmas, and

Joe is looking forward to seeing everyone. One of his favorite cousins is going to be there."

"It won't be the same without you there."

Kelly reached across the booth and patted her mother's hand. "Next year your house will be done, and you can host Christmas there. It'll be my family's turn next year."

June picked up a spoon, looked down at her coffee cup, and absently stirred it with the spoon, which was totally unnecessary, since June had added no cream or sugar to her coffee. Her expression reminded Kelly of a child who had done something naughty. "Mom? What is it?"

Setting down her spoon, she smiled guiltily at her daughter. "I really don't want to host Christmas. I'm hoping Danielle will keep inviting us."

Kelly arched her brows. "Are you serious?"

June shrugged. "It's so much work. Decorating, cleaning the house for company, and all that cooking! And Danielle, she always has the most amazing dinners. I love spending Christmas there. I just wish you were going to be there too."

Kelly laughed. "I agree with you. If Joe's mom weren't such an excellent cook, I might be more jealous of you having Christmas dinner at Marlow House."

THEY HAD FINISHED breakfast and visited one store before Kelly received the phone call. Joe was all right—but he was in the hospital—and they would be keeping him overnight for observation.

Kelly and June's shopping trip ended abruptly. Kelly dropped her mom back at her parents' house and headed to the hospital. When she arrived, she found her husband already checked into a room. He was alone and sitting up in bed, staring at the television and absently clicking the TV remote. When Kelly walked into the room, he immediately turned off the television, set the remote on the side table, and the next moment she rushed to him before giving him a hug and kiss. As soon as the kiss ended, she took his face in her palms, tilting his head toward her slightly as she inspected his head wound.

"They didn't put a bandage on it," Kelly said when she released hold of his face.

Joe briefly touched the tender bump on the top of his head and winced. "It didn't bleed."

"What exactly happened?"

Joe then recounted the morning's events while Kelly sat on the edge of the mattress.

"And there has been no news on Mark?"

Joe shook his head. "Not that I've heard."

Kelly abruptly hugged Joe, resting the side of her face on his shoulder. "Oh, my gawd, that could have been you. It would be hell not knowing where you are! Have they notified the family?" She released Joe and sat back a little, studying his face.

"I haven't heard. I told you everything I know."

Kelly kissed Joe again and then sat back on the side of the mattress. "How did Adam manage to tie up those two guys? You said they had a gun?"

"When he called into the station, he told them someone had broken into his house and had a gun, and they had tied him up, but he escaped. By the time the police arrived, the two men were tied up in the hallway, and the gun was sitting on the dining room table. As close as I can figure, he got untied and somehow got the gun away from them. I have no idea how he tied them both up while still holding onto the gun. But apparently, that's what happened. But not long after the police arrived, I think everything got to him because he just shut down. He refused to talk to us."

"Is he in the hospital?"

Joe shook his head. "No."

POLICE CHIEF MACDONALD was sitting behind his desk, talking on his phone, when Brian walked into the office. Brian paused at the open doorway but was waved in by the chief a moment later. Holding papers in one hand, Brian took a seat facing the chief, waiting for him to get off the phone.

"That was Danielle," the chief said when he ended the call.

"How is Adam?"

"They got him to talk. I guess Heather gave him a smack. That did the trick."

Brian arched his brows. "Really? Where did she smack him?"

"Across the face."

Brian winced. "So how's he doing?"

The chief shrugged and then recounted what Danielle had told him.

"When is Melony returning?"

"Late this afternoon. Early evening, maybe. I'm not sure. I just know she's coming back with Chris, and I'm not sure what all he needs to do in Portland before they head back."

"Have you gotten ahold of Mark's family to let them know what's going on?"

The chief let out a sigh and leaned back in his chair. "It's just a brother. He lives in Portland. Their mom died a couple of years ago, and from what I understand, the father isn't in the picture. I tried calling, but I didn't get an answer."

"Not a surprise if he didn't recognize your number."

"True. I assumed he would answer if he saw the call was coming from Frederickport, since his brother lives here now. But I had to leave a message. I just said who I was and asked him to call me, that I needed to talk to him about his brother." The chief nodded at the papers in Brian's hands. "What's that?"

Brian held up the papers, stood, and then tossed them on the desk, sliding them toward the chief before he sat back down. "It's the results of the fingerprints for our John Doe. We now have a name and know a little more about the guy."

The chief gathered up the papers, holding them in his hands as he glanced over them to Brian.

"His name was Shawn Hoffman. Age forty-five from Beavercreek, Oregon. No priors. He was a nurse."

"Nurse?" The chief arched his brows.

"Yeah. Until about two weeks ago, he worked at a care home in Oregon City."

The chief set the papers on the desk and looked up at Brian. "Was he married, have a family?"

"Divorced, no kids. His emergency contact is his brother. He lives in Vancouver, Washington. You'll find his name and number on the last page." Brian nodded at the papers on the desk. "I talked to his supervisor. He was shocked when I told him what happened, said Hoffman was always conscientious and good with the patients. He told me he had been surprised when Hoffman gave his notice two weeks ago, especially because he didn't have another job lined up. But he suspected it was burnout."

WORD TRAVELED FAST IN FREDERICKPORT—NEWS about an attempted robbery, murder, and the abduction of a local police officer. When Kelly left Joe's hospital room, she heard nurses talking about it in the hallway. Once in her car, she turned on the radio, and while they were discussing what had happened, they said nothing Joe hadn't already told her.

Instead of going home, she headed for the police station. Once there, she headed straight to Chief MacDonald's office.

"Nothing on Mark?" Kelly asked the chief after updating him on Joe's condition.

"I'm afraid not. But they found the car about five minutes ago."

"They did? Where?"

"The south side of town. They're going through it now."

"I'm so worried about Mark. That could have been Joe. Are you getting more help in? I keep hearing how you're understaffed, and now your newest replacement has been abducted."

"We're working on it."

When Kelly left his office ten minutes later, the chief stared down at his desk, looking at the name and number of Hoffman's brother. Before he called the number, they needed to find out what they could about the man. It was possible the brother was the accomplice. And if that was the case, it meant Mark was being held by the brother of the man he probably killed. What had happened?

The chief thought of Brian. While it was technically Brian's day off, he had come in for work and had gone down to where they had found Hoffman's car parked. Kelly was right. They were understaffed, and he needed people to go through the neighborhoods. There was a good chance their escaped prisoner was hiding out in someone's house—hopefully one of the vacant weekend homes. The possibility of a home-invasion hostage situation chilled him, and the man had already shown he was capable of murder, considering he intended to shoot Adam.

Had this happened before Danielle came into his life, he would have reached out to the FBI by now for assistance. Yet there was something he wanted to try first. The chief picked up the phone and called Danielle.

"Hey, Chief," Danielle answered the phone.

"Where are you?"

"We're still at Adam's. We're trying to convince him to come to Marlow House and stay there until Mel gets back. It's going to be a couple of hours before she gets here."

"Talk him into it. That will mean Marie doesn't need to stand guard because you'll be with Walt."

"Umm, you don't want her to stay here in case they come back?"

"I'd like Marie to stay with them when they're both back home. But while Adam is at Marlow House, I wanted to see if Marie would do us a favor. After you take Adam home with you, I would like Heather and Marie to meet up with Brian. Heather can play interpreter."

"What's going on?"

"They found the car abandoned on the south side of town. Brian is down there. No sign of Mark. We need to check the houses in the area and make sure they're not hiding out somewhere. But that takes time, and lives can be at risk if someone is being held hostage, and we're understaffed."

"But a ghost might be able to go through the houses fairly quickly without having to knock or be seen."

"Exactly."

SEVEN

Adam had been in the bathroom when Danielle was talking to the chief. When he returned, she was sitting alone in the living room, no longer on the phone. Unbeknownst to him, Heather was outside telling Marie about the change of plans.

Adam stopped just inside the living room doorway and looked at Danielle. "You don't need to stay and babysit me. Mel will be home in a few hours, and I'm just going to get some sleep."

"You can't stay here alone."

Adam walked over to the chair facing the sofa and sat down. "I'm a big boy, Danielle. I've been living by myself long before Mel and I got married."

"You've been through a lot today. You said yourself your mind is all jumbled and confused."

"I don't think I said jumbled. Confused, yes. But I would rather be alone."

Heather walked into the living room, came to an abrupt stop, and looked at Adam. "You can't stay alone."

Adam frowned at Heather. "Why? Are you going to slap me again?"

"No. But you can't stay here; it isn't safe."

"Why isn't it safe?" Adam asked.

Danielle let out a sigh. "We didn't want to tell you when we first got here. But it's not safe because the men who attacked you—well, they escaped. At least one of them did; the other one is dead. But the one who isn't, he took Mark Summers hostage."

"Holy crap," Adam muttered.

"I just got off the phone with the chief, and he thinks it would be safer if you stayed at Marlow House tonight. We don't know if the guy might come back here."

"How did that happen? How is Joe?"

"Joe got knocked unconscious, but he's okay. They're keeping him overnight for observation at the hospital." Danielle elaborated on the events that occurred after the police took the attackers away.

Adam didn't need to pack a bag for the night. The suitcase he had packed for his stay in San Francisco was still standing in the front entry. After hearing about his attackers' escape, Adam didn't require further convincing to leave his home.

BEFORE ENDING her call with the chief, Danielle had asked him to call Walt and tell him what was going on, because she didn't know when Adam was going to come back in the room, and she needed to tell Heather to update Marie on the change of plans. When they arrived at Marlow House, Walt already knew what was going on, and had prepared the downstairs bedroom for Adam and Melony.

Heather left Marlow House minutes after their arrival, but she wasn't alone. Marie sat in the passenger seat. Together they discussed what the chief wanted her to do.

"I wish Eva were here," Heather said. "We could use her help."

"She's attending that play in Portland. She wanted me to go with her, but I've seen that play before, and frankly, it's not my favorite. But I could pop over there quickly and see if she'd come back with me. We could use Eva's help."

"Use my help for what?" came a familiar voice, momentarily

startling both Heather and Marie. Marie turned abruptly in the seat and saw the spirit of silent screen star Eva Thorndike sitting in the backseat. Eva, who bore an uncanny resemblance to Charles Dana Gibson's drawing the Gibson Girl, looked as if she had just come from the theater…from the early 1900s.

"I didn't expect you back so soon," Marie told her friend. "And where's the glitter?"

"Considering the urgency of the situation, I felt glitter might not be appropriate. And you were right, dear; that was a dreadfully boring play. I stopped in on Chris. I remembered he had that meeting in Portland. He told me what happened, so I hurried home in case you needed my help."

WHEN THEY REACHED BRIAN, the other officers in his charge were already pairing off and preparing to canvas the neighborhood. No one questioned why he took Heather aside for a moment to talk privately. It wasn't because they knew she was his girlfriend, but they knew she had been with Adam, and many assumed she was simply updating Brian on the victim's current condition.

The plan was simple. The paired officers would move through the surrounding neighborhoods, talking to residents and telling them what to be on the lookout for, should the suspect return to the area. Unbeknownst to them, Eva would move quickly through the homes before they arrived and would alert Brian if any were about to run into the suspect.

Meanwhile, Brian focused on the immediate neighborhood they considered more critical, taking both Heather and Marie with him. Without Marie, he never would have felt comfortable having Heather accompany him.

SHE WORE a long red dress fringed with white fur. When she first tried the dress on, Jason had teased her and called her Mrs. Santa.

But then he had also told her she was a gorgeous Mrs. Santa, so it became one of her favorite dresses to wear during the holiday season, which included one Christmas where she played Mrs. Santa for a charity event.

She stood by the sitting-room window, pulling open the curtains slightly so she could look outside. Police cars had pulled up on her street, and she watched the activity.

Jason was in the next room, watching television, its volume blaring. Jason hated wearing his hearing aids and often removed them, shoving them in his shirt pocket. Knowing Jason, he probably forgot he had taken off the hearing aids, and after turning on the television, he kept increasing the volume instead of putting his hearing aids back on.

Ignoring the annoying sound from the television, her gaze focused across the street, and she watched as several of the police cars drove off while one police officer walked in her direction. He wasn't alone. Next to him was a young woman who didn't look like a police officer, with her long black hair pulled into two childish braids. She couldn't get a good look at her face, but the woman wore all black, what looked like a long jacket over dark pants and high black boots.

As they got closer, she noticed a third person, an elderly woman who wore a green jogging suit and what looked like a Santa hat. Why were they walking toward her house? The next moment, the police officer turned to step onto the curb in front of her house and in doing so walked through the elderly woman—literally walked through her like the woman was nothing but air. The stunned woman gasped and stepped back from the window, letting the curtains fall back into place.

"BRIAN, YOU JUST WALKED THROUGH MARIE," Heather scolded.

"Oh, Brian! Be more careful," Marie said before disappearing.

Brian came to a stop. "I'm sorry, Marie."

Heather shrugged. "Marie's gone. She's in the house. We might as well wait here for a second until she gives us the go-ahead to knock. And then, while you're talking to the residents who live here, she can check out the next house."

"I never imagined police work would ever be like this," Brian grumbled as he shook his head at the ridiculous nature of his life.

MARIE HEARD the blaring television from the front porch. Yet once she stepped through the wall into the house, all went silent. She immediately understood why. A man who looked to be in his early sixties stood in front of the television, pointing a remote at it. He had obviously just turned off the TV. The next moment, he placed the remote on a nearby table, picked up a magazine, sat down on a recliner, and started to read.

"I don't think our escapee is here," Marie muttered. Her plan was to check the rest of the house, tell Heather what she found, and then check the next house.

From the man's living room, Marie moved through the wall into the adjacent room. There, she found a beautiful woman who looked young enough to be the man's daughter. The room reminded Marie of the parlor at Marlow House. The young woman sat on a chair, reading a book. She wore a long red dress.

"Oh my, you look like Mrs. Santa." Marie giggled aloud. The woman glanced up briefly from her book, let out a sigh, and then looked back down and turned a page.

A few minutes later, Marie returned to Heather and Brian.

"Tell Brian all is clear in that house. I'll go check the next one."

Heather remained on the sidewalk while Brian walked up to the front door of the house, and Marie left to check out the neighbor.

BRIAN RANG THE DOORBELL. A few minutes later, a man he recognized from around town yet hadn't met answered the door.

"Hello, may I help you?" the man asked while fitting a hearing aid into his right ear.

Brian handed the man a business card, introduced himself, and started to explain why he was there when the man interrupted him and said excitedly, "Is this about the break-in at Adam Nichols's house?"

Brian's eyes widened. "You heard about what happened?"

"Oh yes, Carla, the waitress at Pier Café, told me about it." The man pulled a second hearing aid from his shirt pocket and fit it into his left ear.

"How did Carla happen to tell you?"

"I ate there today. It was all anyone was talking about. Carla told me it was Adam. Is he okay?"

"Yes, he's fine. But we're going door-to-door to inform everyone that we have a fugitive on the run, and he is considered dangerous." Brian gave the man the rest of his spiel.

MELONY NICHOLS SAT in the passenger seat of Chris's car as he drove toward Frederickport. If they had stopped along the way, anyone who saw them would likely stare and question their identity. They looked like the perfect couple—maybe movie stars, with beautiful faces and perfect bodies. The blond, blue-eyed, Hollywood power couple, the envy of the red carpet—and yet, they weren't.

Melony's true gift wasn't her appearance. She was a respected criminal attorney and the wife of Realtor Adam Nichols. Chris wasn't a limelight-seeking movie star, but a recluse who spent his time and fortune helping people. They weren't lovers, but close platonic friends.

Melony had just finished listening to the news report on the radio discussing the recent events in Frederickport, which took place in her home and involved her husband. When the news segment ended, she turned off the radio and looked at Chris.

"I can't believe what they said. How did Adam get untied and then get his hands on their gun?" Melony turned, looked back out the front windshield, and slumped back in the seat.

Chris reserved comment. He glanced briefly at Melony and then looked back out at the road. Unlike Melony, he knew exactly what had happened at her house, and it didn't involve Adam playing Superman and capturing two villains.

EIGHT

After identifying Shawn Hoffman, local motels were contacted to see if he had been a registered guest, hoping to find more information on him and his accomplice. A photograph and other critical information were also sent to the local newspaper, the *Frederickport Press*. While the next edition of the newspaper didn't come out until the following morning, the *Frederickport Press* had an online edition, which could post news articles immediately after they were written. However, news of a police officer being taken hostage had spread beyond the local newspaper.

Edward MacDonald sat alone in his office on Monday afternoon. He had just gotten off the phone after calling the hospital to check on Joe when he was told there was someone who wanted to see him. It was Bill Jones, a local handyman who often worked for Adam.

When Bill walked into the office a few minutes later, he carried a piece of typing paper with something printed on one side. Bill placed the paper on MacDonald's desk. It was obviously a printout from Bill's home computer of the news article and photograph now on the *Frederickport Press* website.

"I heard what happened. How's Adam? I tried calling him, but he's not answering his phone," Bill asked.

"He's shook, but physically okay."

Bill shoved the paper he had set on the desk toward the chief, who remained sitting in his chair. "I saw this online. And I'm wondering if the newspaper screwed up and used the wrong picture."

With a frown, MacDonald picked up the paper and looked at it. The picture with the article was the one his office had sent to the newspaper of Shawn Hoffman. He looked back at Bill. "Why do you think it's the wrong picture?"

"According to the article, that's one of the guys who broke into Adam's house, and his accomplice is the one who abducted Mark Summers. But that can't be right."

The chief looked at the picture again and then back at Bill. "Why do you say that?"

"Because that's a friend of Mark's brother. I met them when they helped Mark move in. I don't remember his name. But Mark introduced them to me when I stopped by the house to see if he needed anything. They were in the middle of unloading a U-Haul."

The chief held up the photo for Bill to see. "And you're sure that is the friend of Mark's brother?"

"Yes. Positive."

MacDonald pointed to the chair facing his desk. "Can you sit down for a minute while I check something?"

"Sure." Bill sat down on one of the chairs facing the desk while the chief turned to his computer. Ten minutes later, MacDonald turned the monitor around so it faced Bill. On the monitor was a driver's license picture of a Peter Summers, the name on Mark Summers's emergency contact, the person the chief had been trying to contact on the phone to inform him of his brother's abduction.

"That's Mark's brother," Bill said before MacDonald asked.

MacDonald nodded and then picked up his phone and called the front desk. After someone answered, he asked, "Is Carpenter back yet?…Send her to my office."

A few minutes later, Officer Carpenter walked into the chief's office.

"Yes, Chief?" she asked, glancing briefly at Bill, flashing him a nod and smile, and then looking back to the chief.

MacDonald waved her over to his desk. He had already turned the monitor around, so it no longer faced Bill. When she reached his desk, MacDonald motioned to the monitor.

"That's him!" Carpenter said when she looked at the monitor.

WHEN MELONY and Chris stepped into Marlow House on Monday afternoon, they were first greeted by Chris's pit bull, Hunny, who had stayed with Walt and Danielle while Chris went to Portland on business.

While Hunny excitedly wiggled and brushed up against both Chris and Melony in greeting, Adam silently stepped out into the hallway from the downstairs bedroom, where he had been resting since Danielle had brought him home with her.

The moment Melony spied Adam, she abandoned her suitcase in the entry with Hunny and Chris and rushed to Adam, throwing her arms around him.

THEY SAT in the living room—Walt, Danielle, Chris, Melony, and Adam, along with the twins, who quietly played with a pile of toys atop the center of a quilt spread out on the living room floor. Both Hunny and Danielle's cat, Max, sat on the edges of the quilt, watching the twins, with Hunny occasionally picking up one of the plastic blocks that one twin had thrown before returning it to the pile.

Melony had been doing most of the talking, recounting what she and Chris had learned from the radio. "They said it was unclear how you escaped and got their gun and tied them up before calling the police." She smiled at Adam with pride while Adam stared down at the floor, his expression blank. Melony patted Adam's knee and added, "I understand all this makes you uncomfortable, but it's pretty amazing, and don't be surprised if it's not just Kelly who wants to interview you."

Adam looked to Melony, his expression dark. "What do you mean, Kelly wants to interview me?"

"I'd just be surprised if Kelly wouldn't jump at the chance to interview you for her podcast, but I imagine she won't be the only one." The mediums remained silent while exchanging knowing glances when Melony and Adam weren't looking their way.

Reaching out to place her right hand on Adam's left knee again, Melony turned to her husband and asked, "Adam, how did you get the gun away from them? To tie them up by yourself. I don't understand how you did it." By her expression, it was obvious she did not doubt Adam had indeed somehow secured the gun and tied up his attackers, but she just didn't understand how.

Adam looked at Melony, smiled weakly, and said, "I'm really tired. I still feel a little sick from what I ate last night." He gently removed her hand from his knee, stood, and kissed her forehead. "I'm going to lie down."

Without another word, Adam walked from the room, the eyes of his friends and wife on him. When he was no longer in the room and out of earshot, Melony turned to Danielle and asked, "Did he tell you or Heather how he got away?"

Chris and Walt looked to Danielle. Danielle smiled weakly at Melony. "I think the entire experience was so terrifying that it's difficult for him to talk about. I imagine while trying to get away from his kidnappers, his emotions were all over the place, and it's possible there are parts he can't remember. That can happen with trauma."

Melony glanced briefly at Walt and then looked back to Danielle. She chose not to share her thoughts in that moment but kept them to herself. She had once wondered if Walt would ever get his memory back. Would he someday remember the woman he had been engaged to? Did something in his brain prevent him from remembering his deceased fiancée, the woman some people claimed he had been hopelessly in love with? And while she remembered

Walt had supposedly woken from his coma not only unaware that his fiancée was dead, but unaware of her existence, was it possible that something deep inside him knew she had not survived and because of that, he forgot her altogether?

While Melony understood why Walt would not wish to bring back those memories now, considering the life he had built with Danielle and his two children, Melony believed Adam's inability to remember what had happened—if what Danielle suggested might be true—was not something he should ignore.

WALT HAD MADE chili using Danielle's recipe while Heather and Danielle were with Adam. He had placed it in the slow cooker to keep warm. Not long after Adam retreated to the downstairs bedroom to rest, Walt suggested they all gather in the kitchen for some chili. While he hadn't made cornbread, as Danielle might have, he had a fresh loaf of Heather's sourdough bread ready to serve.

Melony helped Danielle put the twins in the highchairs while Walt set the food on the kitchen counter and Chris set the table. No one asked Adam if he wanted to join them, knowing the idea of eating a bowl of chili was probably the last thing he wanted considering his queasy stomach.

They had just sat down at the kitchen table, with their food and beverages, with the twins happily munching on cut-up pieces of sourdough toast, when Brian and Heather walked into the house through the kitchen door.

"Hey, you're back," Walt greeted. "If you're hungry, join us. There's plenty."

Instead of immediately taking their offer, Brian and Heather stood just inside the kitchen door. Brian glanced around and asked, "Where's Adam?"

"He's resting in the downstairs bedroom," Danielle said.

Brian looked over to Melony and Chris. "Glad you're both back."

"Did they find them? Have you learned anything new?" Melony asked. After she and Chris had arrived at Marlow House, Danielle had told her that the police had been sweeping the neighborhoods where the car driven by the escapees had been abandoned.

"We have the identity of the second man, the one who threatened to shoot Adam. The one who escaped," Brian announced.

"But you haven't found him yet?" Chris asked.

In response, Brian shook his head.

"And the police officer who was taken hostage, is there any news on him?" Danielle asked.

"I guess you could say that," Brian said, glancing briefly at Heather, who in return gave him a shrug before looking back at their friends. They remained seated around the table.

"What?" Walt asked.

"The man who took Officer Mark Summers, the one who threatened to kill Adam, is Officer Summers's brother, Peter Summers. Although we are starting to think Mark might be more accomplice than hostage," Brian said.

"Does this mean the new officer is part of this?" Melony gasped.

Brian shook his head. "I'm not sure what this means. I wasn't there during the arrest, but I asked Arleen and a few others who were about Mark's reaction when they showed up on the call. Did he seem surprised to see who it was, or did he already know his brother was there?" Brian gave a shrug.

"Do you think this means they're no longer in Frederickport?" Danielle asked Brian.

"I don't know what to think."

AFTER DINNER, Danielle prepared two bottles while her friends helped Walt clean up the kitchen. They all returned to the living room, where Danielle and Walt each took a baby, sat down in the recliners, and proceeded to bottle-feed them. Melony sat on the sofa with Heather and Brian, and Chris sat on the floor, leaning against the sofa while Hunny curled up beside him, her head resting on his thigh.

"How's Adam doing? Did he tell you I slapped him?" Heather asked Melony.

Melony arched her brows at Heather. "What do you mean you slapped him?"

"When Danielle and I got there, he wouldn't talk. He hadn't said anything since the police made their arrest. I just wanted to snap him out of it. And well, it did sort of work. He started talking to us."

"Did he tell you how he escaped? How he tied them up?" Melony asked.

The mediums exchanged brief glances while Heather gave a shrug. "Well, Adam didn't really want to talk about that part. It's probably best if we not dwell on the details and just be glad he's okay."

Melony shook her head. "No, this convinces me more."

Chris stopped petting Hunny for a moment and glanced up at Melony. "Convinces you of what?"

"Adam is going to need therapy to process all that happened. While he may not want to talk to us about this, he needs to talk to someone. And I think a professional would be the best way to process his feelings and emotions, help him get through this."

"I am not going to a therapist!" Adam shouted angrily from the doorway.

All eyes in the room turned to Adam, who stood in the doorway. Melony jumped from the sofa. Now standing, Melony said in a soft voice, "Adam, it's okay. You don't need to go right away."

Adam adamantly shook his head. "No, Mel. I am never going. Because they are just going to tell me I'm crazy."

"What are you talking about?"

"I didn't take the gun away. I didn't tie them up."

"Then who did?"

"I don't know. But I watched the rope tie them up with no help from me...from anyone."

NINE

After Adam's outburst, he returned to the downstairs bedroom without saying another word. Melony followed him, and when they were out of earshot, Heather said, "Wow, I've never seen Adam like that before."

"Not even after you smacked him?" Chris snarked.

Heather flashed Chris a glare. "Oh, shut up."

The next moment, Marie appeared in the room. "You're all here. Where's Adam? I stopped by his house, and he wasn't there, so I assumed he's still here."

"Marie's here," Heather told Brian.

"He's spending the night," Danielle said. "Melony's here too."

Brian looked to where he assumed Marie stood, considering both Danielle and Heather had looked in that direction. "Did you or Eva find anything?"

Marie let out a sigh. "Tell Brian we could find no trace of either man." Marie glanced toward the downstairs bedroom. "How is the dear boy doing?"

"He's still freaked," Heather told Marie before recounting Adam's outburst minutes earlier.

When Heather finished the telling, Marie said before vanishing, "I'm going to check on him."

MELONY AND ADAM sat on the end of the bed in the downstairs bedroom of Marlow House, side by side, holding hands. Melony studied Adam's face while he stared down at the floor.

"I'm sorry I yelled like that out there," Adam said in a soft voice.

"You don't need to apologize. We all understand you went through a terrifying experience. I just wish you would talk to me."

Adam let out a sigh and looked at Melony. "Okay, I'm going to tell you exactly what happened." And he did.

When he finished the telling, the two continued sitting on the bed, neither one speaking.

After about five minutes, Melony, her voice barely a whisper, said, "It makes me think of what happened at the Marymoor site."

Adam quickly turned his head, looking over at Melony, who gazed blankly across the room.

No longer holding Adam's hand, she now held her clasped hands on her lap with her thumbs absently fidgeting. "Or what happened to me back in high school at that barn." Melony turned to look in Adam's face. "Or what you told me about the croquet set in the attic above us." Melony briefly glanced upwards.

"What are you saying?"

Melony shrugged. "I'm saying we've both experienced, well… something that doesn't seem to have a reasonable explanation. Something that makes a person question the existence of ghosts."

"Are you suggesting a ghost saved me?"

"Something supernatural saved you. I don't think you're crazy. But yeah, I can see why you wouldn't want to share that experience with a therapist."

They were silent for a few minutes before Adam said, "I need to understand what happened. You can say I'm not crazy, because we've both seen some weird stuff, but this is different from before.

Mel, I am seriously questioning my sanity. It's one thing to see objects move and attribute it to…I don't know…residual energy."

Melony frowned at Adam. "What do you mean, residual energy?"

"Remember what Walt and Danielle said after what happened to us at the Marymoor site? About how we're made up of energy, and how energy doesn't die."

"Which might explain how an object could move," Melony said.

"But this was different, Mel. This was…deliberate, strategic."

<hr>

WHEN MARIE RETURNED to the living room, she found Danielle and Walt standing in the middle of the room, each holding a baby.

"My grandson believes he's losing his mind, and I'm the reason." Marie took a seat on the chair Walt had been using minutes before.

Heather told Brian Marie was back, pointing to the chair she now occupied, and repeated what she had said, and asked, "How is he losing his mind?"

Marie recounted what she had overheard in the downstairs bedroom.

"You saved his life, Marie. It's just going to take him a little time to let his mind come up with an explanation for what happened. Maybe he'll go with my suggestion." Danielle gave a shrug, patted Addison on her diaper-clad bottom, and said, "Walt and I are going to take the babies upstairs and give them their bath. And I would suggest you stay out of the downstairs bedroom, give your grandson and his wife some privacy."

"I'm seriously worried about Adam," Marie told Chris and Heather after Walt and Danielle left the room.

"I can understand," Heather agreed. "He was super shook when Danielle and I first went over there. He was in shock."

Brian looked at Heather. "I'm not sure what Marie just said. But had the chief not known about Marie's role, I'm sure they would have taken him to the hospital to be checked out. And I can certainly understand that what Adam saw this morning is not something he is going to want to explain to people, especially since he doesn't understand what happened."

"Since there is nothing I can do here, I think I'll go back to Adam's. Just in case they come back."

"Marie is going back to Adam's house," Heather told Brian.

"That might not be a bad idea. On the one hand, I can't see why they would return to the scene of the crime, considering what happened. But something about this makes me wonder if they targeted Adam and Melony's house. And if that's the case, maybe they'll be back. While we're patrolling that neighborhood, we're so understaffed we can't keep someone at the house. We already have someone at Mark's, but since word is out about who his brother is, I don't see them going there."

"Tell Brian I'll be at Adam's." Marie looked at Heather and then to Chris. "Are you staying here?"

"We told Danielle we'd stick around in case Mel needs something. Like you say, Adam's pretty upset. They didn't want Mel to come back in here and find everyone gone," Heather explained. "And she didn't want to knock on their door and tell them they were going upstairs."

MARIE DIDN'T ENJOY SITTING in the dark. Unfortunately, when she arrived at Adam and Melony's house, none of the lights were on. The sun had long since set, there were no streetlights, and tonight's sliver of a moon offered minimal moonlight. However, there were random night-lights throughout the house, so she wasn't in complete darkness. While being a ghost gave Marie special powers, one of them was not the ability to see in the dark.

She had been in the house for about an hour, sitting in the dining room, which had been the scene of the crime, when she heard a familiar voice call her name.

Marie perked up. "Eva?"

"Goodness, Marie, why are you sitting in the dark?" Eva

appeared before Marie, a dusting of gold glitter swirling around her, momentarily illuminating the illusion of Eva now dressed in a floor-length white gown, her hair pulled atop her head like the Gibson Girl.

"I didn't want to turn on a light. One of the neighbors might notice and call the police, and frankly, I don't want to cause Adam any more stress."

"I stopped by Marlow House before coming here." Eva, her glitter now gone, took a seat on one of the dining room chairs, sitting next to Marie. The faint glow of a nearby night-light provided minimal illumination. "They told me you'd come over here, and how upset Adam was about what he saw this morning. But, dear, you need to stop beating yourself up over it. You saved his life."

"Are he and Melony still in the bedroom?"

"Yes. When I was there, Melony came out to tell everyone good-night. She told them Adam had already gone to bed, and she had just taken her shower. Walt and Danielle were in the living room with Chris, Heather, and Brian. Danielle told me they had just put the babies to sleep. Max and Hunny were upstairs in the nursery. They're very good nannies." Eva chuckled at the thought.

Marie started to say something when she heard a rattling sound.

"What's that?" Eva asked.

Moments later, Eva and Marie stood outside on the side porch, where two shadowy figures were attempting to break into the house. One knelt by the door, holding a small flashlight on the doorknob, while the second figure, holding a narrow tool in hand, fiddled with its lock.

"Should I go tell Heather, and she can tell Brian?" Eva asked.

"Let's wait until they get inside. I'd like to see what they're up to."

"Bingo!" the man fiddling with the lock called out in a loud whisper.

"Shhh, we don't need to announce we're here," the second man scolded.

"House next door is empty. No one can hear us," the man said while pushing the door open. "Joe mentioned that this morning. He told me it's a vacation property."

The two men walked into the house, gently closing the door behind them.

From the light of the kitchen nightlight, Marie could make out their faces. "That's the one who was going to shoot Adam." Marie pointed to the man who had been holding the flashlight. "And the other one is the new officer Edward hired."

"I don't imagine he'll get to keep his job," Eva snarked. "I must say, they need to refine their hiring practices, considering how the last two men the department hired worked out."

"I'm wondering why they aren't worried about Adam being here," Marie asked. "Have they come here to kill him?!"

"At least one thing is going our way. Nichols is staying at Marlow House tonight," Mark said.

"Maybe not," Eva said, looking from Mark back to Marie. "They apparently know Adam's not home."

"I still don't understand why this all went sideways," Peter grumbled.

"And I don't know why you had to shoot Shawn."

"We didn't need him anymore."

"Yeah, and we sure as hell didn't need to turn this into a homicide, like you did by killing Shawn."

Peter swung around and faced his brother, glaring into his face. "I didn't really have a choice. I told you Nichols saw my face. He wasn't supposed to be here. And then Shawn freaking attacked me when he realized what I was going to do."

"We would have thought of something. I still don't understand why you had to kill Shawn."

"There was no way we could have controlled him. And like I said, he attacked me. If he hadn't done that, Nichols would never have gotten the jump on us."

"Fine," Mark grumbled. "This isn't how it was supposed to happen, but I guess we have to play the hand dealt."

Peter gave a nod. "Good. Now let's get it and then get out of here."

"I wonder what it is," Eva asked.

"Let's see." Marie followed the two men.

"Lead the way," Mark said, stepping aside once they entered the hallway. Peter started walking, with Mark behind him.

Marie and Eva were not prepared for what happened next. Mark quietly pulled a gun from his jacket and pointed it at the back of his brother's head. But before he was able to get off a shot, Peter turned around to say something. The next few minutes were a blur, and with the limited lighting of the night-lights, neither Marie nor Eva could clearly see what was happening. Fists flew, multiple shots fired, and suddenly all went quiet. All that remained were two bloodied bodies sprawled on the hallway floor, and next to them stood two confused spirits, one holding a gun.

TEN

Despite the limited lighting in the hallway, Marie didn't need to check the men's pulses to see that they were dead, considering their spirits stood next to their bodies. However, she suspected the darkness didn't help either spirit process what had just happened to them. She wondered if they even realized those were their bodies on the floor, since the lighting was so poor.

"I can fix that," Marie muttered more to herself than to Eva. The next moment, every light in the house turned on.

"Did you do that?" Eva asked Marie.

"I had to," Marie told Eva, her eyes never leaving the two spirits.

The ghosts of Peter and Mark looked over to Marie and Eva. Until that moment, they didn't realize the two women were in the hallway with them.

"Who are you?" the men shouted in unison.

Mark raised the gun, pointing it in Eva and Marie's direction. "What are you doing here?"

"I would think you'd be more curious about the two bodies at your feet," Marie countered.

Both men looked down at the gruesome scene as if it was the

first time either had noticed. The dead bodies told a story of struggle and competition with no happy ending. The hand of one of the deceased men clutched the muzzle of a gun, while the index finger of the other man looped around the gun's trigger guard. Blood spilled slowly from both bodies.

"Oh damn, we're dead!" Peter blurted. His head jerked up, and he looked at his brother, who held a gun. "You killed me!"

"You obviously killed me too!" Mark angrily waved the gun over his head. "This is all your fault!"

"How is it my fault? I saw you aiming that gun at me. What was I supposed to do, just let you shoot me?"

"You screwed up everything; I had no choice!"

"Exactly how was killing me going to help you?" Peter asked.

Mark's right hand dropped to his side. The gun slipped from his hand, and it disappeared before hitting the floor. He glared at his brother while Marie and Eva stood quietly on the sidelines, watching the drama unfold.

"You messed this up by letting Nichols see you. You could have been more careful. I can't believe you not only let him get the gun away from you, but he tied you up!"

"I told you Shawn attacked me! And I couldn't do anything about it. How was killing me going to help you?"

"I should never have hit Joe over the head to help you get away. And then you went and killed Shawn, making it worse."

"That's why you killed me?"

"Yes. But I didn't think you were going to kill me too. I could have claimed I wasn't involved. That I was in shock when we arrested you and that I was going to tell the chief who you were when we got back to the station. I didn't want to do it in front of all the people I worked with. Joe didn't know I was the one who hit him. I was going to say you did it. I was going to say you killed Shawn to prove to me you would kill me too if I didn't do what you wanted. That I was a hostage. And you made me come over here with you, and I got the gun away from you, and I had no choice but to shoot you."

"How were you going to explain why you turned off on the

wrong street? When you and Joe got out of the car, maybe his back was to you, but we were still locked in the backseat. Who else could have hit him but you?"

"I would have thought of something. And after killing you, I could get what we came here for, and no one would know. I wouldn't be on the run for the rest of my life."

"Now you don't even have a life," Peter scoffed.

"Why don't you tell us what this 'it' is? What you planned to take from this house," Marie interrupted.

Mark and Peter, who had obviously forgotten they had an audience, turned and stared at the two women. Mark opened his mouth as if he was about to say something when the ceiling above them opened with a roar, revealing a dark, ominous space filled with gray clouds.

"Oh dear, I've seen this before," Marie muttered. Her and Eva's gaze fixed on the emerging tornado vortex from above, its rapidly rotating column of air extending from the dark opening in the ceiling as it moved toward Mark and Peter, who stood dazed, their eyes wide and mouths agape. The vortex reached out and pulled them up from the floor, into the dark clouds above. An agonized scream called out from where the men disappeared, and then all went silent.

Several minutes later, Marie and Eva stood alone in the hallway with the two dead bodies and a ceiling that looked as it had when Marie first entered the house.

"That was certainly dramatic," Eva noted.

"I do wish the Universe weren't so impatient. I was hoping to find out what those two were looking for."

Eva shrugged. "The Universe has its own reasons for doing things."

"I suppose." Marie stepped closer to the two bodies and looked down at them. "I imagine that blood is going to be much more difficult to get out than the vomit was."

"What I'm surprised about, you turned on all the lights. I can understand the hall light, but why in the other rooms? That's sure to draw attention."

"Exactly." Marie smiled.

"Ohh…" Eva chuckled. "Now I understand."

Marie gave a shrug. "Brian mentioned the police are watching Adam's house. I figure when one of them drives by tonight and sees it lit up, they will investigate. This way, Brian won't have to manufacture a reason to come over here, and Adam and Melony won't walk in on two dead bodies when they return home."

"Speaking of Brian, we should probably get back to Marlow House and tell them what's going on." Eva glanced over the bodies again. "I don't think there is anything else we can do here."

"There is one more thing I need to do before we leave."

"What's that?"

"I need to unlock the front door. It'll make it easier for the police to enter the house."

WHEN EVA and Marie arrived back at Marlow House, they found Walt and Danielle sitting in the living room with Heather and Brian. Chris and Hunny were no longer there.

"I thought you might show up about now," Danielle greeted the pair.

Marie arched her brows. "Why do you say that?"

"Is Marie here?" Brian asked.

"Yes," Heather told Brian before looking back to Eva and Marie. "Brian just received a call from the station. One of Adam's neighbors called to tell them the lights were all on in the house. The house had been dark earlier. They understood no one was supposed to be there."

"I assume they're sending over a patrol car?" Marie asked.

"Did you turn the lights on and forget to turn them off?" Heather asked.

"Yes, I turned them on. No, I did not forget to turn them off. You might tell Brian his people are going to find the men they are looking for. Unfortunately, they're both dead."

"They're dead? How?" Heather blurted.

"Who's dead?" Brian asked.

Marie told them what had occurred at Adam and Melony's house. When she finished the telling, Heather repeated the story to Brian.

"I'd better call the chief and tell him what happened," Brian said.

"This also answers another question," Walt said. "They didn't choose Adam and Mel's house randomly or because they thought they were out of town. It sounds as though they were looking for something specific. I have to assume it's something of value. But what?"

"Mel's engagement ring is valuable, but if that's what they were looking for, they wouldn't have broken in when she was out of town, wearing the ring," Heather said.

"It must be something very valuable, considering they risked getting caught by going back over there when they had to realize everyone was looking for them," Danielle said.

"I can't imagine what that would be," Marie said.

LATER THAT EVENING, across town, Joanne Johnson looked out her front window and saw it was no longer raining. She walked into her kitchen, where she had left her cellphone charging on the counter. Joanne picked up the phone, unplugged it, and called her next-door neighbor.

"Joanne?" came the cheerful greeting.

Joanne smiled at the familiar voice. "Evening, Jason. I made a chocolate cake, used Danielle's double fudge chocolate cake recipe. There's no way I can eat all of it. I was wondering if I could bring some over to you."

SHE STOOD in the sitting room, the blinds open as she looked outside into the night. Light from the direction of the neighbor to her left caught her attention. A moment later she saw the next-door neighbor, Joanne Johnson, stepping onto their front porch, a flashlight in one hand and what looked like a large Tupperware container in the other. A moment later the doorbell rang, and then she heard Jason call out, "Coming, Joanne!"

JOANNE SAT with Jason at his kitchen table, each eating a slice of chocolate cake and drinking a glass of cold milk.

"This is absolutely delicious," Jason practically purred before taking another bite.

"I'm glad you like it."

"You know how I love chocolate."

Joanne grinned at Jason and took another bite.

After a few moments of silence, Joanne said, "Coming home from Portland, I heard about the break-in at your old house on the radio."

Jason set his fork on his plate, picked up a napkin, and wiped his mouth before saying, "Carla told me about it when I stopped to get something to eat earlier today."

"Who needs a newspaper or the radio when we have Carla? The last I heard, one was killed, and the other one took a police officer hostage. He was new, just started today. Can you imagine something like that happening on your first day on the job? I also heard Joe Morelli was attacked, but he's in the hospital and doing well."

"When you were in Portland today, the police went through the neighborhood, going door-to-door. They found the car the men were driving; it was abandoned not far from here."

"Poor Adam must have been terrified."

"You know Adam fairly well, don't you?" Jason asked.

"I've known Adam for years. And he and his wife are close friends of the Marlows. And Adam's grandmother, Marie, she was very fond of Danielle."

"I remember Marie Nichols. I didn't really know her well. So you still like working for them?"

Joanne smiled. "I do."

***

SHE WALKED INTO THE ROOM, her red gown flowing behind her. In the kitchen she found Joanne and Jason sitting at the kitchen table, each with an empty plate in front of them and partially filled glasses of milk. By the crumbs left on the plates and the half of a cake sitting on the counter, she understood they had just eaten some of Joanne's chocolate cake.

After studying Joanne for a moment, she turned her attention to Jason. Shaking her head, she said, "Oh, Jason, you are so blind. What have I done to you?"

ELEVEN

The twins—Addison and Jack Marlow—almost eight months old, had inherited their mother's brown eyes, while their features were a combination of their parents. On some mornings, Danielle imagined she glimpsed Walt in Addison or Jack, while on other days, she saw herself.

They were happy babies, something Danielle didn't automatically attribute to an innate trait. She suspected it had something to do with the amount of attention they received. Many children grow up with not just one parent who left each day for work, but two. Walt worked from home, and he was an active parent. These days, with the bed-and-breakfast on an indefinite hiatus, Danielle considered herself a stay-at-home mother. She understood how lucky they were to be able to afford to stay home to raise their children. But it wasn't the constant presence of both parents in their lives; it was the supportive group of friends who were always there when needed.

Each twin sat in a highchair in the kitchen, happily kicking their sock-covered feet and eating French toast their mother had cut into bite-size pieces and placed on the highchairs' food trays. Danielle and Walt sat at the kitchen table, each with a cup of coffee, sharing a cinnamon roll, with Walt reading the morning's edition of the *Frederickport Press*. While doing so, Walt discussed with his wife the article about yesterday's events. The discovery of the two bodies in the Nichols home had not made the morning paper, but Danielle assumed it was probably now on its online edition.

"Knock, knock," Lily Bartley's voice called out as she opened the kitchen door and walked into the house.

Danielle and Walt glanced over to the door and watched as their neighbor from across the street—who was also Danielle's best friend—walked into the house, closing the door behind her. A petite redhead, Lily wore denim leggings and an oversized Christmas sweatshirt, with her long red hair pulled into a high ponytail. Unlike Danielle, she was still breastfeeding her infant daughter. And unlike Danielle, Lily had been busty even before the pregnancy, which was one reason she had taken to wearing oversized sweatshirts.

"Morning, Lily," Walt and Danielle chimed as Lily walked all the way into the kitchen.

"Morning. Did Mel and Adam go home already?" Lily walked to the twins, gave them both a quick kiss, and then went to the counter, where she poured herself a cup of coffee.

"Cinnamon rolls are in the bag." Danielle pointed to a paper sack on the counter near the sink. "No. They're still here. Marie checked a few minutes ago. They're sleeping. I suspect they had a rough night."

Full coffee cup in hand, Lily snagged a cinnamon roll from the bag and headed for the table to join Walt and Danielle. "Their car wasn't out front."

"Their car's not here. Remember, we picked them up yesterday morning, and I brought Adam back here in my car. Chris brought Mel directly here from the airport," Danielle explained.

Lily stood by the table, holding her coffee cup and cinnamon roll, and looked at the two empty chairs. "Which one is Marie in?"

Walt smiled at Lily. "Marie left for your house a minute ago to visit Connor and Emily Ann; you must have missed her."

Lily giggled. "Which is easy to do." Lily sat down and glanced toward the doorway leading to the hallway and downstairs bedroom. "How are they doing? Did anyone tell them about the dead guys?" Danielle had called Lily last night and told her what had happened.

Danielle picked up her coffee cup. "No. We haven't seen either of them since Mel said goodnight. They haven't come out of the room."

"Well, Kelly already stopped by this morning." Lily snatched a napkin off the table, set her cinnamon roll on it, and tore the sweet roll in two.

"Did you tell her what happened?" Danielle took a sip of her coffee.

"I didn't have to. Kelly visited Joe this morning to find out when he could come home. Brian was there at the hospital, telling Joe what had happened. Of course, Brian told them the abbreviated version, leaving out Marie and Eva. But I wanted to give you the heads-up on something." Lily pulled off a small piece of the cinnamon roll and popped it into her mouth.

"Heads-up about what?" Danielle asked.

After Lily chewed and swallowed her food, she said, "Kelly is all hot on interviewing Adam for her podcast. She's hoping for an exclusive."

Danielle groaned, and Walt said, "Well, Mel predicted that one."

"Adam has so much to process, I wish she wouldn't try interviewing him," Danielle said.

Walt let out a sigh. "If not Kelly, someone else will try."

"Is she still at your house?" Danielle asked.

"No. They told Joe he should be able to go home before they serve lunch over there. He's supposed to rest today, and Kelly wants to get everything all comfy for Joe for when he comes home." Lily shrugged. "She was going to Old Salts on the way home to buy some goodies for him. But I suspect after she gets Joe all settled in, she's going to ask Adam for an interview. Knowing Kelly, once she finds out where he is, she'll try talking to him in person. So if Adam is still here, expect to get a visit from Kelly later this afternoon."

Danielle let out a sigh. "Poor Adam, worried he's going crazy. I'm not sure how he'll handle the interview."

"It would actually be easier if he had the truth." Lily popped another piece of cinnamon roll into her mouth.

Walt and Danielle looked curiously at Lily. "Why do you say that?" Walt asked.

Lily considered the question for a moment. Finally, she said, "Adam remembers what he witnessed, but it doesn't make sense to him. Which I get." Lily looked at Danielle. "You tried to give him an out by giving him permission to tell others it was all a blur. But that won't take away his memories."

"Yeah, he made that clear last night," Danielle agreed.

"While he may choose to go with what you suggested if he can't avoid sitting down for an interview, he'll know it's not only a lie, but he'll remember what he actually witnessed."

"How would knowing the truth help Adam?" Walt asked.

Lily cocked her head slightly as she looked at Walt. "It's simple. So he doesn't question his sanity. It's easy for you to claim you have amnesia and not worry something is wrong with you. Because you have the truth. Adam could agree to an interview and do what Danielle suggested. Say he simply doesn't remember. But is that going to take away his dread as he imagines he's losing it? And if he dares to tell someone what he remembers, everyone else will look at him like he's lost it, and there goes his reputation. And if he sees a therapist, that could be worse."

"You're saying we need to tell Adam about Marie?" Danielle asked.

"I'm saying you should tell Mel and Adam about Marie," Lily corrected.

LILY'S VISIT lasted less than twenty minutes. After she left, Walt and Danielle cleaned the twins up after breakfast and returned to the parlor to give them each a bottle. They were each sitting on a recliner, bottle-feeding a baby, when Melony wandered into the room, wearing her robe, her long blond hair looking as if it had barely been brushed after getting out of bed.

"Morning," Danielle called out.

Combing her fingers through her hair, Mel stumbled to the love seat and sat down, facing Walt and Danielle. "I don't remember the last time I slept this late."

"Is Adam up?" Walt asked.

"Yeah. He's in the shower. Any news?"

Walt and Danielle exchanged quick glances before Danielle updated Melony on what happened after she and Adam turned in the previous night.

"Damn," Melony muttered.

"From what the chief told us, one of your neighbors called the station when they noticed the lights on. The chief called Brian, who was still here. He drove over there and arrived right after the squad car got there. The front door was unlocked, and the chief told them to go in," Danielle explained.

"They actually killed each other in the hallway?"

"That's what it looks like. There was some sort of struggle. Both of their prints were all over the gun."

"Oh gawd, in our house," Melony groaned.

"The chief doesn't want you going over there until they finish processing the scene. And he also wants you to let him arrange for a cleaner."

Melony frowned at Danielle. "A cleaner?"

"There was a lot of blood on the floor," Danielle explained.

Melony groaned again.

"You both can stay here for a few days. If you need something from the house, let Brian or Edward get it for you. You don't need to see your home like that," Walt urged.

Melony considered Walt's suggestion for a moment. "I appreciate your offer. Let me talk to Adam about it."

"Okay. Are you hungry? Danielle and I haven't had breakfast yet."

Melony stood. "Hungry? Food doesn't sound terrific right now. But I should probably eat something."

"I'm so sorry, Mel," Danielle said.

Melony smiled sadly at Danielle. "Thanks. And I really appreciate everything you guys have done. I wish they could have found those guys somewhere else."

"How is Adam this morning?" Danielle asked.

Melony shook her head. "Umm, not great."

When Melony left the room, Walt turned to Danielle and said, "Lily may be right."

"About telling Adam and Mel?"

Walt nodded.

"I don't know. Maybe." Danielle set the now empty baby bottle on the end table and picked up her cellphone while she repositioned Addison, who had fallen asleep while taking her bottle.

Walt frowned at Danielle. "What are you doing?"

"Calling Lily."

"I REALLY DIDN'T WANT to burden Adam with this knowledge," Marie muttered. When Danielle had phoned Lily minutes earlier, she had asked her to call out to Marie and tell her Walt and Danielle needed to talk to her, and if possible, find Eva first and bring her.

"Unless you want your grandson to convince himself he has gone insane, this might be the best thing," Eva said.

"I suppose you're right," Marie reluctantly agreed.

"But when and where do you plan to tell him?" Eva asked.

"Or how," Danielle groaned.

"It might be best if we do this with the mediums present," Walt suggested. "And at Chris's house immediately."

"Why immediately?" Eva asked.

"We should do it before Kelly shows up and starts asking her questions. Which is why we need to do it at Chris's house instead of here," Walt said. "We don't need Kelly knocking on the door while we're in the middle of trying to explain something like this to Adam and Mel. And from what Lily said, it's very possible Kelly will be over here in a couple of hours."

Voices came from the hall—Adam and Melony.

"Please go talk to Heather and Chris about this. They're at work," Danielle said in a rushed whisper just before Melony and Adam walked into the parlor.

TWELVE

The twins had been put down for a morning nap in their portable cribs in the living room. Before leaving the room, Walt turned on the baby monitor. It sat on a nearby table. In the kitchen, Walt and Danielle sat with their houseguests at the table, eating a late breakfast of waffles, bacon, and scrambled eggs Danielle had prepared. The baby monitor's receiver emitted a faint hum from where it sat on the kitchen counter.

"Don't you ever worry about Max alone in the room with the twins? I've heard you're not supposed to leave a cat alone with a baby," Adam asked before taking a bite of bacon. When passing by the open doorway to the living room before coming to breakfast, Adam had noticed the black cat napping on the floor between the two portable cribs.

Danielle smiled at Adam's question. While tempted to tell Adam the truth, that Max was watching over the babies, she instead said, "No. I'd be more concerned with them hurting him."

"But you're not worried he might…umm…jump into one of the cribs while they're sleeping? He could scratch them."

"Not really." Danielle's cellphone rang, preventing her from elaborating on her answer to Adam's question. Instead, she stood, excused herself from the table, walked to the kitchen counter, and picked up her cellphone, which had been sitting on the docking station. She looked at the phone to check the caller. Danielle flashed her husband and friends a quick smile, excused herself again, and stepped out into the hallway to answer the call.

"Hey, Chris," Danielle greeted, keeping her voice low. As she talked, she strolled down the hallway and peeked into the living room to check on her sleeping babies.

"Marie and Eva stopped by the office. Heather and I agree; it's time Adam and Mel learned the truth."

"About everything?" Danielle asked.

"We should take the Eddy Junior approach. We don't need to hit them with everything at once." Chris was referring to Police Chief Edward MacDonald's oldest son, who earlier in the year had learned that not only was his younger brother, Evan, a medium, but there were other mediums and spirits in Frederickport. Yet he hadn't been told about Walt's past life.

"That would probably be best. And we need to do this as soon as possible."

"I agree. But there has been a change of plans."

"What do you mean?"

"Eva mentioned Walt suggested we do this at my house. But it would be better if we did it here at my office in the private conference room. That way, we won't have any interruptions. Eva and Marie are already here. How soon can you get here?"

"After we finish breakfast and I get the twins up and dressed. They should wake up pretty soon."

"That would be perfect. It would give time for the others to arrive."

Danielle frowned. "Others?"

AFTER DANIELLE RETURNED to the kitchen, she informed them they needed to go to Chris's office directly after breakfast because Chris had something he needed to discuss with Adam and

Melony. Adam didn't pump Danielle for more information so he could decide if he wanted to go or not. It was Chris, and Adam would have probably done just about any favor for Chris. As for Mel, she was simply happy the distraction seemed to put Adam in a better frame of mind.

ON THE DRIVE over to the Glandon Foundation Headquarters, Adam wondered why Danielle hadn't simply offered to loan them her car instead of driving them over. At the very least, why hadn't Walt driven them over and left Danielle home with the babies? Not only did Adam and Melony have to sit in the rear seat of the Flex because of the baby car seats in the seat directly behind the driver's and front passenger seats, it wasn't necessary for them all to go, and it seemed like a major hassle to take two babies anywhere.

But he didn't ask, as his mind continued to be all over the place. Still trying to process what he had seen, remembering those moments when he feared he was about to die, and now curious why Chris had summoned him to his office.

When they arrived at the Glandon Foundation headquarters, it wasn't Heather sitting at the front desk, but one of the other foundation employees. The moment they stepped into the office, the woman greeted them by asking, "Is this the Adam Nichols group?"

Adam didn't consider them a group, but he said yes and was confused when she told them to follow her. He had expected Chris to step out of his office. She led them down a hallway to the private conference room. Walt and Danielle trailed behind him and Mel, each carrying a baby. He wanted to stop and tell them, "It's okay. I've got this. You can wait for us out front." But something kept him from saying that, probably because of all they had done for him in the last twenty-four hours.

The moment they entered the conference room, both Adam and Mel looked confused. An oval conference table occupied the center of the room, and sitting around it were five people— Chris Johnson, Heather Donovan, Ian Bartley, Brian Henderson, and Edward MacDonald. Next to the table was a baby playpen filled with an assortment of toys. What they couldn't see were the spirits of Eva and Marie, who stood on the other side of the playpen. The woman who had led them to the room stood quietly until they were all inside, and then she silently stepped back into the hallway, shutting the door behind her.

Chris stood up from his seat and motioned to the empty chairs. "Please sit down."

Adam and Mel exchanged confused glances before each took a seat, sitting next to each other. Walt and Danielle walked to the chairs closest to the playpen. Danielle looked over to Heather and mouthed, *Thank you*, before placing Jack in the playpen. She took Addison from Walt and set her next to her brother. Once the babies were settled, Walt and Danielle took their seats at the conference table.

For several moments no one said anything, but all looked at Adam and Mel.

"What is this about?" Adam finally blurted.

"It's sort of an intervention," Heather said.

Adam stared at Heather dumbly, but then, as if something clicked in his brain, he stood quickly, almost tipping over his chair. "You're all convinced I'm crazy, aren't you? This is what this is about, isn't it? You want me to check myself into a mental ward, don't you? You want me to submit to voluntary institutionalization; is that what this is about?"

"I didn't realize how dramatic that boy can be sometimes," Marie muttered from the sidelines. Danielle, the only medium who had heard her, suppressed a giggle.

Chris let out a sigh. "No, Adam, that is not what this is about. Please sit down." He glanced at Heather with narrow eyes and said, "You certainly have a way with words."

Heather shrugged sheepishly. "I'm sorry. But it is sort of an intervention, but not the kind Adam is talking about."

"Then what kind of intervention is it?" Adam snapped.

"I'm confused. What is going on?" Melony asked.

Chris looked over to Danielle and motioned to her with one hand. "Perhaps you should do this."

Danielle gave Chris a solemn nod and looked over to Adam and Melony, flashing them a smile. "Perhaps I need to start this by saying something like, *We called you all here today*, or *I imagine you're wondering why we called you here today*. While both are cliché, I suppose they're also accurate."

"Why did you bring us here?" Melony asked.

Danielle smiled softly at Mel and Adam. "Because two dear friends are in a lot of pain right now. One of those friends is convinced he's going insane. Which I can promise you both, he isn't. And the other friend is worried about her husband because she's not sure what's going on."

Adam furrowed his brow. "Is this, like, a pep talk?"

Danielle grinned at Adam. "No. It's an explanation. Everyone in this room knows what you witnessed yesterday. We also understand —except for Mel—what actually happened at your house. We have the answers to your questions, but before we tell you, we want you both to understand that those answers cannot leave this room."

"I don't understand. If you know what happened, why must it remain a secret?" Melony asked.

"For one thing, it could destroy the reputation and career of one of your oldest friends."

With a frown, Melony looked over to MacDonald and back to Danielle.

"It wouldn't help my career either," Brian said.

"Although it could be a boost to mine," Ian added. Walt chuckled at the comment.

"Please tell us, what did I see?" Adam asked, his tone sharp.

"It's no secret that when I was a child, my parents sent me to a therapist because I claimed to have talked to my grandmother at her funeral, and later with a child who had died. Cheryl told people. Joe found out," Danielle said. "Adam, Mel, I want you both to remember what you experienced at the Marymoor property. Of the conversation we had at Pier Café when you both ran into Walt and me after a pipe tried to kill Mel."

"We talked about Mel's experience in high school and Adam's encounter with a croquet set in Marlow House's attic not long after Danielle moved here," Walt reminded them.

"I get what you're going to say," Adam interrupted. "Mel and I already talked about it."

"And what's that?" Danielle asked.

"We talked about how people are made of energy and how energy doesn't die. And if some of that energy is from a conflicted soul who hasn't completely moved on, then we might experience what some call paranormal activity. That's why doors might slam shut on their own in houses that are supposedly haunted. We talked about how there is much in this world we don't understand," Adam said.

Danielle nodded. "Exactly."

Adam shook his head. "But this isn't the same thing. What happened at our house was more than some random object flying or a door slamming. Someone or something took the gun away from the man who intended to kill me and threw the two of them together. I said they were fighting, but it wasn't fighting. It was like something slammed the men together, holding them down until it could tie them up. They kept yelling, wanting to be released and…" Adam didn't finish his sentence; he shivered at the memory.

"And you are right, Adam. It was different. But not in the way you imagine. That pipe that attacked Mel, the croquet set that flew at you and Bill, and what happened yesterday weren't a product of random energy. Yes, energy moved those things. But it was more than that. Each of those things happened because a ghost could harness their energy," Danielle explained.

Adam stared at Danielle for a moment and then shrugged. "So I'm simply supposed to accept the theory that a ghost…what did you call it? Harnessed their energy…and moved those things? So a ghost saved my life yesterday? What ghost? Oh, I bet it's Grandma's ghost, right? She saved me yesterday." Adam snickered at the idea, but when he glanced around the table, he noticed no one was laughing, not even Mel; they all stared at Adam.

Finally, Danielle spoke, her voice calm and resolute. "Yes, you're right. It was Marie. Your grandmother saved your life yesterday."

THIRTEEN

Silence filled the room following Danielle's announcement that Marie had saved Adam. Melony sat, stunned. She had not been prepared for Danielle's words. Her eyes searched the faces of her friends, trying to understand what this was really all about. While she had embraced the possibility of paranormal activity and understood there were things about the world beyond her comprehension, it seemed a far leap to imagine Adam's grandmother a guardian angel capable of disarming and restraining two men. Instead of asking questions, Melony waited for Danielle or one of the others to say more, to explain what this was actually about and why Danielle had said what she did.

Adam, however, did not remain silent. After a moment he stood abruptly and angrily asked, "What are you trying to do? Is this your way of showing me how crazy I sound? I won't argue; what I saw sounds crazy."

Chris stood, looked at Adam, and in a serious tone said, "Adam, please sit down and listen."

Had anyone else made that demand, Adam might have argued. Instead, he sat down, his eyes focused on Chris.

"I'm going to tell you and Mel something about myself—something that everyone else in this room has known for a long time. Something you are unaware of. Trust me when I say it is all true. When I am done, the rest of us will each stand up and do the same. We will tell you and Mel something that we have kept from you. And if either of you leaves this room and shouts to the world what we said, we will probably deny it all."

Adam and Mel glanced at each other, exchanging questioning frowns, yet said nothing. Instead, they turned back and gave their attention to Chris.

Seeing they were listening and not intending to interrupt, Chris continued, "We've all heard of mediums. In fact, you met a famous medium when Danielle's former mother-in-law visited Marlow House. Fin Walsh. Many in this room were convinced he was a charlatan. Now, we're sure he is the real thing. But why were we so convinced he was fake back then? Because there are several people in this room who are also mediums, and our gifts differ from Walsh's. We just didn't understand at the time."

"Are you saying you're a medium?" Adam blurted.

Chris gave a nod and continued, "As Danielle reminded us, when she was a little girl, her parents took her to a therapist because she claimed to communicate with the spirits of people who had died. But it wasn't the overactive imagination of a child, nor was she crazy. You see, Danielle and I have something in common; we're both mediums."

"You can see ghosts?" Adam asked.

"I have been able to see ghosts—or as some people call them, spirits—since I was a child. It is a gift—or curse—passed down from my biological mother. My brother is also a medium. Fin Walsh's gifts work differently from Danielle's and mine and my brother's. The best I can explain it; he's on a different frequency. Walsh communicates with spirits who have moved on. When I say moved on, I mean they are on a different plane of existence from where we are now. I suppose some might call it Heaven. Whereas I and the other mediums in this room communicate and can see spirits who have not yet moved on—which we call ghosts."

"Are there other mediums in this room besides you and Danielle?" Adam asked.

Chris looked at Heather and motioned for her to stand.

Heather stood as Chris sat back down. "I'm not like Chris or Danielle. I haven't been seeing ghosts since I was a child, yet I've always embraced the possibility of the paranormal. All of us probably have the potential, yet some people are more sensitive, or it comes more naturally to them. One of the first ghosts I ever encountered was at Presley House before it burned down. Over time, my ability grew stronger. So now, like Chris, I can see ghosts." Heather looked at Chief MacDonald. "Okay, Chief, you're next." Heather sat down.

"Are you saying Eddy is a medium?" Melony blurted.

"No," Edward MacDonald said as he stood. "But Evan is. Just as Chris's gift came from his mother, I suspect my son's gift came from my grandmother. I first learned about Danielle's ability not long after she moved here. She mentioned meeting my grandmother in the local cemetery, but what she didn't realize was my grandmother had passed away."

Both Melony and Adam looked over to Danielle briefly and then back to Edward.

"Evan would sometimes talk about seeing people who weren't there. I was naturally concerned that it was more than some childish imaginary friend. After I realized Danielle's gift, I told her about Evan. Since then, she and the rest of the mediums have been incredibly helpful. I've carried this secret for a long time, and over this period I have witnessed things—things I only discuss with a few people. And Adam, yours isn't the first life your grandmother has saved." Edward looked over to Ian. "But not everyone accepts so easily. Ian, your turn."

MacDonald sat down as Ian stood and said, "No, I'm not a medium, either. But Lily has known about Danielle's ability since they moved to Frederickport. Lily didn't want to continue keeping this secret from me after we married, so before we were married, she shared what she had experienced and learned about the spirits, or as Chris calls them, ghosts, spirits who have refused to move on. She told me about my friends who were mediums. As much as I loved Lily, I refused to accept what she was saying. It went against everything I was—the skeptical investigative journalist. I saw it as an elaborate mocking prank. Adam, remember when Lily and I broke up for a while? When I gave my notice and was moving? This was during that time. But then I saw the truth, and, well, here I am. And like the chief, I have seen things that repeatedly confirm Lily's claim. And I know it was Marie who saved your life yesterday. This is the one story I would love to write about. But I understand I can't." Ian looked at Brian, and before sitting down, he said, "Your turn."

Brian stood. "Like Ian and the chief, I'm not a medium. But when Walt, Heather, and I were kidnapped by those crazy women who thought they were witches, well, let's just say I learned a lot that weekend, and your grandmother, Adam, helped bring us home. She also has an annoying habit of tugging on your earlobe if she's irritated with you. So if you can recall any times it felt like someone tugged on your ear, it was probably your grandmother." Brian sat back down.

Adam absently touched his right ear for just a moment, and by his expression some might wonder if he had just remembered an instance where it felt as if his ear had been tugged.

Walt glanced around the room. He was the only one who hadn't yet spoken. He stood and looked at Melony and Adam. "I am a medium. But Clint Marlow wasn't. However, I won't go into the why and how of all that. What we have already told you is a lot to take in all at once. I think it's best if we give you time to adjust and accept what you learned today before you dive any deeper into, as Eva says, the mysteries of the Universe."

"Eva?" Melony asked. "Eva who?"

Walt smiled. "There are two spirits who frequent Marlow House. They each have their own reasons for not moving on yet. One of them is Adam's grandmother, Marie. The other is Eva Thorndike; you have seen her portrait in the museum."

"The silent screen star?" Adam squeaked.

Walt nodded. "Actually, your grandmother knew Eva as a child. You see, there is something we didn't mention. Children, especially very young children, often can see spirits or ghosts. Eva would visit your grandmother when she was a baby, sing to her. But over time, Marie lost the ability to see Eva. It's difficult for a child to continue believing when the adults around them insist it is all make-believe or an imaginary friend."

"Connor sees your grandmother," Danielle interrupted. She remained sitting. "To him, she is Grandma Marie. He adores her. It's getting a little awkward, because I suspect with so many adults around him who can see Marie and reinforce her reality, I imagine he'll continue seeing her, but I'm not sure."

"We've learned Lily's imaginary friend as a child was actually the ghost of a little boy," Ian said. "She never realized that until last year. And today, Lily normally can't see spirits, although there have been a few times she has."

"Do you really expect us to believe all of this?" Adam asked in a loud voice.

"Not right away," Walt said. "Ian certainly didn't."

Heather stood. "Perhaps Adam needs a visual."

Everyone looked to Heather. "What is that supposed to mean?" Walt asked.

Heather smiled at Walt. "You can sit down. I think Adam and Mel have heard enough for now. But what they need to help them understand is a visual." Heather looked to Mel and Adam. "We didn't mention this, but the spirits—or ghosts—of Marie and Eva are with us today. They are standing near the playpen."

Melony and Adam automatically looked at the playpen, and of course, neither saw the ghosts. They looked back at Heather.

"Another thing," Heather continued. "Not all spirits or ghosts can move objects. Marie can, Eva can't, but Eva has other gifts. One of Eva's gifts, I guess you could say, she understands more than the rest of us how some of this works. Mel, when that pipe attacked you on the Marymoor property, it was being moved by an unhappy ghost. But according to Eva, spirits—or ghosts—can't harm an innocent. Now, had you been a murderer about to kill Adam, it's possible that ghost could have whacked you over the head and done some actual damage."

Melony frowned. "An innocent?"

Heather shrugged. "Someone not evil. If cranky ghosts could go around randomly hitting people with heavy objects, we'd have dead bodies all over the place."

"I am waiting for you to get to the part about a visual," Chris called out.

"Oh, that." Heather flashed Chris a grin and then looked back to Adam and Melony. "As Walt mentioned, children and babies can normally see spirits. The twins can. Like Connor, they're familiar with Marie. But let me explain something: sometimes a medium— or very young child—will see a ghost and assume it's a living person. They can look just like a real person. But what we see is only an illusion; it's not an actual body. Marie can pick up a baby and look as if she is holding it. But it is not actually her body that is picking it up, because she has no body. So as not to scare the baby, she will make it look like her body is picking it up. Otherwise, the baby will think it's flying on its own. So maybe Marie could carry Addison over to me to show you what I mean. A visual."

Adam rolled his eyes at Heather's suggestion and reluctantly glanced toward the playpen. But he froze when Addison floated up out of the playpen, giggling, as she moved across the room toward Heather while suspended some four feet from the floor.

"Oh, my gawd," Melony muttered, her eyes wide as they fixed on the flying infant.

Next to Melony came a thump, as Adam fell out of his chair and landed on the floor.

Adam Nichols had fainted.

FOURTEEN

Those sitting closest to Adam rushed to his side first, as he sprawled on the floor in the conference room, his chair now pushed out from the table. Adam wasn't out for more than a minute when he regained consciousness. He started to sit up. Melony, who knelt by his side, had placed her hand on his shoulder and gently guided him to a sitting position. His right hand touched his forehead, which had hit the side of the table when falling. A bump started to form.

"Are you okay?" Melony asked.

"What happened?" Adam gently touched the tender bump on his forehead again and then winced.

"You fainted," Melony told him.

As soon as Adam fell from his chair, Marie had handed Heather the baby so she could go to her grandson's side. Heather walked with Addison toward the crib but handed the baby to Danielle, who was now standing. Walt had already picked up Jack, as the baby had stood up after Marie took his sister, and had been holding onto the side of the playpen, bouncing up and down, demanding attention.

Melony stood up from the floor while Chris and Ian helped Adam get to his feet. She walked over to MacDonald and stood directly in front of him. She looked up into MacDonald's face as she searched his eyes. "Eddy, is this really true?"

MacDonald nodded solemnly. He reached out and briefly touched Melony's cheek before slipping a lock of her blond hair behind her ear. "You know deep down it's true. This isn't something I'd lie about."

FIFTEEN MINUTES LATER, they all sat back around the conference table. Heather had left the office for a moment and had returned with a damp washcloth holding an ice cube, which she handed to Adam, who now held it to his forehead. The twins hadn't been returned to the playpen, but instead each sat on a parent's lap, each drinking from a bottle.

Adam sat rigidly on his chair, not looking at anyone in the room, but staring blankly across the table. His right hand continued to hold the washcloth with the ice cube on his tender forehead. "If this is all true, I have two questions."

No one asked him what those questions were but waited for him to continue.

"First, why didn't you tell me before? And second, why tell me now?" Adam looked around the table at all his friends, each sitting quietly, their expressions blank as they looked in his direction.

"I can answer that." Danielle repositioned Addison on her lap as the baby held her own bottle. Danielle looked at Adam. "I learned long ago that sharing this with other people can…well…it rarely works out. My parents couldn't fathom the idea their daughter spoke to dead people."

"That's rather a rude way to put it," Marie grumbled.

Danielle ignored Marie's comment and continued, "Over the years, Cheryl used the knowledge as a weapon. I'm not suggesting she believed it was true. At least, not while she was still alive. And so I learned to be careful whom I told."

Adam glanced around the room briefly and then looked back to

Danielle. "It seems you didn't have a problem telling everyone in this room."

Danielle smiled at Adam. "True. But sometimes, like today, it's inevitable. While at other times, we would like to tell someone, but we know it will cause more problems. For example, Kelly. Ian would like to tell her, considering some things that have happened in the last few years. But he decided not to share the information with his sister for one reason. He's concerned about her marriage. He doesn't want to do anything that would interfere with her and Joe's relationship, because he believes his sister really loves Joe, and she's happy in her marriage."

"How would that interfere with her marriage?" Adam asked.

"Oh, I understand," Melony said, answering for Danielle. "Kelly would tell Joe, he would never believe it, and it would put a wedge between them, considering how Kelly feels about Ian."

"Exactly. Certain people have been led to believe I dabble in magic—sleight of hand." Walt spoke up. "If Joe walked in and saw Addison flying across the room, he would sooner believe I'm the next David Copperfield than he would ever believe Marie's ghost is in the room with us."

"Adam," Danielle began again, "back when you and Mel told Walt and me about what happened at the Marymoor property, we knew you and Mel could handle the information. We understood you would disbelieve at first, but you had already seen things. Yet it was your grandmother who didn't want us to tell you."

Adam frowned. "Why would she want to keep it a secret?"

Danielle glanced briefly at Marie and then back to Adam. "For the mediums, when Marie comes to visit, we can see her. But if Marie goes to visit—let's say Connor—Lily and Ian can't see her. They may suspect she's there because of Connor's response. In that case, they might ask Marie to move something to show she's there. Marie was afraid that if you knew about her, it might freak you out, wondering if she was at your house when she wasn't, always looking over your shoulder, feeling your privacy was invaded. She thought it might be uncomfortable for you. And while Marie checks in on you, like she went over to your house after discovering you had food poisoning to make sure you were alright, it's not like she hangs out at your house spying on you and Mel." Danielle wasn't certain about the truth of her last sentence but thought she would throw it in anyway.

Addison finished her bottle, handed it to her mother, and squirmed. Danielle set the empty bottle on the table and checked the baby's diaper. She needed changing.

"While Danielle takes care of Addison, I'll answer your second question, Adam. The reason we felt it best to tell you both now is simple. We didn't want you to feel you were going crazy. Because you're not. Marie arrived at your house just as that man was about to kill you. Had she had more time to consider her options, she might have handled the situation differently so you wouldn't have seen all that you did. But she didn't have that time, and she didn't want you moving to her side," Chris explained.

"She took the gun away from him?" Adam asked.

Chris nodded. "She initially put it in the lamp to keep it out of their way while she restrained them. You must understand that when Marie manipulates energy—or as Danielle calls it, harnessing energy—it's not like she can easily move multiple objects simultaneously. It takes focus and practice. And after she tied them up, she took the gun out of the lamp and set it on the table because the police would ask how it got into the lamp, especially without breaking the glass."

"I wondered that myself," Adam muttered.

"But how does our knowing what happened help Adam explain to people how he managed to escape?" Mel asked.

"Like Kelly. She's already planning to ask Adam for an interview," Ian looked from Melony to Adam. "After picking Joe up from the hospital today, she wanted to go over to Marlow House and talk to Adam. That's one reason Danielle and the others thought we should talk to you both immediately."

"But you still haven't answered my question. How does our understanding of what really happened help Adam explain?" Melony said.

"Because now that you know what really happened, Adam can

stop obsessing about his sanity, and he can focus on coming up with a believable story—or in layman's terms, a believable lie," Heather explained.

"And Danielle's pretty good at coming up with those," Walt said with a chuckle.

"Which means Adam doesn't need to come up with a story, just memorize what Danielle tells him." Heather winked at Walt.

"Is he supposed to lie to the police, too?" Melony looked at the chief. "I'm thinking of Joe."

Brian chuckled. "It wouldn't be the first time. But yes. And since the only two people able to contradict the revised version are on Marie's side, Adam doesn't have to worry about that."

"I wouldn't actually say they are on my side; at least one of them isn't. Not exactly sure where they took him," Marie said, but only the mediums could hear her.

"You said ghosts are spirits who haven't moved on. Why isn't Grandma in Heaven?" Adam asked.

"Marie is free to move on if she wants," Walt said. "I suspect she initially stayed because of you. She wanted to make sure that you were happy. I think she wanted to see you married."

"And have children," Adam muttered. "Is she really disappointed in me?"

"Adam, your grandmother still adores you." Heather spoke up. "And it's true, at first, she didn't understand why you and Mel didn't want to have kids. I sort of helped her through that, made her understand. And she's thrilled you married Mel."

"I am," Marie said.

"And she's accepted the fact that you and Mel don't want children. And frankly, if you had kids now, I doubt she would have much time to enjoy them, considering all the time she spends with Connor, the twins, and now there is Emily Ann," Heather finished with a laugh.

"I think Marie initially stayed for you, Adam," Brian said. "But frankly, I think she stuck around because she was having too much fun."

Now finished diapering Addison, and placing her back in the

playpen, Danielle looked at Adam and said, "Adam, remember your grandma's divinity I've been making you the last couple of years for Christmas? Truth is, I didn't make it; your grandmother did."

Wide-eyed, Adam looked at Danielle.

"Remember the time you sent Bill over to paint Connor's nursery, and it had already been painted? That was Marie," Ian said with a grin.

"Tell Adam that the times when he dreamed about me and told Mel how real the dream felt, it was really me visiting him in his sleep," Marie said.

Danielle repeated what Marie said, and Adam's eyes teared up in response.

"We can talk about this more later. But we should probably get back to coming up with a story for Adam to tell about his escape," Chris said.

"I've given it a lot of thought, and I've come up with an alternate story that should work." Danielle sat back down in her chair. All eyes were on her. "It's always best to stick as close to the truth as possible. Marie has already told us what happened, so I'll give her version a few tweaks."

"I'm not sure how you can tweak it to sound believable," Adam said.

"Keep to the truth right up to when you are tied up in the chair and the two guys are arguing about killing you. At this point, say you're tugging on the ropes, trying to get untied while they were distracted, and in doing so, you realize the guy did a lousy job tying you up. As they continue to argue, not realizing you are just about out of the ropes, the one guy who doesn't want to kill you knocks the gun from his partner's hand. It falls on the floor, and since they are still arguing with each other and don't realize you're no longer tied up, you get the gun. You then turn the gun on them, make them walk into the hallway, where you tie them up with the rope they used on you. It all happened so fast, and your adrenaline was pumping, and most of this is a blur, and you aren't sure how you managed to get them tied up—but they were probably afraid the gun in your shaking hand, the one pointed at them, might go off at any moment. Once they are tied up in the hall, you go back in the dining room, pick up your phone from the table, where they had set it, and call the police. You rush outside, leaving the gun on the table. Later, after you come back in the house with the police and see the gun sitting on the table, you realize you were really stupid to leave the gun, because had they gotten untied, like you did, they could have gotten ahold of the gun again and killed you. Thinking of that, and everything that just happened, you mentally shut down, which is why you just sat there for a while, not talking."

"But didn't Adam initially tell the cops the guy threw the gun in the light fixture?" Heather asked.

"Adam can say he doesn't really remember saying that but admits he might have because everything seemed to happen so fast, and he was confused and terrified. And obviously the guy didn't throw the gun in the light fixture, because it was sitting on the table when the police walked in." Danielle flashed Heather a self-satisfied smile.

FIFTEEN

Kelly stood in the middle of her living room, cellphone in hand, and opened her Reminders app. That morning, after leaving Joe at the hospital, she had created a list in Reminders of all the tasks she needed to complete before picking Joe up in the afternoon. One by one, she checked off the items she completed. She smiled, seeing there was nothing more she needed to do. The house was clean, she had changed the sheets, and she had stocked the refrigerator and pantry with some of Joe's favorite treats. After closing the app, Kelly glanced at the time. She had completed her to-do list sooner than expected, and she had an hour before she needed to go to the hospital.

Pleased with herself, she thought aloud, "I have time to talk to Adam before I pick up Joe." Kelly walked over to her purse sitting on the nearby coffee table, picked it up, and dropped her phone in its side pocket. She never considered calling Adam instead of asking him in person. She felt it was more difficult for someone to turn down an interview request when she approached them face-to-face. But she wasn't sure where she might find Adam.

Ten minutes later, Kelly sat in the driver's seat of her car, still parked in her driveway. She grabbed her purse, opened it up, and instead of getting her car keys and starting the vehicle, she pulled out her phone again and called Joe's cellphone.

"You ready to come home?" Kelly greeted cheerfully when he answered his phone.

"I am. But like I told you, it probably won't be for another hour."

"Yeah, I figured as much. But I was calling to ask if you've heard from Brian or the chief about Adam."

"What about Adam?" Joe asked.

"I want to talk to him about an interview."

"Kelly, I'm not sure that's a good idea, at least not right now. From what I've heard, he's barely talking. Like he's still in shock. It's too soon."

"He must not have been that bad; the chief didn't think he needed to go to the hospital."

"I know. I'm just saying that what he experienced was traumatic. And you need to talk to the chief first; make sure he even wants him to talk to the press right now; it's still an open investigation."

"True, but it's not like the bad guys are still out there. I mean, they're dead. And I consider Adam a friend. How about if I just see how Adam is doing, and if he seems okay, I'll ask him about an interview, and before we have the actual interview, I'll check with the chief."

Joe was silent on the other end of the phone for a moment before saying, "Okay, I think that would work. You can talk to Adam, but don't upset him. And if he agrees to an interview, don't do it until you talk to the chief."

"I promise. Now, the reason I called. Any clue where Adam is? I'm not sure where to find him, not after what happened last night at his house. Do you think he's still at Marlow House?"

***

KELLY PULLED her car in front of Marlow House and parked. She didn't see any vehicles parked in front of the house, but she assumed Walt and Danielle's cars were in the garage, and she didn't expect to see either Melony or Adam's vehicle parked on the street, since she understood Danielle had brought Adam to her house and Chris had brought Melony to Marlow House from the airport.

Kelly got out of her car and started up the front walkway to Marlow House. She spied Max sitting in the living room window, watching her, his tail twitching.

KELLY USED her key to let herself into her brother's house. Sadie, the golden retriever, greeted her at the door, her tail wagging. Kelly had called Lily a minute earlier to tell her she was coming over, to which Lily told her to use her key and come into the living room. Kelly had tried calling her brother first, but the call had gone to voicemail.

When Kelly reached the living room, she found Lily sitting on the sofa, nursing Emily Ann, while Connor played nearby on the floor. When he saw his aunt, Connor showed her one of his trucks, inviting her to play with him.

"I saw you pull up across the street a minute ago and go up to the door," Lily said, making no attempt to stand up or disrupt her daughter. Lily still wore what she had on that morning, yet her hair was no longer in a high ponytail but fastened in a messy bun atop her head by a scrunchy.

Kelly dropped a kiss on Connor's head and flashed a warm smile to the nursing infant before saying, "No one was home. Any idea where they are?" Kelly sat down on the floor with her nephew and picked up one of his toy trucks before absently pushing it around.

"No," Lily lied. "What did you need?"

"I wanted to talk to Adam." Kelly smiled down at her nephew, who pushed his toy truck around the one she held.

"Ahh, that's right. That interview you mentioned."

Kelly glanced up from the toy trucks to Lily and Emily Ann. "I wonder where they are."

"Maybe they went out to get lunch or something," Lily suggested.

"Oh, probably." Kelly let out a sigh before asking, "How is your mom doing?"

"Great. Not thrilled they can't come for Christmas now."

"Laura's not coming either, right?"

Lily shook her head. "No, she's being a dutiful daughter and staying home to take care of Mom." Lily's mother had fallen the prior week and had broken a hip, which resulted in her having hip-replacement surgery.

"Have you guys considered going down there for Christmas?" Kelly instantly thought better of the question and added, "Don't tell Mom I even asked the question."

Lily laughed. "I won't. But no. We really don't feel up to driving down to Sacramento with a toddler, an infant, and all our Christmas gifts. No, we're staying home."

Kelly glanced around and then looked back at Lily. "Where's Ian?"

"He's running some errands," Lily lied again.

Kelly let out a sigh. Still sitting on the floor, she leaned back against the recliner, now holding the toy truck on her lap. Connor didn't seem to mind. His attention had shifted to a small pile of wooden blocks. "Have you heard how Adam is doing?"

"I stopped over there this morning. Adam and Mel were still asleep. I didn't see them. At that time, they still hadn't been told about what happened at their house last night, but I imagine Danielle told them when they got up."

"I wonder if they're over at Mel and Adam's house now."

Lily glanced down at her nursing daughter and moved her sweatshirt slightly before shifting the baby to the other nipple. After getting comfortable, Lily looked back at Kelly and said, "I seriously doubt it. Danielle said the chief wanted Mel and Adam to stay away from the house until the police were done with it and after the blood was cleaned up. He didn't think either of them needed that image forever burned in their brains. I think they may stay at Marlow House again tonight, so if you want, I'd be happy to call you when I see them come back." Lily smiled sweetly at her sister-in-law.

"Would you?"

"Sure."

BACK AT THE GLANDON FOUNDATION, Adam tried to wrap his brain around what he had been told, while Mel sat silently in her chair next to him, her expression a mixture of curiosity and disbelief.

"So Grandma is here right now?" Adam asked Danielle.

Danielle glanced behind Adam, where his grandmother stood. "Yes."

Eva had remained by the playpen, where she had been singing little songs to the twins to amuse them, while trying to keep her voice low so as not to be too distracting to the mediums who could hear her.

"This all sounds crazy. Crazier than what I saw yesterday," Adam told her.

Danielle shrugged. "Yeah. I know."

"Where is she?" Still sitting in the chair, Adam glanced around the room. Before Danielle could point to Marie, the ghost moved from behind Adam and stood in front of him, in the middle of the conference table, her legs hidden beneath the tabletop. Marie looked down at Adam and smiled.

"She's standing right in front of you," Danielle said. "And from my perspective, it looks like the tabletop is cutting her in half, but ghosts can walk through walls—and furniture."

Adam turned toward the table. Part of him expected one of his friends to shout, "We're just kidding," at any minute, but another part knew that was not about to happen.

"Maybe Walt really is the next David Copperfield, and this is all a magic trick," Adam said. "So tell me, if Grandma is really here, ask her who cut my hair in third grade. Unless David Copperfield is also a mind reader, he won't have the answer."

"You can ask her yourself," Heather said. "She can hear you. You just can't hear her answer; we'll have to tell you what she says."

Marie didn't call out the answer; instead, she removed a pen from Chris's shirt pocket and picked up a legal pad of paper that sat on a table by the entrance to the conference room. Pad of paper and pen floated toward Adam. The pad dropped in front of him while the pen hovered a foot above the table. Both Adam's and Melony's eyes widened at the sight. The next moment, the pen lowered to the paper and wrote a name. When done, the pen dropped to the table. Adam stared down at the name written.

"Is it the right answer?" Heather asked.

Still staring at the paper, Adam nodded in disbelief. The next moment, the top sheet of paper ripped from the pad and floated off the table, landing on the floor. The pen then lifted from the table and began writing on a blank sheet of legal paper. Instead of one word, it wrote several paragraphs that only Adam could clearly see. When done, the pen dropped back to the tabletop. As if mesmerized by the sight, Adam's hands trembled as he lifted the pad of paper up, silently reading.

"It's…it's…Grandma's handwriting." Tears slid down Adam's face. He turned to Melony and handed her the pad of paper. She read it quickly, and when she finished, she clutched the legal pad to her chest as she pulled Adam into her arms—the two embraced, silently sobbing.

The others looked away from the pair; the scene felt too intimate, as if watching would be an invasion of privacy. No one but Melony and Adam knew what Marie had written on the paper, but from Adam's behavior, they didn't doubt he now believed it. They could hear the sobs, but it was not a cry of sorrow or loss, but of someone who suddenly believed magic was real.

SIXTEEN

Eva and Marie said their goodbyes and left the Glandon Foundation headquarters. Danielle stood next to her car in front of the building, holding Addison, while Walt secured Jack in one of the baby car seats in the back of the Ford Flex. Ian had already left for home, and Danielle stood with Brian and MacDonald as they watched Melony and Adam drive away with Heather and Chris in Chris's car.

"Heather mentioned Chris was going to stop someplace so they could have lunch before they go back to your house," Brian said.

"What are you guys doing now?" Danielle asked Brian and the chief just as Walt took Addison from her arms so he could put her in the car seat.

The chief glanced briefly at his watch. "I think Brian and I will grab something quick for lunch. We're supposed to meet Bill Jones over at Mark's house in thirty minutes."

"You haven't gone through the house yet?" Danielle asked.

"After Bill stopped by the office yesterday and we learned Mark's connection to the two men, some of our people went through it. But now, Brian and I are going to go through it again. See if we can find something to help us figure out what they were looking for."

"You know, Chief, you should probably take a medium along with you. While I don't imagine you'll run into Mark's or his brother's spirits there, considering what Marie and Eva saw, it's entirely possible the partner Mark's brother killed might be there. Especially if he was staying there, and it sounds like he might have been."

"Danielle, I appreciate your offer, but I'm not sure how that would look if we brought you along. In situations like this, some nosy neighbor will inevitably show up to see what's going on, and I don't know how I'd explain you and the twins."

Danielle laughed. "I wasn't talking about me. Or taking the twins."

"Chris and Heather are already gone, and we can't wait for either of them," MacDonald said.

"I was talking about Walt."

"What about me?" Walt asked, having missed the first part of the conversation and having just finished securing Addison in her car seat.

Danielle glanced at Walt and back to Brian and the chief. "I don't know why I didn't think about it before. Walt should go with you. If anyone asks why he's there, tell them he asked to accompany you, you know, for research. Tell them he's working on a book and wants to get a better feel for how the police investigate crimes. Sort of like in *Castle*."

The chief looked at Walt. "If you wouldn't mind, that would be great."

"I wouldn't mind. Let me take Danielle home, and I'll meet you over there."

"We can pick you up," Brian said.

SADIE GREETED Ian at the front door when he returned home. The golden retriever didn't bark; she just wagged her tail and nudged Ian affectionately. When Ian walked into the living room, he found Lily lounging on the sofa, reading a book. She looked up, flashed him a smile, and then laid the book, still open, on top of her stomach.

"You look relaxed." Ian walked over to Lily and dropped a kiss on her forehead.

Lily sat up, set her book on the table, still open but placed the cover side up, and put her feet on the floor. "Emily Ann is napping. And Connor is in his bedroom, playing with Marie."

"So Marie came here after she left us?" Ian sat on the sofa next to his wife.

Lily leaned over the coffee table and picked up what looked like a white sheet of paper. She handed it to Ian. When he turned it over, he found two words written on the paper in Marie's handwriting. It read, *Adam knows.*

"I didn't realize Marie was here until this floated into the living room. I think she found the paper in your office. Connor saw her, and the next minute he went running into his bedroom, saying something about playing with Grandma Marie. I checked on them a few minutes ago; looks like they've lined up all Connor's little people and animals into a parade. So what exactly does Adam know?"

Ian tossed the paper back on the coffee table, next to Lily's book, and leaned back on the sofa. After he recapped what had happened at the foundation offices, Lily said, "Actually, I heard a little of that already. Dani called me. Said she and Walt were on their way home, and that Adam and Mel went with Chris and Heather. I guess they're getting something to eat before they go back to Marlow House."

Lily's cellphone rang. She picked it up from the coffee table, looked at it, and before answering told Ian, "It's your sister. I promised to let her know when they're back. She wants to talk to Adam about an interview."

"Here, let me talk to her." Ian reached for Lily's phone, but she pulled it out of his reach.

"She doesn't know you were with them. She stopped by, and I told her you were running errands, and that I didn't know where any of them were."

Ian reached for her cellphone again, this time snatching it from

Lily's grasp. "Yeah, I know. She left me several voice messages and texts." Ian answered the call with, "Hey, Kelly."

"Ian? Well, glad to see you're answering the phone, even if it's Lily's. I've been trying to get in touch with you all afternoon." The volume was so high on Lily's phone that Lily could hear her sister-in-law's voice.

"I accidentally put it on silent," Ian lied.

"Well, you shouldn't do that. What happens if Lily has an emergency at home? Alone with a baby and toddler?"

"Fortunately, they survived my absence." Ian flashed Lily a smile.

"Where were you?"

"Out running errands. What's up?"

"I was calling Lily to see if Walt and Danielle got home yet."

Ian glanced at the front window but didn't bother standing up to get a closer look. "It didn't look like anyone was there when I drove up. Why?"

"I want to talk to Adam and see if he'll agree to an interview."

"You asked if Walt and Danielle are home. But I don't think he's there either. I just got home, and Lily mentioned talking to Danielle, and she said something about Adam and Mel going somewhere with Chris and Heather."

"Where?"

"I don't know. But I think you should at least give it another day before you bombard Adam with this."

"I am not bombarding anyone."

"IS MARIE HELPING DANIELLE?" Brian asked Walt after he and the chief picked him up on their way over to Mark's rental house.

"No, she's alone." Walt sat in the back seat and fastened his seatbelt before Brian pulled the police car out into the street.

"Joanne's not working today?" the chief asked.

"No. Since the BnB isn't open, her schedule is pretty flexible since we don't need her as much. This week she took off Monday, Tuesday, and Wednesday. So she'll be back on Thursday."

Brian sat in the driver's seat, his gaze staring out the front windshield as he drove the police car down the street toward Mark's rental. "You know, it was her neighborhood where Mark and his brother dropped Shawn's car."

Walt looked out the side window, watching the houses pass by. "I wondered about that."

"She wasn't home," Brian said.

"I seem to remember Joanne mentioned she was going into Portland yesterday to see some friends," Walt said.

A few minutes later they pulled up at Mark's rental. Bill was already there, sitting in his truck parked in the driveway. When Bill noticed the police car pull up and park along the sidewalk, he got out of the truck.

"Surprised to see you here," Bill told Walt when Walt and the others reached the driveway.

"I asked the chief if I could tag along. Promised to stay out of their way. It's a little research for something I'm writing."

Bill nodded. "Cool. How's Adam doing? I understand he and Mel are staying at Marlow House."

"I suppose as good as expected, considering what he went through yesterday." *And what he learned today*, Walt silently added.

Bill quickly exchanged greetings with MacDonald and Brian before starting for the front door, the three men trailing behind him. Bill reached the front door first, unlocked it, and then turned to the others. "Chief, just lock it when you're done. I'm assuming someone from Mark's family will come to get his stuff." Bill pushed open the door, yet didn't enter the house. He remained standing on the front porch and handed the chief the set of keys he used to unlock the door.

The chief accepted the keys. "Thanks, Bill. Until I tell Adam differently, I don't want anyone going into the house. But if you have to, contact me or Brian first. As for who will claim Mark's belongings, at this point I have no idea. His emergency contact was his brother. If someone suddenly shows up, claiming to be a relative, have them contact me, and don't let them in the house."

"Gotcha, Chief." Bill nodded.

The chief peeked through the doorway, which opened into the living room instead of a formal entry. He noticed the artwork decorating the walls and furniture. He looked back at Bill. "Did the house come furnished?"

Bill shook his head. "Just the beds in the guestrooms, nothing else. Mark had us remove the bed in the main bedroom, he had his own, and like I mentioned, his brother and that other guy showed up with a U-Haul, with all his furniture."

"And the artwork on the wall? Those are all Mark's?" the chief asked.

Bill looked into the house and then back to the chief. "They don't belong to the house. It didn't come furnished or decorated aside from the beds. But I'll get out of your way. Give me a call if you need anything else."

FIVE MINUTES LATER, Walt and the chief stood in the living room of Mark's rental, glancing around, while Brian took off to check out the rest of the house.

"Why were you so interested in the artwork?" Walt asked while walking over to take a closer look at what hung over the fireplace. It was a framed lithograph protected by glass. The print was of a painting, a quaint tackle store. Parked in front of the store was a Woody Wagon, and in front of that stood a man and a young boy proudly holding up a fish. In the background was a lake, several canoes pulled up on its shore, and a mountain.

"I had wondered if, whatever Mark and his brother were trying to do, did he plan to stick around afterwards? I think I have my answer. Why bother going to so much trouble decorating your rental if you weren't planning to stay for a while?" The chief walked over to Walt and looked up at the framed picture. "That's a Wysocki."

Walt glanced over to the chief and smiled. "You recognized the artist?"

Edward grinned. "Yes. Charles Wysocki. And by the looks of that, it's a signed lithograph."

"I didn't realize you were an art aficionado," Walt teased.

The chief chuckled. "I'm not. I can just recognize a Wysocki. He was one of Cindy's favorite artists. One year for Christmas I splurged and bought her a signed lithograph of one of his paintings, *'Twas the Twilight Before Christmas.* I'd forgotten about it." The chief continued to stare at the artwork.

"What happened to it?"

The chief shrugged. "It's in our attic."

"Why in the attic?"

"We hung it up every Christmas. After her last Christmas, I was taking it down to take back to the attic, and she suggested we just leave it up. But, well, I thought it was silly to hang a Christmas picture up year-round. After she died, well…"

"You never hung it up again?"

Edward continued to stare at the picture as he said, "It was just too painful."

Before Walt could respond, Brian stepped out from the hallway and announced, "It looks like both Mark and Shawn were staying here."

Walt and the chief turned to Brian. But Brian was not alone. A man walked into the living room with him, and it was obvious to Walt why neither Brian nor the chief seemed to notice the man.

SEVENTEEN

"Shawn?" Even if Walt had not seen Shawn's photograph, he knew who the ghost was, considering the bloody stain on the center of Shawn's T-shirt. MacDonald and Brian froze, looked at Walt, and then turned to look at the corner of the living room where Walt focused his attention. They silently listened.

Shawn stared at Walt. "You can see me?"

"Yes, I can. Please don't leave. I can help you."

Shawn glanced nervously at the chief and then at Brian, both obviously police officers considering the uniforms they wore. Shawn nodded to the two men. "Can they see me too?"

Walt shook his head. "No. Only I can. I'm a medium."

Shawn looked from Brian to the chief, back to Walt. "They act like they can see me. Those women could see me."

Walt nodded. "Yes, Heather and Danielle. They're like me, mediums. They told me they saw you. That's why I'm here. I was hoping you'd be here so we could help you."

Shawn laughed bitterly. "Help me? I'm dead. How can you help me?" He stopped laughing and then looked back at Brian and the chief. Glaring, he said, "If they can't see me, why do they keep looking at me like that? It's creepy."

Walt suppressed a smile and said, "Brian, Edward, please leave the living room so I can talk to Shawn alone. You're making him uncomfortable."

Brian and Edward started to comply, but Walt quickly stopped them. "Wait." He looked at Shawn and motioned to the left. "Move a few feet over there. You don't want them walking through you. It's not a pleasant feeling."

A few minutes later, Walt and Shawn stood alone in the living room. Shawn frowned at Walt. "They know you can see me?"

"Yes. But we don't have time to explain all that now."

"You said you wanted to help me. Can you bring me back to life?"

Walt shook his head. "No, I'm afraid I can't do that."

Shawn dug his hands deep into the pockets of his hoodie and began pacing the room. "Then how do you expect to help me? I'm dead. That's about as bad as it can get."

"Oh, it can get much worse," Walt said under his breath.

Shawn frowned at Walt. "What is that supposed to mean?"

"You need to tell us why you broke into Adam Nichols's house."

"Why, did Mark and Peter find it? You trying to find them to get it back?"

"Is that why you're here, waiting for them?"

Shawn stopped pacing, twirled around, and faced Walt, his hands still buried in the pockets of his hoodie. "You're damn right. I've been waiting here for them to get back. I'm dead, I might as well haunt those two jerks. Figure there's some way to make my presence known. I'll make them pay. Even if it means finding some way to drive them insane."

"They aren't coming back here."

Shawn arched his brows and curled his lips into a smile. "They got their butts arrested?"

Walt shook his head. "No. They're dead, too."

Shawn's eyes widened. Absently he removed his hands from his pockets and stumbled to a nearby chair and sat down. He looked up at Walt. "What happened?"

"They went back to the Nichols house. Apparently, to get whatever you were there for the first time. But it seems Mark had another idea. He was going to shoot his brother, then claim his brother forced him to go to the house, pretend he wasn't involved with whatever it was you were doing—but then his brother turned around. From what I understand, there was a scuffle, and they ended up shooting each other."

Shawn let out a snort. "Serves them right. So where are they now? Why aren't they here?"

"Before I go into that, I need you to tell me what you were looking for at the Nichols house. Why were you there in the first place?"

Shawn stared at Walt for a moment and then shook his head. "No one needed to get hurt. This was supposed to be so freaking easy. In and out, no one would even know we had been there. Mark knew the doorbell cam was the only security camera on the property. All we needed to do was avoid that camera. With all the trees on either side of the property, we weren't worried about the neighbors. All we had to do was pick the side door's lock. But then he just showed up."

"How did you know there was only one camera?"

Shawn chuckled. "The minute Mark accepted the job, he knew he had to get cozy with Nichols. That was fairly easy, since he has a rental business and Mark needed a rental. Mark asked him if it was okay if he installed security cameras—it's not like Mark actually wanted to install them, but he wanted to start a conversation about them. Everyone has a camera these days. And that was one thing we worried about. Being caught on camera. Obviously, there was more we should have worried about."

"Adam told you he only has one camera?"

Shawn shrugged. "I have to admit that part of the plan went super smoothly. Mark didn't even need to ask Nichols what type he had, like he had intended to do. When Mark asked permission to install them, Nichols just volunteered the information. He told Mark he'd installed a doorbell cam on his own house but didn't bother putting cameras on the rest of the property because it was a safe neighborhood. Told Mark the house he was renting was in a safe neighborhood too, and a doorbell cam should be enough." Shawn stood abruptly and started pacing again. "I can't believe we're all dead. It wasn't supposed to go this way."

"Tell me, what were you looking for at Adam's house?"

Shawn stopped and stared at Walt. "I was a fool to tell Peter. I shouldn't have told anyone."

"What did you tell Peter?"

Shawn didn't answer Walt's question; instead, he said, "Peter said it was a sign, the fact his brother had mentioned an opening at the Frederickport Police Department. If he applied for the job and got it, the whole thing would be a piece of cake. Not saying we wouldn't have tried even if Mark hadn't gotten the job. But Peter kept saying it was a sign. Some sign. Well, no one will find it now, because everyone who knew it was there is dead." Shawn vanished.

WALT STOOD with Brian and MacDonald in the kitchen of the rental, telling the two what Shawn's spirit had told him.

"There is obviously something in Adam and Mel's house they were looking for, but what?" Brian said.

WHEN CHRIS and Heather brought Melony and Adam back to Marlow House, they found Danielle in the living room, sitting on the floor atop the quilt with the twins. The babies wore matching Christmas-themed footie sleepers. Addison sat on Danielle's lap while Jack lay next to her, his feet kicking and hands waving as he giggled up to his mother, who played a game of peek-a-boo with him and his sister.

After exchanging greetings, Heather joined Danielle on the quilt while Melony and Adam sat on the sofa, and Chris sat across from them in one of the recliners.

"How was lunch? Where did you go?" Danielle asked.

"Pearl Cove," Heather said.

"Ooh, fancy." Danielle glanced over to Melony and Adam, who sat quietly on the sofa while Chris apologized for not offering to bring her something back.

"That's okay. Hey, Adam, Mel, you guys doing alright?" Danielle asked.

"Just trying to wrap our heads around all this," Melony said.

Adam stood up and walked to Danielle. He sat down on the floor next to the quilt and said, "I want to ask you something." In the background, Chris said something to Melony and then leaned forward, now talking to her, while Adam spoke to Danielle, and Heather sat quietly, listening to what Adam wanted to ask.

Danielle studied Adam's expression, which now looked more curious than confused. "Sure. What?"

"Remember today when you told me the pipe that attacked Melony was moved by the energy of a ghost? Just like Grandma's energy saved me yesterday."

Danielle nodded. "Yes."

"And you said it was a ghost who used his energy to throw that croquet set at Bill and me."

"Umm, yes."

"Do you know whose ghost that was? The one who threw the croquet set at us in the attic."

Danielle stared at Adam for a moment before answering. Finally, she said, "Yes. It was the ghost of Walt Marlow. The grandson of Frederick Marlow, who built Marlow House."

Adam nodded, as if he already knew the answer. "But his ghost isn't here anymore, is it?"

"Why do you say that?"

"Is it?"

Danielle smiled at Adam. "No, the ghost of Walt Marlow is no longer haunting Marlow House."

"When did you first see him?"

"The first day I moved in."

"He was the one turning the television off and on upstairs, wasn't he?"

Danielle grinned. "Yes. While not all ghosts learn to harness their energy like your grandma, they can usually mess with the electricity. Make a lightbulb explode, turn off the television, computer…"

"Computer?" Adam interrupted, his eyes wide.

Danielle frowned at Adam. "Yeah…What is it?"

"Could a ghost mess with a computer search? Disconnect the internet?" Adam's voice practically squeaked.

"Sure. Why?"

Adam groaned and stood up. He walked back to the sofa and flopped down next to Melony, practically throwing his head back on the sofa cushion as he stared up at the ceiling. He remembered how he had stopped visiting adult websites before he got married. But he hadn't stopped because he was getting married—he stopped because adult searches started getting weird, resulting in internet interruptions and bizarre search results. Now he understood why. It had been Grandma.

EIGHTEEN

Chris helped Danielle take Addison and Jack upstairs to their bedroom while Heather stayed downstairs with Melony and Adam. Each holding a baby, they made their way slowly up the staircase, side by side, with Danielle clutching a handrail with her right hand, Chris clutching a handrail with his left.

"You're a heavy little dude," Chris told Jack and then asked Danielle, "How do you do this all day?"

"It's not like I'm constantly going up and down the stairs carrying them, and it's easier when Walt or Marie are here."

Chris chuckled. "Yeah, much easier."

"But these two are getting cranky, and I don't think they're going to take a nap in the living room with everyone here."

They reached the second-floor landing and headed for the nursery.

"Are your brother and his girlfriend still coming for Christmas?" Danielle shifted Addison in her arms.

"I was going to talk to you about that. But then all this happened with Adam."

"Oh no, they aren't coming?"

"He's coming; she's not. They broke up. Not sure what's with the men in my family. Destined to remain single."

They walked into the nursery, and Chris set Jack on the floor with his toys while Danielle proceeded to change Addison's diaper on the changing table. Jack immediately picked up a stuffed animal off the floor. "Heather tells me you haven't been going to Portland as much as you were."

"I was in Portland yesterday, remember?" Chris took a seat on one of the rocking chairs next to where Jack played.

"I wasn't talking about your business trips. I was talking about your social life." Danielle lifted Addison from the changing table, set her in the crib, and handed her a stuffed animal before kissing her nose.

"I need to make Heather sign an NDA," Chris grumbled.

Danielle chuckled and picked up Jack, who then accidentally dropped the small stuffy he had been holding; it fell to the floor. Jack squirmed and reached for his fallen toy. Still holding onto her son, Danielle scooped up the stuffed animal, handed it to Jack, and then laid him on the changing table while he clutched the soft toy in his small hands. "I don't think you can make Heather do anything."

"True." Chris let out a sigh. "I have no right to complain. But I bet Adam would be shocked to discover I envy him."

Danielle paused mid-diapering and glanced briefly over at Chris. "You envy Adam? Yeah, that would shock him, for certain."

"You know why. He has a great partner in Mel. I also envy Walt; he has you. And I envy Ian, Lily. Damn, I even envy Brian because he has Heather. I'd like to find what you all have."

Danielle didn't bother telling Chris he was a great guy, that any woman would be thrilled to have him. He already knew that. The problem, Danielle understood he wanted a relationship with a woman who wanted him not just because he had a pretty face and a prettier bank account.

Addison was no longer lying passively in her crib, prepared to nap, but stood on the mattress, jumping up and down while holding onto the side of the crib.

"Chris, can you grab Addison?"

Five minutes later, Chris and Danielle each sat in a rocking chair while holding a baby. Their conversation lowered to a whisper as they rocked in unison, the babes on their laps yawning while eyes fluttered closed.

"I was sort of hoping Christopher might come for Christmas," Chris whispered while looking down into Addison's face, her eyes closed and lashes gently fluttering against her pink cheeks as she breathed steadily.

"How is he doing?"

"He sounded great the last time I spoke to him. Rosalyn has him in therapy, and she told me he loves his school and has lots of friends. His school is putting on a Christmas play, and he's excited about that. They have a lot going on during the holidays. I'm happy for him."

"I imagine his grandmother wants to stay home for Christmas so they can start their own traditions."

"I totally get it." Chris looked over at Danielle, who smiled down at the babe in her arms. He studied her a moment before saying, "I appreciate you and Walt including Noah and me at Christmas."

"Of course. You guys are family."

DOWNSTAIRS, Ian had just arrived and joined the others in the living room. "How are you two doing?" Ian asked Melony and Adam as he took a seat on one of the chairs facing the couple.

"I think I'm probably doing better than Adam here." Melony reached over and gave Adam a pat on his knee. He flashed her a dull smile and said nothing. "Of course, I wasn't tied up and facing the muzzle of a gun. But the truth is, it's not like I didn't already believe in...well...woo-woo stuff. And to be honest, in some ways what I learned has made me feel a lot better."

"Why do you say that?" Heather asked. She sat in the chair next to Ian.

"Because it was pretty terrifying when a freaking pipe tried to bash my head in. Back then, Danielle tried to convince me I wasn't really in danger. I just figured she was trying to make me feel better. It's unsettling to think an inanimate object can come to life and attack you—like Adam experienced in the attic." Melony glanced briefly at the ceiling before continuing, "But somehow knowing where the energy really came from—and how the rules of the Universe work—it's kind of comforting."

Adam glanced around. "Is my grandma here?"

Ian shook his head. "No. She's over at my house, helping Lily. Mostly keeping Connor entertained."

"Is it weird, having her there when you can't see her?" Adam asked.

Ian chuckled. "I suppose it was at first. Connor adores your grandma."

"I once heard Grandma wanted more kids. But there was some reason she couldn't have any more. When I was little, I remember when she'd babysit me and my brother, she didn't just sit us in front of a TV or tell us to go into the other room and play, like Mom did. She always played with us. At her house, she had a trunk with old clothes and costumes, and we'd play dress-up. I remember there was a cool pirate costume in that trunk. At our house, we'd set up all my Fisher-Price people like they were having a parade."

Ian laughed. "She does that with Connor."

"When I babysit with Marie, she can be pretty bossy," Heather noted.

"What do you mean bossy?" Melony asked.

"I suppose bossy in a good way. Marie is super careful with the little ones. When Joanne first watched the twins, Marie stuck around to make sure she was doing it right."

Melony laughed. "That sounds like the Marie I remember."

Ian turned his attention to Adam. "The reason I came over, I wanted to talk to you about my sister. Kelly has been trying to see you. She wants to interview you on her podcast, and I think she's hoping to get to you before one of the regular news outlets does. I'm surprised no one has contacted you yet."

"I called Leslie when we were at lunch," Adam said. "I guess there have been a few calls down at the office, people wanting to interview me. Frankly, I don't want to. How am I going to keep Danielle's version straight during multiple interviews?"

"I think you should let Kelly interview you," Melony blurted, "and tell her it's an exclusive. That way, you only have to do it once. If someone else asks for an interview, tell them you gave an exclusive to your friend, so you can't."

"That might not be a bad idea," Ian agreed.

WALT, MacDonald, and Brian arrived at Marlow House a few minutes after Ian left for home. Before coming to Marlow House, they had first stopped by MacDonald's to pick up his car and his sons, who were home from school. On the way to Marlow House, the chief explained to Eddy and Evan what they had told Melony and Adam earlier that day.

Just as they arrived, Chris and Danielle were walking down the stairs after getting the babies down for a nap. Once in the living room, Eddy Junior walked over to Melony and Adam, who remained sitting on the sofa, and said, "Welcome to the club!"

Adam raised his brow. "Club?"

Evan joined his brother and stood next to him, facing Melony and Adam. Evan rolled his eyes and said, "Dad told us what happened. And how they told you about the ghosts and stuff."

Melony looked at Evan, who looked so much like his mother— her best friend. "Your dad also told us you're a medium."

Evan nodded.

"Does that mean you've seen…" Melony didn't finish her sentence, as she thought better of it. But Evan understood what she wanted to ask and answered the question anyway.

"You were wondering if I can see Mom. But it doesn't really work that way. When a spirit moves on, well, a medium like me, we can't really communicate with them, at least not like we do with Marie and Eva."

"You've seen my grandma? And Eva Thorndike?"

Evan flashed Adam a grin. "Yeah. Your grandma's the GOAT." Evan turned back to Melony. "While I can't see Mom like I do Marie, she's visited me in dream hops."

"What's a dream hop?" Melony asked.

"It's when a spirit—either one on this side or one who has moved on—visits you in your dream. Two Christmases ago, we spent Christmas with Dad, Eddy, me and Mom. It was just as if she were really here. It was the best Christmas ever."

"It felt real, yet the next morning I woke up and thought it had all been a dream. But after I learned about Evan, I realized it really happened. It was pretty dope. And like Evan said, the best Christmas. One I'll always remember," Eddy added.

As if he knew what they were about to ask next, Evan said, "The thing is, I wish Mom could be with us every Christmas. But she can't."

"Why not?" Adam asked.

Evan shrugged. "It just doesn't work that way."

Edward placed a hand on Evan's shoulder and said, "I'm sure Mel and Adam will have more questions for you, but right now, we need to ask Adam and Mel some questions."

EVAN AND EDDY retreated to the parlor to watch television, Hunny tagging along behind them, while the chief filled the others in on what they had found at Mark's rental.

"So you have no idea what they were looking for?" Melony asked.

"No. We couldn't find anything at the house that gave us any clues. We have their phones, and hopefully we'll find some text messages in there. But we have to assume someone hid something in your house, and they want it. My question, who lived in the house before you bought it?"

"There was only one other owner before me. But after he moved out, he started renting it. He had several full-time renters, but after the last one moved out, he put it in my rental program. It's been rented hundreds of times before Mel and I bought it."

"And any of them could have hidden it," MacDonald muttered. "Whatever it is."

NINETEEN

Melony walked into the kitchen at Marlow House on Wednesday morning and stopped abruptly when she saw the twins sitting in their highchairs, watching a spoon that hovered in midair—over a bowl, which also hovered in midair—while Danielle stood at the pantry, her back to her and the twins.

"Uhh, what the…" Melony stammered out.

Danielle turned from the pantry, holding a box of cereal. She glanced at what had caught Melony's attention and then looked back at Melony. "Marie's here." Danielle closed the door to the pantry and walked to the counter, where an empty bowl sat next to a carton of milk. "She offered to feed the twins."

Melony gasped when the floating spoon, now empty, did what looked like a wave in her direction.

Danielle noticed the spoon wave and set the box of cereal on the counter and turned around, facing the twins. She folded her arms across her chest and let out a sigh before saying, "That's Marie's way of greeting. Part of me thinks she shouldn't use the same spoon for both of them, but considering how much spit they share anyway."

"That sounds crude, dear," Marie scolded as she scooped up another spoonful of oatmeal.

"Oh, my…I guess, good morning, Marie?" Melony shook her head and stumbled toward the coffeepot on the end of the counter.

"Good morning, Melony. You look lovely, dear. That's a beautiful sweater. Burnt orange suits you."

"Marie just returned your good morning and complimented your outfit. She likes that color on you." Danielle turned to the counter and picked up the box of cereal. "You hungry?"

Melony had just grabbed a clean coffee mug and started to fill it. "Not really, and I'm starting to think I might need something stronger than coffee this morning to deal with this new reality."

Danielle giggled. "You mean like Walt's brandy?"

Filled coffee mug now in hand, Melony grinned. "No, maybe a cinnamon roll?"

Danielle laughed. "I can help you there. You'll find one in the sack next to the coffeepot. But you want me to make you eggs or something?"

Melony set the mug back on the counter and reached for the paper bag. "Thanks, Danielle. I'm not really that hungry. Where's Walt?"

Danielle had just filled a bowl with cereal and added the milk. She returned the carton of milk to the refrigerator, grabbed a spoon from a drawer, and carried it and the bowl of cereal to the table. "He's in the basement, getting the rest of the Christmas decorations. Is Adam up?"

"Yes, he's getting dressed for his interview with Kelly." The night before Adam had called Kelly and told her he was willing to do an exclusive interview with her, and explained that because of everything that happened, he didn't intend to do more interviews, so he would only be answering questions this one time for the media.

"You think Adam is going to want any breakfast before he goes over?" Danielle remembered the interview was scheduled for 10 a.m. at Kelly's home office studio.

"He'll probably just want a cinnamon roll and coffee. And I want to thank you for letting us stay here. Eddy says he thinks we should be able to go home Friday afternoon. He scheduled the cleaning for the carpet tomorrow. That was really sweet of him. I assume our insurance will pay for it, but if they don't, I'm just grateful Adam didn't get killed." Melony glanced at where she imagined Marie was. "Thank you."

"You are most welcome, dear," Marie responded, adding a spoon wave, since Melony wouldn't be able to hear her words.

Before taking a bite of cereal, Danielle asked, "You mentioned at breakfast on Monday that you were planning to take the rest of the month off after you came back from San Francisco. Is that still the plan?"

Melony set her mug of coffee on the table and picked up her cinnamon roll. "Yes. In fact, Adam is talking to Leslie this morning to see if she might be willing to take over the office for the rest of the month. A few weeks back she told him if he and I wanted to go anywhere in December, she'd be more than happy to pick up some extra hours. I guess her plans for Christmas fell through, so she's staying home and spending it with her aunt and uncle who live here."

"If he takes off, you planning to go somewhere?"

"No. Umm…" Melony looked up at Danielle from her cinnamon roll. "One reason he wants to take time off, he feels he needs to process all that happened, and he isn't in the right head-space to go back to work right now."

"And the other reason?"

"It's been five years since he spent Christmas with his grand-mother, and he just wants to enjoy it this year."

The spoon paused in midair.

ACROSS TOWN, Chief MacDonald sat in his office, talking to Joe Morelli.

"How are you feeling?" MacDonald asked, looking across his desk at Joe, who sat in a chair facing him.

"No headache, and the doctor said I can go back to work

today." Joe lightly touched the top of his head. "It's still a little sore up there if I touch it."

"Then don't touch it."

Joe laughed and moved his right hand back down to his side, resting it on the chair's arm. "Yeah, that's what Kelly told me."

"So how is Kelly? Is she ready for her exclusive?"

"She's excited. I told her to make sure it was okay with you."

"And she did. It was Mel's idea for Adam to give the interview to Kelly. Between you and me, I think Mel is worried about Adam, considering what he went through."

"I can understand that. While I still don't remember getting in the squad car with Mark and our prisoners, or how we ended up on that street, or how I got hit, I do remember being in the house before we left, and how Adam was totally out of it."

They discussed Adam for a few more minutes before Joe said, "Brian told me about going over to Mark's place. And I've been thinking about it."

"What about it?"

"When I heard Mark and his brother killed each other at Adam's, for a moment I wondered if maybe Mark wasn't part of it. Can you imagine walking in and finding your brother tied up, accused of trying to kill someone? Would you immediately expose his identity, or would you switch to protective-brother mode and try to figure out some way out of it? But then I remembered how Mark reacted when we got the call."

"To go to Adam's house?"

Joe nodded. "Yeah. Mark's expression reminded me of someone who had never been called to a live crime scene before. For a moment, he looked terrified."

"I suspect Mark looked afraid because he knew exactly who he'd find at Adam's house."

They talked for about ten more minutes before Joe said goodbye and left to start work. The chief was alone in his office for about fifteen minutes, making phone calls, when he got an unexpected visitor. It was Geoffrey Drewnowski, who had initially given Mark a referral for the job.

After Geoffrey took a seat across from the chief, the office door closed. "I can't believe what I've been hearing on the news. Mark and his brother are really dead?"

The chief leaned back in his seat. "I'm afraid so."

"And Peter tried to kill someone? At the house they broke into?"

MacDonald nodded. "Yes. And we believe Mark was in on the plan."

"I can't wrap my head around that. I've known Mark for years. He was a hardworking, straight-shooting guy. I would never have recommended him for the job—or told him about the opening—if I had questioned his character. Now his brother, that's another story."

"I don't blame you, Geoffrey. I've been in situations where someone I trusted—really trusted—turned out not to be the person I thought they were. Can you tell me what you remember about Mark and his brother?"

Geoffrey gave a nod and leaned back in his chair. "Umm, sure. I lived next door to them when they were growing up. They were raised by their mom. Their dad took off when they were in grade school. He was never in their lives. Their mom was a hard worker; Mark used to try to help her by looking after his brother. But Peter, he used to get in trouble a lot. Their mom died about a month after Peter graduated from high school. Mark was living in an apartment, and he let Peter move in."

"And you kept in touch with them all these years?"

"Not really. But I'd run into Mark around town. Back when he applied for a job at the local police station, he asked me for a referral because of my connections. From what I heard, he seemed to be doing a good job. But a while back I ran into Mark at the hardware store, asked how things were going, and he made some crack about his life would be great if he could just get his little brother to move out and get his own place. I told him if Peter wouldn't move, perhaps he should, and then I told him there were openings in Frederickport. While it was true there were openings, I was teasing, and Mark understood. He laughed and didn't seem interested, but then after Veterans Day, he contacted me and asked if I knew if there was still an opening."

KELLY'S podcast studio consisted of lighting and a green screen backdrop set up in one of their spare bedrooms. Two chairs sat side by side, one for Kelly and one for her guest. The green screen allowed her to change her backdrops using scenic images and images promoting each episode's sponsor. Kelly's online career had begun with her blog and later moved into audio and then video podcasts.

Kelly sat in her chair, with Adam sitting quietly next to her. She had just finished recapping the harrowing events on Monday that had already been discussed in the local newspaper and on the radio, and then asked, "I know what our viewers are curious to hear; how did you manage to escape two intruders, one who was armed? And you even tied them up before calling the police."

Adam smiled weakly while staring at the camera. He took a deep breath. "One had tied me up while the other held a gun on me. After I was tied up, the guy holding the gun said something about how they had just wasted a rope because he intended to kill me anyway."

"Oh my!" Kelly gasped.

"The guy who tied me up, he started arguing with him. I doubt he wanted to face a murder charge. While they were arguing, not paying attention to me, I tried pulling on the ropes. Turns out the guy who tied me up didn't do a terrific job. While they were arguing about killing me, fate intervened. My guardian angel, I guess."

"Your guardian angel?"

Adam shrugged. "It's the only thing that makes sense. What are the chances the guy drops his gun at the same time my ropes come undone, and I manage to grab the gun because it slides across the floor toward me? That had to be divine intervention."

"And how did you tie them up by yourself? I can't imagine how you could hold the gun on them and at the same time tie them up."

Adam smiled at Kelly. "To be honest, everything's pretty much a blur after they dropped the gun. Everything happened so fast. Maybe it was my adrenaline pumping, me believing I was about to die seconds earlier. It's almost like the rope just tied them up without my help. The next thing I remember, I'm sitting in the dining room, and Heather slaps the crap out of me."

"Uhh…Heather Donovan?"

Adam nodded. "Yeah. In Heather's defense, I was in shock and not saying anything. She was just trying to snap me out of it." Adam rubbed his cheek as if it still hurt. "But that girl, she has a mean slap."

TWENTY

"Morning," Melony and Adam greeted when they walked into Marlow House's kitchen on Thursday. They found Joanne Johnson making waffles. Nearby, the twins sat in their high-chairs, eating breakfast. Instead of being spoon-fed oatmeal as they had been the previous day, they each chewed on a piece of blueberry waffle sans the syrup. Walt and Danielle sat at the kitchen table with five place settings, drinking coffee, and reading the daily news. Danielle read hers from her iPhone while Walt read his from the morning newspaper. They both looked up and greeted their houseguests before looking back down to finish what they had been reading.

"I'm making blueberry waffles and bacon, hope you two are hungry," Joanne greeted.

"Sounds delicious." Melony walked to the counter and poured two cups of coffee while Adam sat down at the table with Walt and Danielle.

"It does sound good," Adam agreed. Silently, Walt handed one section of the newspaper to Adam. Adam accepted the offering and folded the paper in half to make it easier to hold and then proceeded to read.

"Are we still making chocolate chip cookies today?" Melony asked Danielle.

"If you want to."

Adam laughed. "Mel, have you ever made chocolate chip cookies before?"

"I think. Maybe." Mel shrugged. "But Danielle says it will help put us in the Christmas spirit, and considering this past week, I'll happily give it a try."

Joanne glanced at Adam. "I watched Kelly's podcast yesterday afternoon. You must have been terrified."

Adam glanced up from the newspaper. "Yeah, not something I want to go through again." Adam didn't mention his grandmother's role in his escape, as both he and Mel had already been told Joanne knew nothing about the mediums.

"Last night I played bunko, and everyone was talking about the podcast," Joanne said.

Danielle glanced up from her iPhone. "And the divine intervention?"

Melony stifled a grin. Joanne, her back to the table as she worked at the counter, said, "Yes. A good number of my friends agreed there had been a divine intervention. One even suggested Adam has a guardian angel."

Danielle flashed Melony a smile. "Really?"

Turning toward the table, now holding a plate with a stack of waffles and a platter of bacon, Joanne told Adam, "One even suggested your grandma Marie was your guardian angel."

Adam grinned. "I wouldn't be surprised."

Joanne carried the plates of food to the table and set them down. "I noticed all the Christmas decorations you put up since Thanksgiving. Danielle told me you two helped. It looks great." Joanne returned to the counter and retrieved the syrup and butter.

"It was fun. Adam and I need to get decorations for our house."

Walt folded his newspaper, stood, and tossed it on the nearby kitchen counter. Adam folded his newspaper and handed it to Walt, who placed it on the counter with his. Before sitting back down,

Walt pulled a chair from the kitchen corner to the table, making room for Joanne to join them.

Several minutes later, the five sat around the table, eating breakfast while the twins remained content in their highchairs, each squishing in their hands a fresh piece of waffle their mother had just handed them.

"Mel and Adam have agreed to join us for Christmas dinner," Danielle told Joanne. Adam and Mel had already been told Joanne was spending Christmas at Marlow House.

"The more the merrier." Joanne helped herself to a second piece of bacon.

"Are you going to bring anyone this year?" Walt asked Joanne. When discussing Christmas during Thanksgiving week, Danielle had reminded Joanne she was welcome to bring someone to Christmas dinner with her.

Setting her bacon on her plate, Joanne looked to Walt. "I've asked my neighbor. It's not the first time I've asked him. Unfortunately, I doubt he'll accept the invitation this time either. I hate that he's always alone at Christmas."

"Oh, I remember you've mentioned him. You invited him another year, and he didn't come," Danielle reminded her.

"He's pretty much a recluse." Joanne let out a sigh and took a bite of her bacon.

"He doesn't have family?" Danielle asked.

Joanne shook her head. "No. He never had kids, and he's never mentioned any extended family. He used to be married, and they attended my church. I was acquainted with his wife. She always seemed like the devoted spouse, but appearances can be deceiving."

"How so?" Danielle asked.

"She just packed up and took off with another man. She didn't even tell him it was over or say goodbye. Totally blindsided him. One minute he's married to the love of his life, and the next minute she's gone." Joanne picked up a napkin and wiped the bacon grease off her fingers. "After that, he stopped going to our church. I never ran into him around town, but then he moved next door. I took him over a plate of cookies after he moved in, as a welcome-to-the-neighborhood gift. At the time, I didn't realize we had met before, that he used to go to my church. We became friends after that." Joanne started to take a bite of waffle and paused a moment. She looked up at Melony and Adam and said, "He used to own your house."

"Oh, you're talking about Jason Aldridge?" Adam asked.

Joanne took a bite of waffle and nodded.

LATER THAT AFTERNOON, across town, Chief MacDonald received a surprise visitor, Stu Hoffman, the brother of Shawn Hoffman.

"I can't believe my brother is dead," Stu said as he sat in the chair facing the chief's desk. Rubbing his eyes with his right hand, Stu shook his head in disbelief. "How could this happen? I doubt Shawn has ever had so much as a parking ticket, much less gotten involved with something like this—a home invasion. He spent his life helping people."

"In your brother's defense, he was not on board with killing someone. I suspect that's what got him killed."

Stu looked up to the chief. "Why do you say that?"

"From what the man they were trying to rob told us."

Dropping his hand from his face, Stu leaned back in his chair and shook his head. "I never cared for Peter. You say that's who shot my brother?"

"We aren't certain. It could have been Peter's brother, Mark." Actually, the chief knew his brother's killer, but he couldn't tell Stu that because that information had come from Eva and Marie.

"I spoke to my parents this morning. They live in Montana. They're both in shock. I promised my mother I'd come here, talk to you, try to find out what Shawn had gotten himself into. It doesn't make sense to any of us."

"You said you didn't like Peter? Did you know him well? Did you know his brother, Mark?"

Stu shook his head. "I didn't know Peter well, but he was sort of obnoxious. I heard his brother was a cop but never met him. In fact, the last time I saw my brother, he was with Peter. It was Veterans Day. He had the day off, and I stopped by his apartment to drop something off. Peter was there; they had both been drinking. They kept talking like they had some inside joke."

MacDonald frowned. "Inside joke?"

MACDONALD HAD MORE visitors that day—Melony, Danielle, and Lily. They came bearing a large tin of homemade chocolate chip cookies. Today, Melony didn't look like a fashion model or a polished professional woman, but wore her blond hair pulled up into a high ponytail, while she wore denim leggings and a cashmere sweater. She reminded MacDonald of a college coed heading to a party.

Both Lily and Danielle wore oversized Christmas sweatshirts with their leggings and boots, and Danielle had fashioned Lily's hair into a French braid that day, matching her own.

"What are you three up to?" MacDonald asked when Danielle set the large Christmas tin on his desk. He had stood up briefly when they first arrived but had just returned to his seat behind the desk.

"Mel and I spent the afternoon making cookies," Danielle announced. "Lily came over and helped too."

The chief glanced over at Mel, who stood to the right of Danielle. He raised his brow. "You got Mel to bake cookies?"

Melony rolled her eyes. "Why do you sound like my husband?"

The chief laughed in response.

"Danielle told me it would put me in the Christmas spirit. But what I didn't tell her; I did it for the cookie dough. Yummy." Melony grinned and licked her lips.

"You're not supposed to eat raw cookie dough," the chief scolded. "A good way to get sick."

"Not if you use pasteurized eggs," Danielle corrected.

"Where did you get pasteurized eggs?" Edward asked.

"I pasteurized them myself using my sous vide machine," Danielle told him.

"Another one of Dani's new kitchen gadgets," Lily teased.

"Hey, you seemed to enjoy the raw cookie dough too," Danielle countered.

Lily shrugged. "True."

"How did you two get away from home? Is Adam helping Walt and Ian babysit?" MacDonald asked.

"When Ian and Walt do it, it is called parenting," Lily corrected.

"Adam help take care of babies?" Melony laughed at the notion. She then sat down in one of the chairs facing the desk. Lily and Danielle followed suit. "That would utterly terrify him."

"Actually, Joanne's working today, so she'll help Walt with the twins if he needs it. And Marie is over at Lily's, helping Ian," Danielle explained. "As for Adam, he's with his grandmother. He wanted to observe how Marie interacts with Connor."

"That will be interesting, considering he can't see Marie," Edward muttered.

Melony sat up straighter in the chair and looked at the chief. "We didn't just stop by to drop off cookies. I wanted to find out if Adam and I can go home tomorrow." She glanced briefly at Danielle and added, "Not that I haven't enjoyed staying at Marlow House, but we've run out of clean clothes."

Danielle nodded. "I understand."

"Yes, you can," Edward said. "In fact, I was just talking to them before you got here. They finished and sent me a picture. It looks good as new. But they had to repaint part of the wall in the hallway. You'll want to wait until tomorrow so it'll be completely dry."

"I don't want to ask what got on the wall and why they had to repaint it," Melony grumbled.

"I imagine you already know." The chief let out a sigh and said, "I also talked to someone else today, Shawn Hoffman's brother." The chief then told them about their conversation.

Danielle looked at Melony. "From what Eva and Marie overheard, there is definitely something of value hidden in your house. But the good news, from what Shawn's spirit said, it doesn't sound like anyone—at least from the living world—knows about it. From what's been released in the news, it's always been presented as a random break-in, not like they were looking for some hidden treasure. Which means you don't have to worry about someone else trying to break into your house again, looking for whatever they were trying to find."

Melony groaned. Her friends frowned at her, and Danielle asked, "What?"

Melony looked at Danielle. "Have you met my husband? When we go home tomorrow, he'll probably start pulling up our floorboards."

TWENTY-ONE

On Friday morning, Melony didn't have the chance to ask Danielle if she wanted her to remove their sheets and put them in the washing machine. By the time she and Adam finished packing their suitcases, Joanne had already stripped the bed in the downstairs bedroom and taken the sheets to the laundry room. Melony stood with her now-closed suitcase while Adam wrestled with his, trying to zip it up. It seemed his dirty clothes shoved into his suitcase took up more space than when clean and neatly folded. With her hand on the handle of her suitcase, Melony stared at the doorway Joanne had just walked through and sighed. "We really need a Joanne."

Finally getting his suitcase zipped, Adam looked up. "We already have someone who comes in once a week."

"But she doesn't do all the things Joanne does."

"And we don't have two babies," Adam reminded her.

"True."

DANIELLE HAD INSISTED Melony and Adam have breakfast before they go home. Afterwards, she drove them back to their house while Walt and Joanne stayed home with the twins. When they arrived, Police Chief MacDonald was there, waiting for them.

"We should walk through the house, make sure everything is okay," the chief told them.

They were still standing on the front porch several minutes later when Chris and Heather arrived, bringing with them an enormous Christmas gift basket filled with an assortment of gourmet goodies.

"Heather insisted you needed something Christmasy to brighten this place after what happened," Chris said as he handed Adam the basket in the entry hall.

"What I said is you needed something Christmasy to help cast off all the bad energy left behind," Heather corrected. "But that was before I watched the podcast and Adam told the world I slapped him." She looked at Melony. "The basket is yours now. You don't have to share it with Adam."

Melony flashed Heather a smile and said, "Thanks."

"Well, you did slap me," Adam reminded her as they all walked toward the dining room.

"And it's a good thing I did, or you'd still be sitting at your dining room table like a zombie," Heather countered.

After Adam set the basket on the dining room table, they walked to the hallway and looked around, trying to figure out what part of the wall had been repainted. All but MacDonald wondered where in the hallway the men had died. He didn't tell them.

Melony, Heather, and Danielle huddled together, chatting among themselves, while Chris and MacDonald talked, and Adam slipped away unnoticed, heading toward his bedroom.

A few minutes later, Melony asked, "Are they here?"

"They?" Danielle asked.

"The ghosts of the men who died here."

"No, they're gone," Chris said. "Sometimes, if a spirit has really messed up during their lifetime, the Universe…well…let's just say they grab them up fairly quickly. That's what Eva and Marie saw."

Danielle gave a shiver. "Yeah, I've witnessed that before. Not pleasant. Yet that doesn't happen to all of them. Stoddard Gussarov was pretty evil, but the Universe allowed him to stick around for a while and haunt me."

"True, but the Universe obviously had some lessons for Stoddard before he moved on," Chris reminded her.

"I'm so confused," Melony muttered.

MacDonald laughed and wrapped an arm around Melony's shoulder. "Mel, you have stepped into the twilight zone."

The sound of pounding interrupted the conversation, and they all glanced to where the sound came from—down the hallway toward the bedroom. Melony frowned and looked around at the people standing with her in the hallway. "Where did Adam go?"

"I suspect if we follow that pounding, we'll find Adam," Danielle said.

A minute later, the group huddled by the open doorway leading into the main bedroom. They looked into the room and watched Adam, now on his hands and knees, crawling along the wall, periodically knocking along the baseboard every few inches.

Melony walked into the room, her hands now on her hips as she looked down at her husband, her friends following her into the room. "Didn't I say something about him tearing off the baseboards?"

Adam glanced up at his wife as Danielle said, "Well, in fairness to Adam, he isn't tearing them off yet."

Adam stood up from the floor. "Those guys were obviously looking for something. And if they were willing to kill for it, it must be worth a lot of money."

Heather shrugged. "Not necessarily. There're people out there willing to kill for a pair of trendy tennis shoes."

"What are we all doing in the bedroom?" Marie asked when she appeared the next moment, only visible to the mediums.

"Marie's here," Heather announced and looked toward Marie and said, "And in answer to your question, your grandson is treasure hunting."

"Grandma's here?" Adam glanced around. The next moment, something gave his right ear a gentle tug. He froze for a moment and moved his right hand up to his ear, touched it, and smiled. "This is so weird," he muttered, still grinning.

"Eddy, don't you have any clue what they were looking for?" Melony asked.

MacDonald shook his head. "I'm sorry. The only thing we're certain about, Mark and his brother had no interest in Frederickport or what might be hidden in your house until Shawn told them something. Probably around Veterans Day."

"I have an idea," Heather interrupted. "Remember after they discovered the hidden tunnels at Marlow House, and how Eva and Marie checked to make sure there weren't more? Can't Marie do that now and find whatever is hidden?"

"What are you talking about?" Adam asked.

"A ghost can move through walls. So if Marie steps through that wall"—Heather pointed toward the wall separating the bedroom from the attached bathroom—"and there was a secret room tucked between your bathroom and bedroom, she would find it."

"I doubt our ability to walk through walls would help in this situation," Marie said.

"Why not?"

"Why not, what?" Melony asked.

"Marie said that her ability to walk through walls probably wouldn't help in this situation," Danielle explained. "And Heather asked her why."

"Let me check," Marie said before vanishing.

"Marie just left," Heather said.

"This is weird," Adam muttered.

Edward patted Adam on the shoulder. "I get it, buddy."

"What Marie meant, if something is hidden in the house, it's probably tucked away in some dark place. While a ghost can move through walls—or dark spaces—they can't see in the dark," Chris explained.

Heather nodded. "Oh, I see what you mean."

"I wish I did," Adam muttered under his breath.

"I was right," Marie announced when she reappeared back in the room. "I moved through the walls in the house and the ceiling, and there is nothing noticeable. No secret rooms or tunnels. Unfortunately, what might be behind floorboards or wallboards I can't see; it's too dark."

Heather repeated what Marie had said for the non-mediums.

"Chief, didn't you tell us his brother said Shawn and Peter kept acting like they had some inside secret when he saw him on Veterans Day?" Danielle asked.

Edward nodded. "Mark contacted Geoffrey about being interested in the job here after Veterans Day."

"It sounds to me, Shawn learned about this mystery treasure before Veterans Day. He also told Walt that everyone with knowledge of whatever is hidden is now dead," Danielle said. "Shawn worked at a care home with elderly residents. Did someone there— someone who recently died—tell Shawn about this treasure?"

"I've read about deathbed confessions. Perhaps a bank robber lived at the care home and told Shawn where he hid his ill-gotten gains," Heather suggested.

"Hmm…I have an idea. Ask Edward if he knows the name of the care home," Marie asked.

"Chief, what was the name of the care home Shawn worked at?" Heather asked.

After Edward said the name of the care home, Marie vanished.

"WHY DID you want me to come with you?" Eva asked when she and Marie arrived at the care facility in Oregon City. Marie had stopped by the cemetery, looking for Eva, after leaving her grandson's house.

"I didn't want to come alone. The last time I stayed in one of these places, I had a horrible experience."

"Murder normally is."

Together, Marie and Eva stood outside the facility, trying to decide where to go. One entrance to their right said assisted living, while another door to the left had a sign that said memory care unit.

Marie pointed at the door leading to assisted living. "Perhaps we should start there."

A few minutes later, Marie and Eva stood in what appeared to be the common area of the facility, with sofas and armchairs situated around a large-screen television hanging on one wall. An old John Wayne movie played on the television while about seven or eight residents sat on the furniture, watching the movie.

"I assume you're hoping we come across some lingering spirits," Eva said after glancing around.

"There were a few lingering at the place I was murdered," Marie said. "And perhaps they can tell us something that might help."

Together, Marie and Eva wandered the halls and rooms of the assisted-living section of the care home, saying hello to everyone, waiting for someone to respond. They had gone through about half of the rooms when a woman asked, in response to their hello, "You can see me?"

Several minutes later, Eva and Marie sat at one of the empty tables in the recreation room with the ghost of a woman named Mary.

"Oh yes, I remember Shawn. He came here after I died. I wish he had been one of the nurses when I lived here. Some of the people who work here have no patience and are too rough. Shawn, he always seemed attentive and kind with the residents, especially those who needed help bathing and dressing."

"Do you remember the last time you saw him?" Marie asked.

"Yes. He left after Roman died. I haven't seen him since."

"Roman?" Marie asked.

"Roman, he arrived after I died, too. Got my room. No one ever visited him. I always felt a little sad for him. No visitors. No one seemed to care. But Shawn, he always spent extra time with Roman. Shawn always did that with residents who didn't have visitors. Usually, he would just sit and watch TV with them or play cards. After Roman was put on hospice, Shawn spent even more time with him. I remember his last day. They talked a lot, Shawn holding his hand, Roman doing most of the talking."

"What did they talk about?" Eva asked.

Mary shrugged. "I never paid attention. I didn't stick around to listen in. But what happened after Roman died, that…well…frankly…scared the bejesus out of me." Mary shivered at the memory.

"What happened?" Marie asked.

"I wasn't in the room when Roman died. But I was by the nurses' station when Shawn called to tell them he had passed. When I went to his room, I found Roman standing next to Shawn, looking down at his own body, as if trying to figure out what had happened. I was about to say hello, like I always do. I like to greet them when they pass. Seems to make it more comfortable for them if someone from their family hasn't shown up yet. But before I could say anything, something happened that I had never seen before."

"What was that?" Marie asked.

"The ceiling literally opened up, exposing dark clouds in what should be the attic, and what looked like a small tornado dropped down from the clouds, and the next minute Roman was sucked up into the ceiling. For a moment, I heard an agonized scream and then…nothing. Silence. And the ceiling was back to normal, and no sign of Roman. Except for his body. It was still there, of course. In his bed. Dead."

TWENTY-TWO

Walt sat in the front passenger seat of the car with Chief MacDonald on Saturday morning while the two drove from Frederickport to Oregon City to visit the care home Marie and Eva had been at the day before. They hoped to find more information on Roman along with any other patients of Shawn's who might have had ties to Frederickport and, more expressly, to Adam and Melony's house.

MacDonald's sons, Evan and Eddy, had stayed at Marlow House with Danielle. Walt had offered to pay Eddy to finish hanging the Christmas lights around the fencing at Marlow House, with Evan and Marie's help. Eddy happily accepted and told Walt he didn't need to be paid. Hanging Christmas lights with the help of a ghost sounded dope to the teenage boy. Danielle had also baked a batch of sugar cookies and invited the boys to help her decorate them after they finished hanging the lights.

When they arrived at the care center, the chief checked in with Walt at the front desk and got permission to interview some of the staff and residents regarding Shawn. Once inside the assisted-living area, the chief stopped at the nurses' station to chat with the staff while Walt strolled through the public areas, such as the dining room, library, and TV room.

Unlike Marie and Eva, saying hello to a spirit and having them respond was not going to help Walt distinguish between a living person and a ghost, since both could see him, and both would likely return his greeting. Instead, he looked for other telltale signs, such as someone moving through a wall, furniture, or other people.

After about fifteen minutes of walking around the public area and not encountering what might be a ghost, he spied a coffee station with a sign that said *Help yourself*. Walt walked over to the station, considering pouring himself a cup of coffee, when he noticed a woman sitting alone on the other side of the room, a tissue clutched in her right hand. It looked as if she had been crying. He guessed she was in her sixties, and he assumed she wasn't a resident, but visiting someone.

On impulse, Walt filled a cup with coffee, grabbed a couple of creamers, a packet of sugar, and a napkin, and headed to the woman. She didn't notice him at first, not until he asked, "Would you like a cup of coffee?"

The woman looked up into Walt's blue eyes; hers were red-rimmed; she smiled weakly. "Actually, that sounds wonderful."

He handed her the coffee and set the cream, sugar, and napkin on the table next to her. "This is if you want anything in your coffee. Do you mind if I sit down?"

She smiled. "Please do. Thank you for the coffee."

Walt sat down in the chair next to her, with the end table holding the condiments and napkin between them.

"My name's Walt."

She held the cup of coffee with one hand while her other hand continued to clutch the tissue. "I'm Melissa. Nice to meet you, Walt."

"I assume you're visiting someone here?"

"Yes, my mom. She's been here for about six months. But she's on hospice now." Melissa took a sip of coffee.

"I'm sorry."

Melissa shrugged. "This probably sounds horrible, but I wish she would move on. I'm glad she's no longer in pain, but all the drugs they have her on to manage the pain…it's like she's not there anymore."

"It's not horrible wanting her to move on to a better place where her pain is removed and her mind has clarity again."

Melissa looked up at Walt and smiled. "Are you confident there's a better place after this? Something more?"

"Yes." Walt chose not to add the caveat that someone who had been an evil person might not find the place after this better.

Melissa grinned, set her cup on the table, and wiped away the last of her tears. "So who are you visiting?"

"No one. I'm here with my friend Police Chief MacDonald from Frederickport. He has some business here. I kept him company on the drive."

"Frederickport? Really? My mom and dad lived in Frederickport for years."

Walt perked up. "They did? Where?"

"Actually, Mom still owns the house. Not long after Dad died, Mom got sick and moved in with my husband and me. She lived with us for about twenty years before we had to move her here. I couldn't take care of her anymore. It required more than I was capable of. It was probably the hardest thing I ever had to do, putting her in here."

"I'm sure she understood."

Melissa shrugged, picked up her cup, and took another sip of coffee.

"Where in Frederickport is her house?"

Melissa told him the street name; it was across town, blocks away from Adam and Melony's house. "Mom didn't want to sell it or rent it out. Now it's used by family. Every summer we go there with our kids. Until this last summer, before Mom's illness progressed, we'd take her with us. And my sister and her family come up from California and use the house."

Walt was about to say something when Melissa blurted, "You said you came up here with the police chief. Is this about Shawn, who worked here?"

"You know about that?"

"One of the nurses here told me he was involved with a robbery in Frederickport and was killed. Which I find impossible to believe. He was a nice guy. So sweet with my mom. He was one of her favorites here."

"You knew him?"

"Obviously not that well. The Shawn I met was always kind, thoughtful, and good to Mom. When I visited Mom, and she'd talk about the people who work here, she always spoke fondly of Shawn. I appreciated that he was good to her."

"Do you visit your mother a lot?"

Melissa set her coffee cup back on the table. "I visit her every week. I try to stay most of the day. At the moment they're giving her a bath, so I came out here to get some coffee." Melissa glanced briefly at the cup now sitting on the table. "But I didn't quite make it over to get myself a cup. Decided to have my own pity party."

Walt smiled. "My wife once told me we are entitled to a pity party occasionally, as long as it doesn't become our entire identity."

Melissa grinned at Walt. "Wise woman. Tell me, do you have any kids?"

"Twins. They're almost eight months old."

"Oh my, twins! I'm not sure whether I should congratulate you or give my condolences! It sounds like so much fun and also exhausting."

"It is, both." Walt chuckled.

"And you left that poor thing at home alone with two little ones?"

Walt grinned. "No. She's not alone—in fact, we are very blessed to have an excellent support system, which allowed me to come today without worrying about my wife."

"Good for you, and for her." Melissa glanced over toward the doorway of her mother's room. "Mom was great when mine were little. It would have been difficult trying to raise a family without her help."

"How many kids do you have?"

"Not exactly kids anymore. I have two—a son and a daughter.

They're probably older than you." Melissa chuckled and then continued, "We have two grandchildren, almost teenagers. Now that's what makes you feel old, when your grandbabies become teenagers." Melissa looked back toward her mother's room and said wistfully, "Enjoy your little ones, Walt. It goes so incredibly fast. We don't realize how fast until it's gone. This will be the first Christmas that my husband and I have been alone. Just the two of us."

"You aren't spending Christmas with your kids?"

Melissa turned back to Walt with a wistful smile and shook her head. "No. Not this year. But we've spent some wonderful Christmases together. Of course, some of my favorites were when they were little, and we spent it with my sister's family, my husband's parents, my parents, even my sister's in-laws, and my crazy aunt and uncle."

Melissa laughed at the memory and said, "Young parents often complain about how difficult Christmas can be, each side's family wanting them to come for Christmas. Which grandparents to spend Christmas with, but in our family, we spent them with all the grandparents. But now…now…most of the grandparents, at least from that generation, are gone. The only ones left are my mother and my sister's mother-in-law, who is in a memory care home down in California, near my sister and her husband."

"I suspect Christmas is always—more magical—when you spend it with children."

Melissa nodded. "When I was little, at Christmas it was not just my sister and me, but my cousins and grandparents, aunts and uncles. Surrounded by family and friends. I remember once my grandmother telling me she wasn't going to put up a Christmas tree one year, and I was horrified. As a child, I couldn't imagine not putting up a tree! I told myself I'd make sure Grandma would have a tree every year. And here I am, sixty-nine years old, and I finally understand why Grandma was talking about not putting up a tree one year." Melissa laughed again, this time sounding like wistful resignation. "It's been years since my sister and I spent Christmas together. We haven't since our kids were little, before my dad died. But now, she's in California, has her boys and grandkids there, and we've both been taking care of elderly mothers. In her case, a mother-in-law."

"And you're not going to spend Christmas with your kids." It was more of a statement than a question when Walt asked this time.

Melissa shrugged. "This year our son and his wife are spending it with her mother in Washington. In fairness, they spent the last two with us. Our daughter and her family, they live in California, and the kids want to stay home this year. I get it. Since they were born, it has been difficult for us to travel over the holidays, taking care of Mom. And my daughter and her family always made an effort to come up here to spend Christmas with us. I totally appreciate their efforts. It's not easy to pack up a family of four, a dog, a pile of wrapped Christmas gifts, and drive twelve hours to spend a couple of days in a cramped space."

"But you're going to miss them?" Walt asked gently.

"Yes, but it's my mom I'm going to miss the most this year."

Walt frowned. "Your mom?"

Melissa nodded. "The hospice nurse says Mom is…well, she will likely be gone before Christmas. And even if she lingers, my mama isn't in there anymore. She's totally out of it with all the medication." Tears slipped down Melissa's face. "I understand I will never spend another Christmas with my mother. I can't imagine that. I've spent every Christmas of my life with her."

Walt handed Melissa another tissue.

After wiping away her tears, she said, "Dang. I'm sorry. I didn't mean to dump all of this on you. You'll rethink offering a stranger coffee again."

Walt smiled gently. "It's okay. Honest."

Putting on a smile, Melissa changed the subject. "One of Mom's neighbors here was also from Frederickport. He passed away right before Veterans Day. His name was Roman Sellars. Any chance you knew him since he's from Frederickport?"

"No. I didn't. Was he one of your mother's friends from Frederickport?"

Melissa shook her head. "No. She hadn't met him before she moved here. He was already here when we moved Mom in. I only found out he was from Frederickport because on that first day I stayed to have lunch with Mom, and Roman was sitting at the table we sat down at. Shawn walked up to the table, and he introduced Roman and Mom and mentioned Roman was also from Frederickport."

"Did they become friends after they were introduced? Having Frederickport in common?"

Melissa laughed. "Hardly. As soon as Shawn mentioned Mom was from Frederickport, Roman abruptly stood up and moved to another table. Shawn looked somewhat embarrassed and apologized to Mom and me. But after that, Mom and I sort of made a joke about it."

"A joke, how?"

"Roman lived in the room right next door to Mom. So I would always ask her how her friendly neighbor was. We'd both laugh. She told me he never spoke to her. Roman, according to Mom, stayed to himself. And the only one he seemed to talk to—I mean, in an actual conversation—was Shawn."

TWENTY-THREE

Melony was sitting in her favorite spot on the sofa, her stocking feet up on the cushion, tucked under her backside, reading the day's news on her tablet and enjoying a cup of coffee, when Adam's cellphone rang. He sat on a nearby recliner, scrolling through his iPhone while his cup of coffee sat untouched on the side table, growing cold.

Melony had just turned on the sound to a video when Adam answered the phone call, and then the doorbell rang. Stopping the video and tossing her tablet next to her on the cushion, she got up from the couch to answer the door, leaving Adam alone in the living room, talking on the phone.

When Melony answered the door, she found Bill Jones standing on her front porch, wearing his trademark blue work shirt, faded denims, and work boots. He held something—the size of a cellphone—in his right hand.

"Afternoon, Mel," Bill greeted, handing her what he had been holding.

Melony took what Bill handed her and looked at it a moment before looking back up at Bill. "Hey, Bill. What's this?"

Bill glanced at his watch as if in a hurry. "Adam asked me to drop it off. I can't really talk, I have a job, and I'm going to be late. But I'm glad you and Adam are okay. That was wild what happened. But we can talk later." Bill turned and rushed down the walkway, heading to his truck parked in front of their house.

Frowning down at the small tool-like object, Melony turned back into her house and shut the door behind her. She stepped away from the door and then remembered she hadn't locked it. Keeping the door locked at all times had never seemed like an issue—until now. Melony turned back to the door and locked it before returning to the living room. She found Adam still on the phone. He wasn't really talking, more a series of head nods, which the person on the other line obviously couldn't see because it wasn't a video call. He uttered a few *yes, okay, yeah,* before finally ending the call. When he did, he looked up; he seemed surprised to find Melony standing over him.

"Bill left this." Melony handed Adam the object.

"Oh, thanks."

"What is it?"

"It's a stud finder." Adam set the stud finder on the table next to him.

"Why do you need a stud finder?"

"That was Mom on the phone," Adam blurted.

Melony's eyes widened. It had been months since Adam had spoken to either of his parents. She sat down in the empty recliner next to his. "What did she say?"

"She found out what happened to me and wanted to see if I was okay." Absently, Adam picked the stud finder up again and started turning it over in his hand.

"How did she find out?"

"She didn't say. I didn't ask. Probably some friend who still lives here called her. I don't imagine the story would have been on the news where she lives."

"Well, that's nice. She was worried about you." The words didn't even sound convincing to Melony. "Did she mention Christmas?"

"Only that my brother is getting married on Christmas Eve, and she and Dad are going to the wedding. It's in London." Before Adam and Melony married earlier that year, Adam's brother had taken a teaching job in London. "I didn't realize he was seeing anyone, much less considering marriage again."

"Are you invited to the wedding?"

"Doesn't sound like it. Mom said it's just an intimate ceremony with the parents and a couple of friends. She mentioned nothing about us being invited."

"Maybe you should reach out to him. Just to wish him a Merry Christmas and congratulate him on his wedding."

"Like they did ours?"

Melony winced and said nothing.

Adam set the stud finder back on the table next to his phone and glanced around. "Hey, Grandma, are you here?"

Nothing happened.

"You can tug my ear if you're here," Adam suggested.

Again, nothing happened.

Adam let out a sigh and slumped back in the chair. "Mel, this thing is weird about Grandma."

Melony chuckled. "If there was ever an understatement."

"It's like she's back, but she isn't. Not like either one of us can see her."

"I thought you said you were looking forward to spending Christmas with her."

"Yes, I said that. But it's not like I can see or hear her."

Melony considered his comment for a moment and smiled. "Adam, what do blind people do? Or deaf people? Or someone who is both deaf and blind, like Helen Keller?"

"What do you mean?"

"Well, if you were suddenly blind, would you think I was no longer…here?"

"I could still hear you."

"That's why I mentioned Helen Keller."

Adam considered Melony's question for a moment and then smiled. "I get what you're saying. You'd still be here, just like

Grandma is. But I'd have to find a new way to communicate with you, like Helen Keller did."

"Exactly." Melony nodded toward the stud finder and changed the subject. "So what is that about?"

Adam glanced at the stud finder, picked it up, looked at Melony, and smiled. "I thought I could use this to see if something is in the wall."

Melony groaned.

Adam laughed at his wife. His phone rang again. He set the stud finder back on the table and answered the call.

"Hey, Danielle," Melony heard him say, still shaking her head over the stud finder while images of Adam dismantling their home in search of a mystery treasure flashed through her mind. Melony sat back on the sofa and picked up her iPad. Instead of looking at it, she absently set it on her lap and listened quietly to Adam's side of the conversation.

When the call ended, Adam looked at Melony and said, "That was Danielle."

"That's what I figured. What's going on?"

"She said Walt went with the chief to Oregon City today, like they mentioned last night. They're on their way home now. She's only talked to him briefly on the phone, and I guess they found out a few things, but he wants to wait until he gets back to tell her everything. She invited us to come over for dinner so we can hear what he has to say. Chris is picking up Chinese food. By that time, Joanne will be gone. She worked today. And I guess she's not part of the cool club."

Melony laughed. "Cool club?"

"I do feel like we've joined some secret society. Perhaps we don't have our own handshake, but…" Adam didn't finish his sentence; he just gave a shrug.

"Dinner sounds good, and I'm curious to see if they learned anything. It would be nice to figure out what those guys were looking for without tearing up our home."

"She also said Grandma wanted to come over here before dinner and wanted to make sure it was okay."

Melony smiled. "She didn't want to just pop in?"

Adam chuckled. "I guess Grandma doesn't want to freak me out by thinking she's lurking in the corner somewhere watching us." Adam then thought of the times in his office when his computer kept acting weird whenever he tried accessing an adult website. But he would not mention that to Mel.

"So she's coming over?"

"Yeah, Danielle said in about fifteen minutes. Said Grandma will knock three times when she gets here."

"This is going to be interesting," Melony muttered. "Your grandma is coming to visit. Not sure how all this is supposed to work."

"Me neither." Adam stood up and started heading for the hallway.

"Where are you going?"

"To get a pad of paper and a pen. My version of Helen Keller."

FIFTEEN MINUTES LATER, Adam sat with Melony on the sofa, a pad of paper and a pen sitting on the coffee table, when they heard three knocks.

"Grandma?" Adam looked around the room.

"Hello, Marie," Melony said, trying to suppress a giggle.

The pen lifted from the table and began to write on the pad. A moment later, the pen dropped to the table, and the pad floated up in the air so that Melony and Adam could see what she had written.

"How are you both doing? Did you sleep okay last night?"

"I slept fine, Grandma."

"I did too," Melony said. "While I appreciated Danielle and Walt's hospitality, it's always nice to sleep in your own bed. And I supposed it helped, knowing the men who broke in are no longer a threat."

The pad dropped back to the table; the pen wrote something else. When the pad floated back up into the air, it read, "Why haven't you started decorating for Christmas? Where are all my old decorations? Did you get rid of them?"

Adam laughed at the question. Since he was a teenager, he had helped Marie bring out her Christmas decorations each year and put them away after the holiday. When he was a little boy, she would gently unwrap each tree ornament from tissue paper and would explain the history of each one before hanging it on the tree. In her later years, Adam had brought her an artificial tree so he wouldn't have to worry about the tree drying up and becoming a fire hazard.

Marie soon learned Adam hadn't gotten rid of her decorations —not even her artificial tree. All of it was now stored in the garage of Melony and Adam's new home. Thirty minutes later, Adam questioned his wisdom in telling his grandmother that he had not only kept all her Christmas decorations, but they were currently stored in the attached garage.

Before Adam and Melony realized what was happening, boxes of Marie's Christmas decorations floated out of the garage and filled the living room. Adam didn't understand how Marie did it, but Christmas music began playing from the nearby Alexa.

Unsure and confused, Adam stood dumbfounded in the living room, watching what looked like a scene from a Disney movie, if Disney had a Christmas movie where the godmother of Christmas decorated someone's home. Artificial garlands floated out of the open boxes, arranging themselves on the fireplace mantel, followed by Christmas candles. Melony's reaction was the flip side of Adam's, as she practically jumped up and down like an excited child who'd just walked in on Santa filling her stocking.

When the box holding Marie's artificial tree floated into the room, Adam inwardly groaned. He had always put the tree together for Marie, and it was never something he particularly enjoyed. Yet Adam soon discovered Marie didn't need his help to assemble the tree this time. Before long, the tree stood proudly in the corner, its cord plugged into the wall and its white lights twinkling. Ornaments floated from boxes, yet instead of moving toward the tree, they floated into Adam's and Melony's hands, as Marie encouraged them to decorate the tree.

When it was time to leave for dinner, Melony and Adam's living room was decked out for Christmas, and all the boxes that had floated into the room floated back to the garage, placing themselves neatly back onto the shelves.

Marie wrote a final note before leaving. It read, "I'm going back to Marlow House. See you there. Love you both."

The Christmas music turned off, and Melony and Adam stood in the living room, taking in the transformation.

"That was without a doubt the wildest experience of my life," Melony said in awe.

Hands on hips, Adam looked around and said, "Well, death has not changed Grandma."

"What do you mean?"

With a laugh, Adam said, "She's still as bossy as ever."

TWENTY-FOUR

Ever since moving to Frederickport, Ian's mother, June Bartley, had insisted on hosting a weekly family dinner. After Emily Ann's birth, Ian had convinced his mother to move the family dinner to their house, claiming it would be more convenient and arguing that after the construction was finished and they moved out of the rental and into the new house, the weekly dinners could return to their home.

June reluctantly agreed, and the weekly dinners transformed into a potluck, which meant June was no longer primarily responsible for the meal. Unbeknownst to her family, June preferred this new arrangement. Hosting a weekly dinner had become exhausting for a woman her age, and she rather enjoyed no longer worrying about cleaning her house before company arrived while preparing a large meal.

The weekly family guest list included just three couples—Lily and Ian, June and John, and Kelly and Joe—along with June's two grandchildren. Each week, a different couple selected a theme for the week's dinner. It was Kelly's week, and she had chosen Italian food. Kelly would be bringing lasagna, using her mother-in-law's recipe and Joe's help. June was bringing a green salad and tiramisu

John had purchased from Old Salt's Bakery. Lily's contribution was two loaves of sourdough bread, which she had made after getting some starter from Heather. Ian's contribution to the evening—he made sure the house was clean for guests.

June and John arrived first. Lily had already made room in the refrigerator for June to put the salad and dessert. When Kelly and Joe arrived, Lily and Sadie greeted them at the front door, opening it before they had a chance to ring the bell.

"That smells amazing. You can put it in the oven," Lily told them as she stepped out of the way so they could enter the house. "Everyone is in the living room already."

Wearing oven mitts, Joe carried the large, covered casserole dish to the kitchen while Kelly and Lily trailed behind him. Sadie had run ahead of them and was already back in the living room.

"Are they having a party across the street?" Kelly asked as Lily opened the oven for Joe.

"I don't think it's a party. Dani mentioned something about Chris buying Chinese food and having some people over."

As Joe placed the lasagna in the oven, Kelly said, "Sounds like a party."

"We're having our own party," Joe said cheerfully after Lily shut the oven door.

"How are you feeling, Joe? It was mean of us to have you make dinner tonight, considering everything," Lily said.

"Hey, I made it. He just sat at the counter and told me what to do," Kelly corrected.

Lily laughed, and Kelly said, "Well, looks like everyone is over there. I saw Adam's car, Brian's, and the chief's."

"Not everyone. We're here." Lily grinned.

"I'm just curious. I want to find out what they're doing over there." Kelly glanced toward Marlow House.

Joe draped an arm around Kelly's shoulder. "Don't be so nosy." He kissed her cheek.

Kelly wrapped her arm around Joe's waist. "I know. I can't help it."

"Maybe it's that reporter in you," Joe teased.

Kelly noticed the two loaves of uncut sourdough bread sitting on the counter. She nodded toward them. "Did you get those from Heather?"

"Nope. I made them myself."

"I didn't know you made sourdough bread," Joe said.

"I will have you know I'm the one who taught Heather how to make it. Although she gave me some starter. I haven't made sourdough bread in ages, and I didn't have the time to make my own starter."

ACROSS THE STREET at Marlow House, instead of taking the food into the living room, they set up the Chinese takeout on the buffet to eat in the dining room. That way the twins could be contained in the highchairs, and they didn't have to worry about spilling food on the furniture. Walt, Danielle, Adam, Melony, Brian, Heather, MacDonald, Eddy, Evan, and Chris sat around the dining room table, while Marie sat in an imaginary chair facing the highchairs so she could keep the twins entertained and help them eat dinner without throwing all their food on the floor.

Walt had instructed Hunny and Max to stay out of the dining room while everyone was eating. However, Adam and Melony were unaware of his instructions—or the fact Walt could communicate with animals—they just assumed the dog and cat were well trained. However, Evan was about to dispel that notion, while not revealing everything.

"Did anyone tell Adam and Mel why Hunny and Max don't come in here when we're eating?" Evan asked as he picked up a pot sticker.

"Because they're well trained?" Adam asked.

"It's easy when you speak the same language." Evan giggled before taking a bite of his pot sticker.

Melony looked at Evan. "Same language?"

MacDonald leaned over to Evan and whispered something in his ear. The boy frowned up at his father. "I know, Dad."

"Ghosts can talk to animals," Eddy blurted.

Evan nodded. "And animals can see ghosts, too."

Adam frowned. "What?"

"It's true," Danielle said. "Animals, at least dogs and cats, we're not sure all animals, they're sort of like mediums, they can see ghosts. Hunny, Sadie, Max, and Bella, they can all see Marie and Eva. And they can also communicate with each other. It's not verbal, more of a telepathy thing."

Melony arched her brows. "What else haven't you told us?"

Ignoring Melony's question, Danielle looked at Adam. "It's why I don't worry about Max and the babies."

"So you're saying Grandma told Max he can't go into their cribs? And he listens to her?"

Heather, who had just opened a soy sauce packet to pour on her rice, looked at Adam. "Max also understands Marie has learned to harness her energy. He's not fond of flying."

Adam frowned. "I still don't get it."

Chris set his chopsticks on his plate and looked at Adam. "If Marie wants to, she can make Max fly across the room and never lift a hand. As Heather says, he's not a fan of flying."

Adam cringed. "That would be kind of creepy."

"It's not creepy!" Evan argued. "It's really cool to fly across the room. Makes me feel like Superman!"

As Adam attempted to process what Evan had just said, Danielle abruptly changed the subject. "What did you learn in Oregon City?"

MacDonald looked up from his plate. "Roman Sellars, the patient Eva and Marie told us about last night, it turns out he was from Frederickport."

"While I didn't know him, now that I hear the last name, it sounds familiar. I think he might have been friends with Ruby Crabtree."

Heather repeated to the non-mediums what Marie had just said.

The chief looked over to Adam and Melony. "Is the name familiar to either of you?" They both shook their heads.

"So what now?" Heather asked.

"News around town, this case is pretty much closed," Chris said.

Melony looked at Chris. "Why do you say that?"

"Of the different people I spoke to today, they have Mark as the victim," Chris explained.

"He is dead; other than that, how is he the victim in all this?" Adam asked.

"The story going around town, Mark's brother, who apparently didn't have a terrific reputation, according to some people the local media interviewed, was visiting Mark with a friend, and they decided to do a little breaking and entering while Mark was out keeping the peace," Chris said.

"I've heard that one too," Brian said. "Supposedly Mark was blindsided when he showed up and his brother and houseguest were the perps, and things went sideways, and they all ended up dead. Case closed."

"Why case closed?" Danielle asked.

Brian shrugged. "Probably because they figure we caught the bad guys, and there's nothing to investigate."

"Chief, I could talk to Ruby. If one of you talks to her, she's going to wonder why you're still investigating this, and someone might start wondering what we've all been wondering. Look what happened when word got out there might be gold hidden across the street." Danielle glanced at Adam.

"Okay, it was not my finest hour," Adam confessed.

"I could stop and see Ruby. Bring her some Christmas cookies. I'll come up with a story to explain why I'm asking about Roman, without bringing Mel and Adam's house into it," Danielle suggested.

The chief looked at Danielle. "You mean lie to Ruby?"

Danielle shrugged. "I like to think of it as stretching the truth—telling a white lie."

Brian looked from Danielle to the chief. "It might work."

"Did you learn anything else in Oregon City?" Heather asked.

"Shawn seemed to have an excellent reputation. The residents all liked him," Walt said.

"Well, he didn't want to shoot me, so I'll give him that," Adam said.

"I also met another woman there with ties to Frederickport." Walt then told them about his encounter with Melissa.

"Poor thing, dealing with possibly losing her mother right before Christmas," Danielle said.

"Well, I lost my grandma right before Christmas. And then got her back right before Christmas." Adam grinned. A moment later, his right hand flew to his right earlobe. Marie had given it a gentle tug.

"I want to tell you all, Adam and I finished decorating our living room for Christmas today. We even have a tree up. Marie helped us. In fact, the decorations are all hers."

"Wow, Marie also helped me put up the lights on the fence today," Eddy bragged. "It was kinda cool."

Eddy, Melony, and Adam began sharing their unique experience of decorating for Christmas with the help of a ghost—one they couldn't see. After several minutes of lively banter, Adam said, "I had forgotten about all of Grandma's ornaments. I've had them stored since she passed away. Some great memories."

Marie smiled proudly. "I had a wonderful time decorating for Christmas today. Those ornaments are more than decorations; they're part of our family tradition."

Evan repeated what Marie had just said to the non-mediums, and then looked at his father and asked, "Dad, do we have any Christmas ornaments that are part of our family tradition? I'm not sure what that means."

MacDonald considered the question for a moment. "Each year we hang the handmade Christmas ornaments you and Eddy have made over the years. I suppose that makes them part of our family tradition."

"Anything else?" Evan asked.

"I know, Mom's Christmas picture you used to hang every year," Eddy answered for his dad.

Evan frowned at Eddy. "What picture?"

"Don't you remember? It was a painting. Well, I guess a picture of a painting. Each year, Mom would make up a new Christmas story about the picture. She would tell us stories about the people and the animals in the painting. That was a family tradition." Eddy looked at his father. "Dad, where is it? Don't we have it anymore?"

"I remember now!" Evan said. He looked at his father. "Dad, what happened to the picture?"

"Was that the Wysocki Cindy told me about?" Melony asked.

Edward nodded. "Yes, and we still have it. It's in the attic."

"Why don't we hang it at Christmas anymore, Dad?" Eddy asked.

TWENTY-FIVE

Rectangular metal cake pans filled with Christmas cookies stretched across Marlow House's kitchen counter. One held chocolate chip, another chocolate drop, and two were filled with decorated sugar cookies. When Lily entered the kitchen that Monday morning, carrying a large Tupperware container, Danielle was already expecting her.

Knowing Ruby Crabtree typically only worked at the Seahorse Motel on Mondays through Wednesdays at this time of year, Danielle had decided to try visiting Ruby on Monday, yet before going over, she wanted to make more cookies. On Sunday, Lily and Heather had come over to join Danielle in the baking, while Walt, Ian, and Brian had watched football in the living room of Marlow House and took care of the little ones. This morning, Lily was coming over to collect her share of the cookies they had baked the day before.

"These are going to be gone before Christmas," Lily said as she filled her Tupperware container with an assortment of cookies.

"Of course they are. We'll bake more." Danielle sat at the kitchen table, drinking a cup of coffee while watching Lily fill her container. Sitting on the kitchen table was a large cookie tin Danielle had filled minutes before Lily's arrival.

"Perhaps this year Marie can teach us all how to make her divinity," Lily suggested as she fastened the lid on her now filled container.

"Adam and Mel could join us. That would be fun." Danielle giggled at the thought and took another sip of coffee.

Leaving her container on the counter, Lily poured herself a cup of coffee, walked to the table, and sat down with Danielle. "Kelly's over at our house. I can stay only a minute. I just finished feeding Emily Ann, and aunty is currently rocking her." Lily sipped her coffee. "When I said I was coming over here to get some cookies, well, one thing led to another, and she found out we were over here baking while the guys watched football yesterday, and I think her feelings were hurt that we didn't invite them."

"It wasn't exactly planned." Which was true. On Sunday morning, when Danielle started to fill a tin of cookies for her visit with Ruby on Monday, she had decided to bake more cookies, and one thing led to another.

"She said she wasn't going to tell Joe because his feelings might be hurt he wasn't invited to watch football, especially since he and Brian are close friends." Lily rolled her eyes and took another sip of coffee.

"I'm sorry."

Lily shrugged. "Don't be."

"So how is your mom doing?"

"I spoke to her this morning. She's still bummed about missing Christmas with the grandkids. Asked me if we were still having our Christmas Eve party."

"And you are?" Danielle asked.

"Of course. And it's still Christmas dinner here?"

Danielle grinned. "Yes. And it's going to be a full house. But I'll have lots of help."

"I think if Kelly had her way, she would rather be spending Christmas dinner here with us instead of with Joe's family. Seems like whenever something's happening over here and she's not invited, drives her nuts. Like on Saturday night."

"She and Joe were invited for Christmas," Danielle reminded her.

"Oh, I know. But they'll spend Christmas Eve at our house and Christmas dinner at Joe's. I don't think June is too thrilled about it either. Since she and John are spending Christmas dinner at Marlow House, I imagine June would like her daughter to be there too. And I'm a little worried about next year, after June and John move into their new house."

"How so?" Danielle asked.

Lily shrugged. "When June has her brand-new house, I imagine she'll want to host Christmas dinner with her family over there. Of course, not sure how Joe will feel. This has become our Christmas tradition."

Danielle let out a sigh. "The thing about Christmas traditions, over time they morph, shift, and evolve. Families grow; some disappear. And then we create our own families, our new traditions."

THEY DROVE the Ford Flex through the Seahorse Motel parking lot, looking for Ruby's car. When they found it, verifying that she was there, Walt pulled into a spot in front of the office and parked. He turned off the ignition, turned, and looked at Danielle. "Ready?"

"You remember the story we're going to use?"

"I think so. But I'll follow your lead." Walt leaned over and kissed Danielle's cheek.

Minutes later, Walt and Danielle stood outside their car, the twins bundled up in red jackets, mittens, and wool caps, tucked into their double stroller. Walt pushed the stroller toward the registration office while Danielle walked beside him, carrying a large tin filled with Christmas cookies.

They found Ruby and Sam sitting on the sofa in the front lobby, not standing behind the counter. Danielle wasn't surprised, because there were no guests in the lobby, which also didn't surprise her. This time of year was slow for the local motel business, especially on a Monday. Business would start picking up closer to Christmas, when locals had family coming in for the holidays and their small beach homes didn't have sufficient accommodations.

Greetings were exchanged; Ruby gushed over the twins, thanked Danielle for the cookies, and Sam brought them all a mug of hot chocolate. Fifteen minutes later, Ruby, Sam, Danielle and Walt sat together on the motel's lounge sectional, with the twins quietly sitting in their stroller next to their parents, each baby drinking a bottle.

"Any plans to reopen the BnB next year?" Ruby asked. "My sources tell me 2020 is going to be good for the BnB business."

"No. We don't have any current plans to reopen." Danielle glanced at her babies. "These two are keeping us busy, and I'm not sure I want strangers in the house right now. Maybe later."

Ruby nodded. "I understand that."

Cupping the warm mug of hot cocoa between her hands, Danielle flashed Ruby a smile before saying, "Even though we're not planning on reopening anytime soon, I really enjoyed the BnB. We had some great visitors. Made friends who keep in touch. In fact, I got a call this weekend from someone who stayed with us when we first opened. Although I'm not sure she would have called if Adam's house hadn't been broken into and those men killed."

"That was just horrible!" Ruby said. "Thankfully, Adam wasn't hurt. But why did that make her call?"

"I guess one of the men who was killed worked in a care home where one of her friends live," Danielle lied. "She told me she had met him, and he seemed so nice, she couldn't believe he had done something like that."

"Well, it's always the ones who are supposedly so nice—those are the ones you have to worry about." Ruby snickered.

"You just never know. She also mentioned that one of the residents at the care home was from Frederickport. She asked me whether I knew him. I didn't recognize the name. But I think he left before I moved here. She said he passed away before Veterans Day.

His name was Roman Sellars. Any chance you knew him?" Danielle took another sip of coffee and then added, "She felt bad about him because he never had visitors."

Ruby's eyes widened, and she set her mug down on the table. "Roman Sellars? Oh my, I haven't heard that name in ages. He's dead? Well, I can't say I'm surprised. Although he wasn't that old. But you can't drink like he did and expect to be around for a long time."

"Drinking problem?" Danielle asked.

Ruby nodded. "Last time I saw Roman, oh my, twenty years ago? Handsome man. There was family money—but I don't remember ever actually meeting anyone from his family. He started dating one of my friends. We ran in the same circle for a while. But after about a year, he broke up with her. It didn't break her heart, and not six months later, let's just say he started spending a lot of time on a barstool."

"He started drinking?" Walt asked.

"Like a fish," Ruby said. "And by the time that year rolled around, he left town. Never heard what happened to him."

"Your friend never saw him again? The one who had been dating him?"

Ruby shook her head. "Sally? No."

Danielle arched her brows. "Sally?"

"My friend who dated him back then. Sally, from Sally and Susan's."

Danielle frowned. "Sally? The Sally from Sally and Susan's the bookstore in town?"

Ruby laughed and then added, "I know what you're thinking. Sally wasn't out of the closet back then. I don't even think she understood at the time. That's why I said I don't think it broke her heart. She's much happier married to Susan."

"Where did Roman live back then?" Danielle asked.

If Ruby thought the question odd, she didn't mention it. Instead, she answered Danielle's question, and according to the answer, Roman had a house right on the ocean, not too far from Adam and Melony's.

"Did he always live there?"

Ruby frowned at Danielle. "What do you mean?"

Danielle took a sip of cocoa and shrugged. "I guess I'm just being nosy and gossipy. I probably need to get out more."

"I imagine you do feel a little confined, adjusting to motherhood with not just one baby, but two. As for any juicy gossip on poor Roman, I always did wonder if he figured out Sally preferred women before she realized it, and that's why he broke it off with her. Maybe it killed his ego, and he started drinking." Ruby shrugged.

"Was he born in Frederickport?" Walt asked.

Ruby shook her head. "No. He had only lived here a couple of years when Sally met him."

"DID WE LEARN ANYTHING?" Danielle asked Walt when they were back in the car with the twins, heading home to Marlow House. She didn't sound as if she expected the answer to be yes.

"According to Ruby, he left Frederickport about twenty years ago. From what the chief found out about Roman, it sounds like he was in the care home for about ten years, and according to Melissa, she thought he was in his late fifties."

"Wow, imagine going into a care home in your forties. That's just around the corner for me. Now I am feeling old."

Walt reached over from the driver's seat and gave Danielle a quick pat on the knee. "What I find interesting, when Shawn introduced Melissa and her mother to Roman, he said Roman was from Frederickport. But if you think about it, he didn't grow up in Frederickport, and he moved about twenty years before he died."

"If he was really hitting the bottle like Ruby said, after leaving Frederickport, he might have just been drifting from place to place the next ten years before he ended up in that care home, and to him, his last real home was Frederickport."

Walt shrugged. "You're probably right."

TWENTY-SIX

"It's entirely possible Roman has nothing to do with any of this," Police Chief MacDonald told Walt and Danielle after he stopped in to see them on the way home from work on Monday. The three sat together in the parlor while the twins napped upstairs in the nursery, a baby monitor receiver sitting on the nearby desk.

Walt and Danielle sat on the sofa, Max sleeping on Danielle's lap, while the chief sat in one of the chairs across from them.

"True," Walt agreed. "It's not like Roman was the only person at the care home from Frederickport. Melissa's mother lived here."

"While it's entirely possible Roman had nothing to do with it, I also think it's entirely possible he does, and we need to find out more about him," Danielle said. "According to Shawn, they were looking for something specific at Adam and Melony's. And whatever it was, he was the one who told Peter and Mark about it. He claimed everyone who knew about it is now dead. Someone obviously had to tell Shawn. This plan of theirs to come to Frederickport seemed to have been hatched around Veterans Day. And Roman died right before Veterans Day."

"And like we have said all along, someone with a tie to Frederickport must have told Shawn about whatever this secret—or trea-sure—might be," the chief said.

Danielle nodded. "Melissa and her mom are still alive, so Shawn wasn't talking about them. I suppose it's possible Shawn knew someone with connections to Frederickport who has since died, that had nothing to do with the care home, and told him about some hidden treasure, but really—"

"It's unlikely," Walt finished for Danielle. "This sounds like something a person shares on their deathbed. And considering what Eva and Marie heard about Roman's spirit's departure after death, sounds like he would have been the type who felt compelled to confess his sins when facing death."

"Not sure it helped," Danielle muttered.

"What now?" Walt asked.

"I think we need to go Christmas shopping. I'm looking for some books for Connor and Evan."

WALT AND DANIELLE weren't able to get away to go shopping without the twins until Thursday. When Walt pulled up to Sally and Susan's Bookstore, Danielle said, "I have to commend you."

Walt turned off the ignition and looked at his wife. "For what?"

"The story you came up with for Sally. It's believable."

"I just hope Sally's working today."

Danielle shrugged. "If she isn't, then I guess you and I get to go to lunch, just the two of us."

IT TURNED out Sally was working on Thursday, along with three employees. The bookstore's staff had been increased in preparation for holiday shopping, but considering there was just one customer in the store when Walt and Danielle walked in, it looked as if talking with Sally would not be a problem. Walt wanted to engage Sally in a conversation, but if she was busy waiting on customers, that would have been difficult.

It was not surprising when Sally rushed to greet Walt and Danielle. Ever since Walt first made the New York Times Best Sellers list, whenever they entered the bookstore, Sally referred to him as her favorite author.

"So what are my favorite author and his lovely wife looking for today?" Sally greeted.

Danielle, who stood with Walt, her small purse in one hand and a shopping list in the other, flashed Sally a smile as she briefly held up the list. "I'm here to do a little Christmas shopping, but Walt here, he was hoping you'd help in a little research for one story he's working on."

Sally beamed and turned to Walt. "I'd love to help you. Are you looking for a certain reference book?"

"I'll leave you two while I browse the children's section," Danielle said as she left them alone.

Walt motioned away from the front entrance to talk in private. "I was hoping I could have about ten minutes of your time. I'm not looking for a reference book, but I was hoping you might supply a little story fodder."

Sally arched her brows. "Story fodder?"

"Real-life events inspire my stories," Walt began.

Sally nodded. "That's why they're so good."

Walt grinned. "Thank you."

"So what story has inspired you?"

Walt briefly repeated the same story they had given Ruby, of learning about Roman through a friend, sharing the story with Ruby, who then mentioned Sally had dated him briefly. "After I got home, I started thinking about Roman, wondering about his story. How he ended up alone in a care home, where no one visited him. Why did the care home say he was from Frederickport when he hadn't been born here, and it sounded like he hadn't lived here for a good decade before he moved into the care home? I wondered if there was an interesting backstory there that might explain it."

"Wow, Roman is gone. I'd wondered what happened to him after he left Frederickport."

"You lost track of him after he left?"

Sally nodded and grew silent for a moment, collecting her thoughts. Finally, she looked up at Walt and said, "There might be some interesting story fodder here. If Roman were still alive, well, you wouldn't be here now, but if you were, I wouldn't say anything. But now that he's gone…I've often wondered myself."

"Wondered what?"

"Umm…" Sally glanced over to the counter. The one customer who had been in the store when Walt and Danielle had first arrived had just checked out, and no one else had walked in after Walt. She turned back to him and asked, "Have you had lunch yet?"

THIRTY MINUTES LATER, Walt and Danielle sat in a booth at Lucy's Diner with Sally. The server had just taken their order, and the three were now alone.

"My mother introduced us," Sally began. "She was determined to play matchmaker, desperate to marry off her spinster daughter." Sally rolled her eyes at the memory and continued, "Mom didn't understand why I wasn't really interested in men; of course, I didn't understand that either at the time. I occasionally dated, but I never dated anyone twice—not until Roman."

"Ruby mentioned you two dated about a year," Danielle said.

Sally nodded. "I really liked Roman. He was fun. Enjoyed books. We liked the same movies and music. Our relationship was comfortable. And for the most part, platonic. Now, for me, it was the dream relationship. As long as we were dating, Mom was happy and not nagging me. Looking back, I should have asked myself why a man in his late thirties was content basically holding hands. But I didn't question it at the time. Then I met Susan, and I finally figured things out for myself and realized what had always been missing. Over the years, Susan and I would occasionally talk about my time with Roman. We both wondered, what was his deal? I think there might be an interesting story there if you could figure it out."

"Why do you say that?" Walt asked.

Sally gave Walt a grin. "Hey, you are the one who approached me because you thought there might be an interesting story with Roman."

Walt laughed. "True. But I wonder why *you* think it."

Sally let out a sigh and continued, "When we live in the moment, we miss things. Things are going on all around us. Then years later, we look back and see things that were there all along, things we ignored. That's how it is with Roman. If I could go back in time, there are questions I'd ask him. Maybe you, with your writer's insight and knack for research, maybe you can find those answers for me."

The server came with their food, and a few minutes later they were alone again.

"Tell me what you remember. And tell me things you now realize you ignored back then," Walt suggested.

Sally picked up a French fry from her plate and popped it in her mouth. After she ate it, she said, "Everything about that time was odd, when I think about it. Roman obviously wasn't interested in me —that way. Susan has her own theory. Not sure I agree with it, but she could be right."

"What's her theory?" Walt asked.

"Susan thinks he was looking for a lavender marriage."

"She thought he was gay?" Danielle asked.

Sally shrugged. "Susan finds it hard to believe that a healthy male of that age would date a woman for a year and be content to be buddies. She wondered if he was gay and then decided against a lavender relationship—which would explain our sudden breakup, which came out of nowhere. And not being able to deal with who he was and unwilling to come out of the closet, he started drinking." Sally picked up her burger and took a bite.

Walt and Danielle considered Susan's theory. After a moment Walt asked, "What do you think about her theory?"

Sally set her burger back on her plate and wiped her mouth with a napkin. "While possible, I'm not sure I buy Roman was gay. I came up with a little more…scandalous version."

Walt arched his brows. "Sounds interesting."

"Story fodder, right?" Sally grinned.

"Go on," Walt urged.

"Now let me clarify, back in those days, I presented pretty feminine. And I certainly wasn't a teenager. I was in my early thirties. I think they called us old maids."

Danielle wrinkled her nose. "I hate that term."

"But I was an attractive old maid. And I suppose I should have been offended because of his lack of intimacy. But I was relieved. Yet I don't think his lack of interest was because he was gay. I think it was another woman."

"Another woman?" Danielle asked.

Sally nodded. "His best friend was married to this beautiful woman. Dang, she was gorgeous. If that's who Roman was having an affair with—and I suspect he was—he had good taste. But she was married to his best friend. I think I was Roman's beard, but not in the traditional sense."

"Why do you think they were having an affair?" Walt asked.

"We often did things socially with Roman's best friend and wife. In retrospect, I remember how Roman looked at her, how attentive he was to her when we were all together. When her husband was out of the room, he became even more attentive. I should have been jealous, but frankly, I enjoyed her company too."

"Did the friend ever find out about Roman and his wife?" Danielle asked.

"He found out she had been unfaithful, but I don't think he found out his best friend was also having an affair with her."

"What do you mean?" Walt asked.

"One day Roman came to me, totally out of the blue, and told me he didn't feel we were right for each other. That while he liked me, he wasn't in love with me. And he apologized. I couldn't really argue with him, because I wasn't in love with him either. I think our breakup was hardest on Mom." Sally picked up her burger to take another bite.

After Sally put her burger back on her plate, Danielle asked, "What happened with the friend's wife?"

"About two weeks after Roman broke it off with me, I heard Jason's wife took off with a lover and left him. And that lover was not Roman."

"Jason?"

"Jason Aldridge, he was Roman's best friend." Sally abruptly set her partially eaten burger back on her plate and cringed. "I said too much. If you make a story about this, don't use Jason's name. Unlike Roman, he's still alive, and while this happened years ago, I don't think he ever got over it."

TWENTY-SEVEN

"Jason Aldridge, that's Joanne's neighbor, the one she invited for Christmas. The one whose wife left him for another man," Danielle told Walt when they got back into their car after leaving Sally.

"The one who used to own Adam and Mel's house." Walt put his key in the ignition and turned on the engine. "We have our connection. But where do we go from here?"

"We can start by talking with Joanne when we get home."

WHEN WALT and Danielle arrived back at Marlow House, they found the twins napping in the living room's portable cribs while Joanne was in the laundry room, putting a load of dirty clothes into the washing machine.

"Did you have a nice time?" Joanne asked Danielle when she entered the laundry room.

"Yes. How were the twins?"

Joanne closed the door of the washing machine and looked at Danielle. "I will confess I didn't get much done while you were gone.

Addison, Jack, and I played a game with Max. We were rolling a small ball, and I swear, Max thought he was a dog! He kept retrieving the ball and bringing it back. It was hilarious. I would have filmed it if those two rascals weren't such fast crawlers and would be into mischief the minute I walked away to get my phone. But I eventually wore them out, and they fell asleep."

"I just appreciate you taking such good care of them," Danielle said. "But could you come into the parlor and talk to Walt and me for a minute?"

"Is something wrong?"

Danielle shook her head. "No, we just need to ask you something."

"Okay, let me finish here, and I'll meet you in the parlor."

TEN MINUTES LATER, Walt, Danielle, and Joanne sat in the parlor with the doors open to the entrance hall so they could hear the twins should they wake up. Danielle sat on the sofa with Walt while they faced Joanne, who sat across from them. "I need to tell you something. We just didn't go to the bookstore to Christmas shop; we wanted to do a little sleuthing."

Joanne arched her brows. "Sleuthing?"

Danielle nodded. "Yes. And I'd really appreciate it if you don't tell anyone what I am about to tell you."

"Umm, okay."

"Those men who broke into Adam's house—some of the evidence suggests they were looking for something specific. Something of value. Something that was hidden in the house."

"What?"

Danielle shrugged. "They don't know, and Adam and the chief don't want this to get out to the public. People do crazy things when they think there's a hidden treasure. Look what happened across the street when the story of the gold coins started circulating."

"Jason, my neighbor, used to live in that house."

Danielle nodded. "That's why I want to talk to you. One of the men who broke into Adam's was a nurse who worked in a nursing home in Oregon City."

Joanne nodded. "Yes, I read that."

"One of his patients was on hospice, and he stayed with him during his last days and was at his bedside when he passed. That patient once lived in Frederickport. Right after the patient died, the nurse quit his job and hooked up with his accomplice. Now, because we don't want it to get out to the public that there might be a hidden treasure, Walt and I sort of made up a story when we talked to Ruby Crabtree about the patient who died—and when we talked to Sally today."

"What do you mean, you made up a story?"

"Let's just say we told them some half-truths. So I would really appreciate it if you also didn't mention any of this to Ruby or Sally."

"Okay, so why are you telling me in the first place?"

"Because the man who died at the care home was best friends with your friend Jason. And we think before he died, he told the nurse about a hidden treasure in Jason's old house."

Joanne sat in silence for a few moments, taking in all that Danielle had just told her. Finally, she asked, "Who is this best friend?"

"His name was Roman Sellars."

Joanne arched her brows. "Roman Sellars? He's the one who died in the care home?"

"Yes, did you know him?"

"I haven't heard that name in years. No, I didn't know him, but I remember him. Mostly because he was a good-looking guy, and… oh, he dated Sally. That's why you talked to Sally."

"Yes. She hadn't seen or heard from him since he left Frederickport about twenty years ago. The only thing she told us that helped was that he was Jason's best friend. Which sort of supports the chief's hunch that those men weren't involved in a random break-in. They were looking for something specific."

"If there's a hidden treasure in that house, I can't believe Jason knows anything. He could have removed it before he sold the property."

"Do you know anything about Roman, his relationship with Jason?" Danielle asked.

"I didn't really know Jason back then. I knew who he was, just like I knew who Roman was. Jason and Roman ran in the same circles. Jason and his wife attended our church, but Roman didn't."

"Jason has never mentioned Roman? According to Sally, they were best friends," Walt asked.

"No. But now that you mention it, I remember a story about Jason confronting Roman in a bar, and there was a fight. From what I understand, Roman had started drinking; this was sometime after Jason's wife left him. Someone said Jason was trying to help him. But some people can't be helped. Not long after that, I heard Roman left town. But Jason has never mentioned him to me. We've never really discussed what happened back then."

"Were there ever any rumors about Roman being involved in anything illegal?" Walt asked.

Joanne frowned. "What do you mean?"

"Like you said, if something was hidden in the house, it's doubtful Jason put it there, because why not retrieve it before selling the house? But if Roman needed to hide something, maybe he hid it at his friend's house, believing no one would look there. And for some reason, he couldn't go back and get it," Walt explained.

"Can't Adam and Melony simply go through their house and find whatever it is?" Joanne asked.

"They're trying," Danielle said, "but it could be hidden anywhere."

Joanne let out a sigh and then said, "I'm reluctant to bring any of this up with Jason. I know how that period in his life devastated him."

"I understand. And I'm not really sure what to ask anyway," Danielle admitted.

"But if you want to find out more, there is one person who might remember something. She's really the only one I remember from Jason's circle back then who is still in Frederickport. It's Jason's former sister-in-law."

"His wife's sister?" Danielle asked.

Joanne shook her head. "No. She was married to the wife's brother. The brother died a few months before his sister left Jason. You might talk to her. In fact, you probably already know her; she works at the library—Allison Bettle."

AFTER JOANNE LEFT for home late Thursday evening, and Walt and Danielle had just finished dinner, Marie popped in to say hello and find out if they had learned anything interesting at the bookstore. The twins were still in their highchairs, happily finishing up their dinner. Danielle gave Marie a quick rundown of everything they had learned today.

"I really don't remember any of those people. But they were all much younger than me," Marie said.

"What have you been up to today?" Danielle asked.

"I've spent most of the afternoon with Melony and Adam, playing a game of twenty questions."

Danielle arched her brow. "Twenty questions?"

"Yes, Adam is full of questions, and I'm seriously considering having a dream hop with him so I can answer his questions face-to-face, because frankly I'm getting writer's cramp."

Walt chuckled. "Marie, how does one get writer's cramp when you don't have a physical hand to cramp?"

Marie shrugged. "Just an expression. And I also watched the dear boy go through each room, looking for likely hiding places. Thus far, Melony has kept Adam from removing paneling and floorboards. At this point, they can't find any clues, and it's conceivable he could remove all the floorboards and find nothing. And then what—start removing the wallboards?"

"Maybe this sister-in-law of Jason's might give us a hint." Danielle glanced up at the counter at the stack of covered cake pans filled with cookies. "Hey, Marie, would you mind helping Walt give the twins a bath?"

"Certainly, dear."

"Where are you going?" Walt asked.

"I want to take some cookies over to Olivia. I've been meaning to, and she's usually home by now. While I'm over there, I can see what she knows about Allison. I know who she is, but I don't really know her. I can't just walk up to someone I hardly know and start the conversation by saying, '*Hi, any idea what treasure might be hidden in the house your sister-in-law used to live in?*'"

<hr>

TWENTY MINUTES LATER, Danielle sat at Olivia's kitchen table while Olivia poured them both a cup of chamomile tea. Danielle watched Olivia, thinking she reminded her of a nice version of the *One Hundred and One Dalmatians'* villain, with her two-toned, black and gray-white hair.

Olivia set the two cups of tea on the table and sat down. Some of the cookies Danielle had brought over sat on the middle of the table on a plate. "I've been meaning to call you about Christmas."

"Will you be coming?" Danielle asked.

Olivia smiled at Danielle as she gently picked up her cup of tea. "I appreciate the offer, but my sister, Shanice, called me the other day, and she told me what my Christmas gift is. She has booked us both a Christmas cruise."

"Really? Wow, that sounds like fun."

Olivia grinned. "It does. I wondered why Shanice kept asking me about my days off around Christmas. I sort of thought she was planning to surprise me. Which she did, but I thought the surprise was her coming here for Christmas, but it seems it's the two of us going on a cruise."

"I'm happy for you."

"I do appreciate your invitation, though. Thank you."

Danielle picked up her cup of tea, took a sip, and then set it back down. "You're welcome. And I didn't just come over here to bring you the cookies, or to ask if you were coming for Christmas dinner." Danielle then went on to tell Olivia everything that had happened since that fateful morning she and Walt had dropped Adam off at his house after he got food poisoning. Unlike Joanne, Olivia knew the secrets of Beach Drive. Olivia had her own secrets, which the mediums knew, and hers was not a secret they had yet shared with Adam, Melony, or Eddy.

"Interesting," Olivia said when Danielle finished the telling. "Coincidentally, just the other day Allison told me about Jason and his wife."

Danielle arched her brows. "Really?"

"Allison is a widow. We've become friends since I started working at the library. In fact, I'm going Christmas shopping with her on Saturday. The two of us go out to dinner every few weeks. The last time we went out, it was on the first Sunday of the month. On that Sunday, as we were sitting there, each enjoying a glass of wine, Allison mentioned it was December first and then proceeded to tell me how her husband's sister had left her husband on December first. She told me the whole sad and sordid story."

"And?"

"Allison and her husband moved to Frederickport after her sister-in-law and Jason moved here. She was close to her sister-in-law and had always been fond of Jason. After her husband died unexpectedly, she relied more on Jason and his wife. But when her sister-in-law left Jason for another man, well, it changed everything. Jason didn't believe Allison when she told him she had no idea his wife had a lover or was planning to leave him. He told her he never wanted to talk to her again. And they haven't. They both still live in this town and haven't spoken to each other in years. I could tell it still bothers Allison. I doubt she would have told me about any of that if it hadn't been the anniversary of the date her sister-in-law left."

TWENTY-EIGHT

Before Danielle had returned to Marlow House the previous evening, Olivia had mentioned that she and Allison planned to have breakfast together at Pier Café before Christmas shopping on Saturday. Olivia suggested Danielle just show up at the same time, and Olivia could invite her to join them. Danielle agreed.

Danielle spent the next day at home. After breakfast, Walt retreated to his attic office to work on his newest project, while Joanne was busy cleaning the rooms on the second floor, and Danielle was in the living room with the twins and Max. Danielle rotated her time, spending some of it giving Addison and Jack attention, or working on her Christmas list. She had managed to find the children's books she wanted to buy for Connor and Evan at Sally and Susan's before leaving with Sally to have lunch the previous day. Like the books, many of the items on her list she would buy locally, and some she planned to buy online. Now sitting on the sofa with her tablet, Max by her side, his black tail twitching, and the twins napping on the quilt spread out on the floor, Danielle noted the date. It was twelve days before Christmas.

"I'd better get this stuff ordered if I want it in time," Danielle told Max. She then proceeded to place her online orders.

Flames flickered and crackled from the living room fireplace. On its mantel, a pine-scented candle burned, filling the air with the scent of fresh pine. From the corner, the Christmas tree's lights twinkled. Danielle had talked Walt into doing something he swore he would never do—they'd bought an artificial Christmas tree before Thanksgiving. While Danielle loved a real tree, she also loved putting up a tree early, and the thought of a tree drying on the first floor while she was on the second floor with her babies concerned her. After they assembled the tree, Walt had to admit it looked better than he expected, and he appreciated how the lights were already on the tree. Danielle pointed out it wasn't as messy, no pine needles on the floor, and it was easier for her to hang ornaments, as it enabled her to bend branches when necessary, allowing certain ornaments to fit that normally wouldn't on a live tree.

THE NEXT MORNING, Danielle prepared for the mock-accidental meet-up at Pier Café with Olivia and Allison. The previous evening, when Danielle had called Heather to see if she could watch the twins on Saturday morning while she and Walt went to Pier Café, she immediately changed course when Heather mentioned that she just didn't know Allison, they had worked together on several humane society fundraisers, and Heather considered her a friend. Instead of Walt going with Danielle to Pier Café, Danielle asked Heather to accompany her.

EVERYTHING WORKED out better than planned. When Danielle and Heather showed up at Pier Café and stopped at the booth to say hello to Olivia and Allison, it was Allison who invited Danielle and Heather to join them. Olivia didn't have to.

After Danielle and Heather joined their table, Allison spent the next five minutes singing Heather's praises, appreciative of all Heather had done for the local humane society. It was after Carla came to their table and took their order that the conversation eventually gave an opening to Danielle, when Allison asked Danielle if she missed running a BnB.

"I miss meeting new people," Danielle replied before recounting the manufactured story she had given Ruby.

"Oh my, I know who that is," Allison said. "Roman is dead?"

"I'm sorry, was he a friend?" Danielle asked.

Allison considered the question a moment before saying, "I suppose at one time I considered him a friend. But not a good friend. He was my ex-brother-in-law's best friend." Allison paused a moment as if something had just popped into her head, and then said, "I wonder if Jason knows Roman died."

"Jason?" Heather asked, but she already knew the answer.

"My former brother-in-law. He was married to my husband's sister." Allison glanced at Olivia. "I told you about her." Olivia nodded and started to say something, but Allison had already turned to Heather and Danielle and said, "I always think about Evangeline at this time of year. She was my husband's sister. They were very close. I often wonder if he hadn't died, would she and Jason still be together?"

"What happened?" Heather asked.

Allison picked up her coffee cup and took a sip before answering, "My husband and I moved to Frederickport about six months before he died. Jason and Evangeline had been living here for a few years, and not long after they moved here, she went on a campaign to convince us to move here too. My husband was in sales and traveled a lot, and at the time we were trying to have children. So we decided it was a good idea to move, because when we had children, and he was off on a business trip, I'd have family here."

Carla interrupted Allison's story when she showed up with the food. After she finally left, Danielle asked Allison to continue.

"The first four months, we were happy here. But then everything changed."

"What happened?" Heather asked.

Allison picked up a packet of strawberry jam and opened it. "My husband was diagnosed with an aggressive form of cancer. He went for his regular checkup, they saw something they didn't like in his blood tests, and he was gone a month later."

"I'm so sorry," Danielle said.

"Thank you." Allison spread the jam on her toast. "My husband died in June. Everything happened so quickly. I thought I was planning a family, but I ended up planning a funeral. Evangeline took her brother's death hard, and Jason back then, he was our rock. When the Christmas season approached not six months later, I knew it was going to be especially hard on Evangeline because she loved Christmas and was so looking forward to having us all together. It was supposed to be the first Christmas we were all together in Frederickport. Instead, my husband was gone, and then on December first, Evangeline left Jason for another man and basically disappeared from Frederickport. I never saw her again." Allison ate her toast and picked up a piece of bacon.

"You never saw her again?" Danielle asked.

Allison shook her head. "I got a letter from her a few months later, telling me she just couldn't live in Frederickport with her brother gone; it was too painful. She said I probably wouldn't understand, but she had turned to someone else in her grief, and she had fallen in love with him. She claimed she hadn't been in love with Jason for years, which, frankly, shocked me."

"You thought they had a good marriage?" Danielle asked.

"Yes. I thought they had a solid marriage. And poor Jason, he was shattered when she left him."

"What happened to Jason?" Heather asked.

"He still lives in Frederickport. His name is Jason Aldridge, but I doubt you've met him; I understand he's become something of a recluse. I haven't seen him for years. Although, one of my friends mentioned seeing him a few times eating alone at Pier Café. After Evangeline left him, he refused to believe I didn't know about her affair. But I didn't. I was as blindsided as he was. But he refused to listen to me. He cut me out of his life."

"What happened to the friendship between Roman and Jason?" Danielle asked.

"Oh yes, Roman. I almost forgot about him—that's what started this trip down memory lane." Allison picked up her coffee cup and took a drink before continuing, "I was there when Roman told Jason Evangeline left him for another man. That day, Jason had driven me to Portland. I had some business with our attorney regarding my husband's estate. When we got back that evening, we found Roman pacing in the living room. He was a mess. Practically crying when he told Jason he didn't want to be the one to have to tell him. According to Roman, when he stopped at the house to ask Evangeline for a favor, she was at the house with another man. She told him she was leaving Jason. Jason refused to believe Roman, but when he went up to their bedroom, he found her wedding rings sitting on her dresser, and her jewelry box, which was kept in the safe, was empty, just as Roman said it was. But she left everything else behind."

"She didn't take her clothes?" Danielle asked.

Allison shook her head. "No. According to Roman, she told him she wouldn't take anything with her that Jason had given her because she didn't want to be accused of stealing from him, and that she was just taking what belonged to her before their marriage. I suspect that hurt Jason the most—that she would say something like that."

"You said she emptied her jewelry box," Heather asked.

Allison smiled and gave a nod. "Ahh, yes, the jewelry box. My husband's maternal grandmother was quite wealthy. Extremely wealthy. She had something like twenty grandchildren, all boys except for one granddaughter, Evangeline. When she died, she divided her estate equally between her children and grandchildren, but she left her only granddaughter all her jewelry, which I suspect would be worth in the millions today."

"Millions?" Danielle asked.

Allison nodded. "After Jason saw the wedding rings Evangeline left behind, he accused me of knowing about the affair. He refused to believe I hadn't known she was seeing someone else. Jason was convinced the only reason I asked him to take me to Portland that day was a ruse to get him out of town so she could leave without having to confront him. He told me he wanted nothing to do with me ever again. One of their neighbors, a friend of mine, told me Roman spent a lot of time with Jason over the next few months. He was always at his house. She told me that Roman seemed as distraught over Evangeline leaving as Jason was." Allison scoffed and added, "Which wouldn't surprise me."

"Why do you say that?" Danielle asked.

Allison picked up a napkin and wiped her mouth. She looked at Danielle and smiled. "Because I always suspected Roman was in love with my sister-in-law. It was the way he looked at her when he assumed no one was paying attention to him. Even when he had a girlfriend. And after he broke up with his girlfriend, Evangeline confided in me once that Roman was getting a little too attentive. She didn't say anything to Jason because she couldn't quite put into words what exactly made her uncomfortable. Anyway, later, after she left Jason, I heard Roman was drinking heavily, hanging out in bars. One of our mutual friends told me Jason tried to get Roman to leave a bar when he'd had too much to drink, and the two got into a physical altercation. Not long after that, I heard Roman left town."

"That letter you received from Evangeline, are you sure it was her handwriting?" Danielle asked.

"Handwriting? No." Allison laughed. "Evangeline never hand-wrote a letter; she always typed letters. My husband used to tell me that when Evangeline was in high school, she typed all of her notes, which apparently some of her male classmates found highly amus-ing. They'd often teased her about it."

"WHAT DO YOU THINK?" Heather asked Danielle as they sat together in Heather's car in the pier parking lot. They had finished breakfast and said goodbye to Olivia and Allison minutes earlier.

"Well, we learned about some priceless jewelry that supposedly left with a woman who later sent a letter to her sister-in-law. A typed letter," Danielle said.

"And what does that remind you of?"

Danielle looked at Heather and nodded. "Maisy's letters."

TWENTY-NINE

On Saturday evening, Lily stood at her living room window with Sadie at her side, looking across the street. Chief MacDonald had already parked in front of Marlow House and was just getting out of his car with Evan and Eddy Junior. Melony and Adam had arrived minutes earlier. Lily turned from the window and looked at her husband, who sat in the recliner, holding Emily Ann while Connor played with his blocks on the floor nearby. "Ian, when did our Sunday family dinners with your parents become our Saturday family dinners?"

Ian looked up at Lily and frowned. "Umm…when we switched them to our house, why?"

Lily turned back to the window. "I kinda want my Saturdays back. I'm feeling like your sister right now."

"What do you mean?"

Lily walked away from the window and plopped down on the sofa. She set her stockinged feet on the coffee table and leaned back against the sofa cushion. "Everyone is over there again. I hate being out of the loop."

"You've already talked to Danielle; you know why they're there."

Lily stubbornly folded her arms across her chest and said, "Yeah, but I just want to be there too."

"If Saturday is family night with your in-laws, that means you have Sundays back."

"Umm…did you forget what we're supposed to do tomorrow?"

He had forgotten. When he remembered, Ian cringed. His mother had insisted that he and Lily and their children, along with Joe and Kelly, come over to her house late Sunday afternoon, as she had hired a photographer to take family Christmas photos.

Ten minutes later, Ian's parents arrived, followed by Joe and Kelly.

***

THE SAME GROUP that had been at Marlow House last Saturday evening, sans Marie, gathered there again this Saturday. But instead of having Chinese food and eating in the dining room, they had pizza in the living room on paper plates. Danielle had just finished recounting most of what had happened since they had all been together. Eddy Junior interrupted her and asked, "What did you mean, Maisy's letters?"

Danielle looked at the teenager. "Remember the bodies they found next door when Pearl was living there? One of them was Maisy, and her twin sister, Daisy, had been impersonating her for years. No one realized Maisy was dead and had never left town. One reason everyone assumed she was still alive and somewhere living her life was because people received letters from her."

"But they weren't from Maisy?" Eddy asked.

Danielle shook her head. "No, they were from Daisy."

"Wow, that's savage," Eddy said.

"Does that mean Evangeline is dead?" Evan asked.

"We don't know if Evangeline's letter to her sister-in-law is fake," MacDonald said.

"But if it is fake, are you suggesting Evangeline is dead and that this Roman took her jewels and hid them at her house and then left them?" Adam asked. "That makes little sense."

"If Allison and Evangeline were close, and they were sisters-in-law through Evangeline's brother and not her husband, I don't understand why she would totally cut off Allison. It's one reason I'd be suspicious of a typed letter followed by years of noncommunication," Brian said. "But it doesn't mean Roman wasn't telling the truth."

About to take a bite of pizza, Heather paused and looked at Brian. "Why do you say that?"

"Allison said the jewels were in the safe, which makes sense if they were worth a fortune. I have to assume Evangeline knew the combination, since it was her home and her property, but why would Roman? If that letter was fake, and something had happened to Evangeline, it could also be she hooked up with the wrong person who manipulated her during her grief, and then after he got his hands on her property, he got rid of her and sent that letter so people wouldn't start looking for Evangeline."

"That's possible, and it would mean her jewelry isn't what those men were looking for," Danielle said. "But I didn't finish telling you guys everything Allison told us. According to Allison, Roman had the safe combination."

"Yeah, I asked Allison about that. I thought the same thing as you, Brian," Heather said. "But Allison told us Roman and Jason weren't just best friends, they were business partners."

"According to Allison, she'd heard they dissolved the partnership after Roman started drinking heavily," Danielle explained. "But Allison remembers being at their home a few times when Roman took something out of the safe. So yeah, he had the combination."

"Another thing Danielle didn't mention yet," Heather continued. "Over the years, Allison tried to reach out to Evangeline. The one letter she received had no return address, just a postmark from Portland. About a year after receiving that one letter, she turned to a private investigator, hoping to find her so she could reach out. But it was like she vanished without a trace. Then, a few years later, while cleaning out her garage, Allison started sorting through some old boxes of her husband's. She found photographs and copies of documents of the antique jewelry

Evangeline had inherited. Allison decided to turn those over to the private investigator."

"Why?" Adam asked.

Heather shrugged. "The pieces were unique and worth a fortune. She figured if her sister-in-law needed money, she might sell something. Because of their value, she figured any pieces Evangeline wanted to sell, she would do through an auction or deal with a reputable collector. If they could find where Evangeline had sold something, they might be able to use that information to find her. But the PI she hired did a deep dive, and there was no trace of the jewelry."

For the next twenty minutes they discussed plausible scenarios while Eddy Jr. and Evan quietly collected the used paper plates, napkins, and empty pizza boxes and took them to the kitchen. When the boys returned to the living room, the adults were no longer having one discussion. They had broken off into several groups, each having its own conversation. Danielle wasn't engaged in any of the current discussions but sat on the sofa, with her laptop pad and laptop computer on her lap, the computer turned on while Danielle's fingertips moved over its keyboard.

Eddy had just stepped a few feet into the living room when Addison floated by. He momentarily froze, watching the gurgling baby wave one hand while shoving a tiny fist into her drooling mouth, her little body some four feet above the floor.

Evan, who had stopped walking when his brother did, looked at Eddy and said, "Marie. She's here."

Eddy gave a nod. "That's what I figured." Eddy didn't return to the game table, where he and Evan had been sitting when eating their pizza, but sat on the floor next to Heather, who sat by the Christmas tree. Hunny followed Eddy over to Heather and promptly wedged herself between Eddy and Heather, snuggling close to Heather.

Evan walked over to the sofa and sat next to Danielle. "Whatcha doing on the computer?"

Danielle looked up at Evan and smiled. "I want to see if I can find anything on Evangeline."

"Like on Facebook or something?"

"I looked on Facebook, but there were dozens of Evangelines, and if she is still alive, I'm not sure what last name she's using."

"So what are you looking for now?"

Danielle shrugged. "I decided to check out the *Frederickport Press*'s online morgue."

Evan frowned at the word morgue. As the son of the police chief, he understood exactly what a morgue was.

Noticing Evan's frown, Danielle laughed. "A newspaper's morgue is just where they have copies of all their old newspapers. I was wondering if the local paper had a picture of her. If I did find something on social media, I would at least have a general idea of what she looked like."

Evan sat quietly as he watched Danielle log into the local newspaper's website. In the background, the chatter of overlapping conversations filled the silence. Several minutes later, the conversations came to an abrupt stop after Danielle yelled, "I found her. I found Evangeline."

"What do you mean?" Chris asked. All eyes in the room were now on Danielle.

"On the *Frederickport Press* website. It's from the Christmas edition of the newspaper, the year before Evangeline left Frederickport. It's her at the annual Christmas tree lighting. She's dressed up as Mrs. Santa. A very young, very beautiful Mrs. Santa."

Danielle turned the laptop around so everyone could see the monitor. Her friends gathered around her, curious about the woman who had been the center of this evening's discussion. Marie waited for the others to move out of the way before she moved closer to the monitor. Still holding Addison in her arms, Marie looked at the monitor and said, "It's possible Evangeline never left Frederickport."

"Why do you say that?" Walt asked.

"Because her ghost is still in Frederickport, and the last time I saw her, she was wearing the very same dress in that picture. It was after they found the abandoned car, and Eva and I were helping Brian look through the houses. She was there, in one of the houses I checked. I assumed she was alive. She must have seen me, but she said nothing."

When Heather finished repeating what Marie had just said for the mediums, Brian asked, "Do you remember which house?"

Marie looked at Brian. "It was the very first house." Again, Heather repeated Marie's words.

"Do you know whose house that was?" Brian burst out. "That was Jason Aldridge's house!"

"The ghost of Jason's wife is with him?" Walt asked.

Adam stood up. "Wait a minute. Are you saying this woman, Evangeline, whom we've been talking about tonight, is really dead?"

"Looks that way," Heather said.

"And in answer to your question, Walt, yes," Marie said.

"Does this mean the men who broke into our house might have been looking for Evangeline's jewelry?" Melony asked.

"It's possible," Edward said. "But we still don't know what happened to her, and if that's what they were looking for, how was Roman involved?"

"And none of this helps us find whatever's hidden," Adam grumbled. "It could be hidden anywhere. I suppose I could tear down the house, board by board, after all, that particular treasure is supposedly worth millions. Of course, I could do that and find nothing, because it's also possible they were never talking about missing jewels."

"Adam has a point," Chris said. "It's possible Evangeline left Frederickport and later discovered she had made a mistake. When she died—which could have been from completely natural causes—she returned to Jason. And perhaps Roman was in love with his best friend's wife, and on his deathbed started talking about her, and during the ramblings of a dying man, Shawn somehow got the idea there was a treasure in her house."

"Sort of like when those guys were looking for a fortune in the tunnels, and they didn't realize it was the name of a man who died in the tunnels?" Danielle suggested.

Chris nodded. "Something like that."

"If she's still with her husband, why doesn't Marie just go ask Evangeline what happened?" Evan asked.

197

THIRTY

elony and Adam had been home for about an hour when
Melony stepped out of the shower, her hair wet from the
shampoo. After leaving the bathroom, she wore her floor-length
fleece robe and her damp hair wrapped in a towel. She expected to
find Adam in their bedroom, but he wasn't there.

She found him in one of the spare bedrooms, walking around its
perimeter as if making an inspection, his hands in the pockets of his
hoodie, which he hadn't bothered taking off since coming home
from Marlow House.

"What are you doing?" Melony asked.

"I'm just thinking about everything."

"Looking for a hiding place?"

Adam shrugged and then sat down on the guestroom bed. "The
crazy thing, having a possible mystery treasure somewhere in our
house is the least of this weirdness."

Melony laughed and sat on the bed next to Adam. "Yeah, I
agree. All of this has been, well, kinda hard to process."

Adam turned to Melony. "Grandma died four years ago. She
was gone, or so I assumed. And all this time, she hasn't only been
watching over us, she's been actively involved with our friends,

and we had no idea. All of this stuff going on in the background."

"I get what you mean. Tonight, I saw Kelly and Joe across the street at Lily and Ian's, and they have absolutely no clue what's been going on. Joe's a cop, but he doesn't realize Brian and Eddy are keeping things from him."

"You know what's especially wild to me?" Adam asked.

Melony shook her head. "What?"

"I remember when Grandma was younger—when I was a kid. And she used to do a lot of stuff; she was pretty active. And then, over the years, I watched her slow down. There were things she couldn't do anymore, things I had to help her with."

"You were a good grandson."

"I tried to look after Grandma; she needed me. And now…" For a moment Melony thought Adam was going to break into tears, but he burst into laughter.

Startled by Adam's sudden outburst, Melony stared at her husband. When he finally stopped laughing, she asked, "What is so funny?"

Adam wore a silly grin on his face as he looked at Melony. "Because Grandma is a ninja now! According to everyone, my life isn't the only one she's saved in the last four years. She keeps herself busy; when she's not saving lives or helping to solve crimes, she's babysitting, painting rooms, and she freaking talks to the animals. And now she's off interrogating some ghost. I have the coolest grandma."

<hr>

AFTER LEAVING MARLOW HOUSE, Marie visited a few of Eva's favorite haunts until she finally found Eva in the museum, standing in the portrait section, observing her likeness under the dim night lighting of the display. Marie told Eva about the evening's events and asked her to accompany her to visit Evangeline.

"Sounds interesting," Eva murmured before she and Marie left the museum for Jason Aldridge's home.

MARIE AND EVA entered the parlor first, where Marie had originally seen Evangeline. But no one was in the room, yet the sound of a television came through the wall adjacent to the living room. When they moved through the wall into the living room, they found both Jason and Evangeline sitting together on the sofa, watching television. Jason continued to watch his program, unaware of his new guests, yet Evangeline startled at the sudden appearance of the two women and stared for a moment before quickly turning away, looking back to the television.

"You can see us, Evangeline. Stop pretending," Marie said.

Evangeline turned back toward Eva and Marie. "Who are you? How do you know my name?"

"We need to talk to you, dear. We mean no harm," Marie said gently. "In fact, we want to help. My name is Marie Nichols."

Evangeline cocked her head slightly and stared at Marie, studying her face. "I remember a Marie Nichols. We weren't really friends, but I knew who she was. But you don't look like her." The next moment, Marie's illusion transformed, now looking like she had twenty years earlier. Evangeline gasped at the transformation and said, "Now I remember you."

Marie motioned toward Eva. "This is my friend Eva Thorndike."

Evangeline turned her attention to Eva. "Yes, I see that now. Eva Thorndike, the silent screen star. I remember reading an article about you in the local newspaper. It included a photograph of your portrait that the city has in storage."

"It's not in storage now," Marie said. "Later we can catch you up on what's happened since you moved over to our side, but at the moment, we need to find out how you ended up here."

NOT WANTING to compete with Jason's television, the three ghosts moved to the parlor. Once settled, the first thing Evangeline asked was, "Why do you want to know how I ended up here?"

Eva looked from Evangeline to Marie. "Perhaps it would be best if you first explained to Evangeline how you and I ended up here."

Marie gave a nod and told Evangeline all that had happened that month. By the time Marie finished her telling, the television in the next room had been turned off, and Jason had gone to bed. The three ghosts sat in the parlor, the room illuminated solely by the moonlight spilling through the windowpane.

They sat for a few minutes in silence before Evangeline said, "Roman, I often wondered if he was still alive. What happened to him?"

"You need to tell us what happened to you," Marie said.

"Roman killed me," Evangeline said plainly. "Oh, he didn't mean to. After he saw what he had done, he panicked. Told horrible lies. Tore apart my family."

"Killed you? How? Why?" Marie asked.

"Allison told you the truth; Roman made me feel uncomfortable. I'm not sure that telling Jason would have changed anything. Perhaps, but I doubt it. It only started bothering me after he broke up with Sally. Before, when he and Sally were still together, I assumed his attentiveness was nothing more than a duty he felt toward Jason."

Marie frowned. "Duty?"

"Yes. There are some men who feel it's their duty to protect the women in their lives. Jason is this way, and I assumed Roman was that way. In the beginning, when Roman became more attentive when Jason wasn't present, I saw it as him making an awkward attempt at gallantry and covering for Jason until he returned. I never imagined he did this because he felt anything personal toward me, because he behaved that way toward me even when he was with Sally. And Sally certainly never seemed offended when Jason gave me a little extra attention; in fact, she was very sweet herself."

Marie smiled but made no comment.

"But it started making you uncomfortable," Eva said.

Evangeline nodded. "Yes. After Roman broke up with Sally, he seemed to be even more attentive, and at first, I wondered if it was my imagination. That's why I said something to Allison."

"So what happened? You said he killed you, but it was an accident," Marie asked.

Evangeline stood up and walked to the window. With her back to Marie and Eva, she looked out into the night, her voice steady and clear as she continued, "Roman had recently moved into his new house. It was about a mile away from ours. It overlooked the ocean, with a steep walkway leading from his backyard down to the beach. He didn't have any close neighbors except for a house on the south, and no one lived there full time. There was a lot of privacy." She turned to face Marie and Eva.

"Is that where it happened?" Eva asked.

Evangeline nodded. "Jason had taken Allison to Portland. Roman stopped by my house right after they left and asked me if I could come with him to his house and give him some advice. He told me he wanted to decorate for Christmas, and he'd never done it before. He knew how I loved Christmas, and he wanted me to walk through the house with him and give him some ideas. I didn't want to go, but I couldn't come up with an excuse without sounding rude. Initially, I had a gut feeling not to go. But I told myself I was being silly because Roman would never do anything improper. I should have listened to my gut."

"Roman didn't want you to help decorate his house?" Marie asked.

"No. Once we were alone in his living room, with me foolishly looking around at the room, trying to decide what space needed garland and where to put the tree, he grabbed my wrist, pulled me into an embrace, and told me he loved me. That he had always loved me."

"What did you do?" Eva asked.

"He started to kiss me, and I pushed him away. He kept pleading. Insisted I felt the same way about him; he could see it in how I looked at him. He told me we were meant for each other. He grabbed my wrist again. I tried to pull away, slipped on the carpet, fell, hit my head. The next thing I know, I'm standing outside my body, looking down at it while Roman is going absolutely crazy."

"I don't imagine he was expecting you to die," Marie said.

Evangeline shook her head. "I often wondered later, after he regained his composure, if he regretted how he handled the situation. He should have simply called the police, claimed it was a horrible accident, that I tripped and fell. People fall all the time on their own. He could have given Jason the same story he gave me, that I was there to give him some suggestions for decorating for Christmas. Instead, he made the tragedy a hundred times worse."

"What did he do?" Eva asked.

"After he realized I was dead, he started pacing the living room, talking to himself, periodically rechecking my pulse. Then he came up with a plan. I wasn't sure what the plan was, not until I saw it played out. But he kept telling himself it was going to work. He pulled my wedding rings from my finger and dragged my body outside, to the pathway leading to the ocean, and I guess you could say he gave me a burial at sea. Fortunately for him, no one saw him."

"He put you in the ocean?" Marie gasped.

"Yes. I stood next to him on the beach as we both watched my lifeless body float away, tossed around in the surf. When it was no longer in sight, he returned to his house, grabbed my wedding rings, and drove to my house. Since he had picked me up that morning, he didn't have to worry about my car."

"And he made up the lie that you had left with another man," Eva said. "And he removed your jewelry from the safe."

"Yes. To make the story believable, he needed to have it look as if I had taken my jewelry with me. If I were really leaving with another man, it would be ridiculous for me to leave the jewelry that I had inherited from my grandmother. Roman didn't want it. In fact, he kept repeating that fact over and over as he fumbled to empty the jewelry box before shoving it back in the safe. Had Jason questioned the story and called the police, they would have found Roman's prints all over the safe and jewelry box. But Jason never called the police. He never reported me missing."

"Roman hid the jewelry at your house, didn't he?" Marie asked.

"Yes. And I can tell you where if you'll help me."

"What do you want?" Eva asked.

Evangeline turned to Eva. "I want Jason to understand I didn't leave him. That I loved him. I love him. I want him to reclaim his life. He's wasting it. Mine was taken from me, and Jason is squandering what he has left."

THIRTY-ONE

Eva and Marie stayed through the night talking with Evangeline and ended up leaving early Sunday morning not long after Jason woke up and started making coffee. They wanted Evangeline to return to her old home with them to show them exactly where Roman had hidden the jewelry. But Evangeline refused, telling them the memories were too painful, and Jason was leaving that morning for Portland, and she intended to go with him. But she told them expressly where to find the hidden treasure. Before saying goodbye, they promised Evangeline they would find some way for Jason to learn the truth about her death.

Their first stop was Marlow House, but when they entered the kitchen, they found Walt and Danielle were not alone. Joanne was busy putting away dishes from the dishwasher, chatting with Walt and Danielle, who each sat in a kitchen chair, facing a highchair, each highchair holding one of the twins, while Danielle fed Jack, and Walt fed Addison.

"Oh dear, I guess this is not a good time," Marie said.

Walt and Danielle smiled at the ghosts but said nothing.

Addison pushed away the spoon her father attempted to put in her mouth as she reached for Marie, while Joanne, her back to the table, continued to chatter away, discussing the menu for Christmas and suggesting some new side dishes for this year.

Marie walked to Walt and Addison, gave the baby a kiss, and encouraged her to eat her breakfast. Danielle glanced curiously from Joanne to the ghosts.

"Come, Marie, we should leave so Addison can focus on her breakfast. We can come back later and tell them what Evangeline told us."

At the same time that Eva made that suggestion, Joanne said, "You'll never guess who I saw at the grocery store."

Danielle, who had been listening to Eva, not Joanne, impulsively blurted, "Tell us now!"

Startled by Danielle's outburst, Joanne paused for a moment and said, "Umm…I was going to." Marie giggled while Joanne told them about how she had run into an old BnB customer at Old Salts Bakery.

Talking over Joanne, Eva said quickly, "Short version. Roman was in love with Evangeline, accidentally killed her, put her in the ocean, and hid her jewelry at her house." The next moment, Marie and Eva disappeared.

THEIR NEXT STOP was Heather's, but when Marie saw Brian's car parked in her driveway, and it didn't look as if anyone at the house was up yet this morning, Marie let out a sigh and said, "I don't want to barge in on them."

"I'd rather go to Chris's anyway," Eva said.

Marie rolled her eyes. "Of course you would."

The next moment, the ghosts stood in Chris's living room. All was quiet, and the blinds were closed.

"Chris is sleeping in this morning too?" Marie scoffed. "Like a bunch of teenagers."

The next moment, Hunny came running into the living room, her tail wagging excitedly. She told Eva and Marie she was getting ready to wake Chris up because she needed to go outside, and she wanted breakfast.

"You do that. We'll wait in here," Marie told Hunny.

Chris stumbled out of bed a few minutes later. Marie and Eva sat quietly in the living room, and they could hear his grumbling as he asked Hunny why she had to get up so early. But Chris left his bedroom, let Hunny out the front door, and waited for her to finish her business. When he shuffled into the kitchen, his blond hair in disarray, his feet were bare, and he wore midnight blue fleece pajama bottoms, no shirt, and a powder blue cotton robe, its front hanging open, worn like an afterthought.

He fed Hunny, flipped on the coffeepot, and while it warmed up, he stumbled toward the living room to open the blinds. Chris abruptly froze upon seeing Marie and Eva sitting casually on his sofa, watching him.

"Good morning, Chris," Eva purred. "You look absolutely adorable this morning."

THIRTY MINUTES LATER, Chris sat at his dining room table, drinking a cup of coffee and finishing a cinnamon roll from Old Salts Bakery. Eva and Marie sat with him at the table, and Hunny napped by Chris's bare feet. Marie had just finished recounting what they had learned from Evangeline.

"No one else knows yet?" Chris asked before taking a sip of coffee.

"I gave Walt and Danielle the abbreviated version, but like I said, Joanne was there. And Heather was still in bed. I didn't want to disturb her; she had company."

"Obviously, Adam and Mel haven't been told yet." Chris considered his own words before chuckling.

"What's so funny?" Eva asked.

"Oh, I'm imagining Adam's expression. First when he learns there really is a treasure hidden in his house. And then his expression when he gets his hands on the jewels. I have to say, this is going to be one magical Christmas for Adam." Chris chuckled again before finishing the last of his coffee.

"The jewelry might be hidden at his house, but it's not his. I doubt the treasure trove law would apply in this case, and Adam knows that," Marie said.

Chris shrugged. "He could keep it. Jason never reported the jewelry missing."

"Chris, Evangeline made us promise to find some way to let Jason know what really happened. And that will ultimately mean that the jewelry needs to go back to him," Marie said sternly.

"Oh, I understand." Chris let out a sigh. "It was just fun imagining Adam's initial reaction. And I'm sure Mel will make sure he does what's legal."

BEFORE CONTACTING ADAM, Chris called the other mediums and MacDonald. When Chris phoned Adam, he didn't tell him what Eva and Marie had told him, just that they needed to meet at Adam's house that afternoon, and he would explain everything to them.

Joanne offered to watch the twins when Walt and Danielle mentioned they needed to go over to Adam and Melony's. "They don't need to go out in this weather," Joanne insisted. "Let them stay with me." They accepted her offer.

THEY GATHERED in Adam and Melony's living room, sitting on the large sectional—Walt, Danielle, Heather, Brian, Melony, Adam, MacDonald, Evan, and Eddy Junior. MacDonald's sons, who weren't at school because it was a Sunday, wanted to come along. Both were invested in the story of a possible hidden treasure and what Evangeline's ghost had to say.

Chris stood in the middle of the living room, facing them; in his right hand he held a cordless electric hand drill. Marie and Eva stood in the corner of the living room, observing, while Hunny curled up under the coffee table. Chris had just recounted to the group what Eva and Marie had learned from Evangeline. While he had told them what Evangeline had asked for, regarding finding some way for Jason to learn the truth, he didn't mention who might legally—or morally—own the valuable jewelry.

"So there really is a treasure hidden in our house?" Adam asked.

"Assuming it's still here, and someone didn't find it years ago. You said yourself, this house has been a rental for years and was remodeled several times," Chris said. "According to Evangeline, Roman hid it in the master bedroom, under the hardwood floor under the bed. So let's go see if it's still there."

"That room is carpeted now," Melony said.

"We pull back the carpet," Adam said.

Five minutes later they gathered in the hallway and doorway leading to Adam and Melony's bedroom. Marie moved the bed and pulled up the carpet. Once the bed and carpet were out of the way, Chris walked to the exposed hardwood floor. He noticed where the boards looked as if they had been pulled up and screwed back into place. Before kneeling to unscrew the boards, he asked, "Wasn't Roman afraid Jason would see this?"

"From what Evangeline told us, Roman didn't think this out very well. It was all spur of the moment," Marie said. "And apparently there used to be a very heavy four-poster bed on that spot, so he probably didn't expect anyone was going to move it."

"His plan was good enough that he got away with it," Heather reminded her. "Although I guess he didn't really get away with it, considering what that ghost told Eva and Marie."

"I bet nothing's there," Adam said as Chris lowered the electric drill to the floor.

"Why do you say that?" Eddy Jr. asked from the hallway, his head peeking in the doorway with his brother.

"Because after Jason moved out and took his bed, any of the subsequent tenants who lived here before they put in the carpet would have seen this floor and wondered why those boards had been screwed down. A shoddy repair," Adam said. "They'd wonder what had been hidden under the floorboards."

Danielle laughed. "Adam, you're looking at this from your perspective. Not everyone sees floorboards that have been screwed down and wonders if someone hid something."

"That's my husband, always looking for hidden treasures," Melony teased while giving Adam a playful pat.

If Adam was insulted by Danielle's or Melony's comments, he didn't say. Instead, he, along with the rest of the room, fell silent as Chris slowly removed one screw after another from the floor before prying up a piece of the flooring.

Heather appeared by Chris's side, holding a flashlight she had pulled out of her purse. She turned on the flashlight and shone the light toward the now exposed opening. No one saw what was in the opening aside from Heather and Chris. But when Heather let out a gasp after Chris pulled a velvet pouch from below the floorboards, everyone moved closer.

Ten minutes later they all gathered around Adam and Melony's bed. Spread out on the bedspread were ten velvet pouches that Chris had retrieved from under the floorboard. One by one, Chris emptied the contents of each pouch onto the bed, each time eliciting a gasp from the onlookers.

When he had emptied the last pouch, Melony whispered, "There must be a fortune there."

Adam reached down and gently picked up one of the pieces, closely inspecting it—a gold brooch encrusted with impressive diamonds and rubies. He stared at it for a moment before looking at Danielle. "Do you have room for all this in your safe-deposit box at the bank?"

Danielle looked at Adam. "Yes, but why?"

"We need to keep them somewhere safe before we return them to Jason. And from what Evangeline told my grandmother and Eva, he's in Portland and not coming back until the end of the week."

Danielle arched her brows. "You intend to return them to Jason?"

Adam smiled at Danielle and set the brooch back on the bed.

"They don't belong to me, Danielle. We need to keep them safe until their rightful owner returns. I don't have a safe-deposit box; it would be easier if we could use yours for a few days instead of opening a new one. Of course, the bank is closed today, but I have this super ninja grandma who I'm sure will keep any thieves away from the jewelry until we put them in the bank vault."

"We can also put them in the safe at Marlow House until the bank opens," Walt suggested.

"He called you a super ninja grandma," Eva whispered to Marie, her voice teasing.

Marie didn't react to Adam's ninja comment, nor to Eva's remark. Instead, she stared intently at her grandson, paying no attention to what everyone else in the room was currently saying about the treasure and its fate.

Eva frowned at Marie's response and whispered, "What's wrong?"

Marie broke into a smile, her gaze still on Adam. "He has grown up so much in the last four years. I'm so proud of the man that boy has become."

THIRTY-TWO

After breakfast on Monday morning, Lily and Ian walked over to Marlow House, bringing Emily Ann, Connor, and Sadie with them. They were both curious to see the treasure before Danielle and Adam took it to the bank. After arriving, Ian and Lily headed upstairs with Danielle while their children and Sadie stayed downstairs with Walt and Marie.

The three gathered in Walt and Danielle's bedroom, where they found the king-size bed neatly made. Once in the room, Danielle walked to the wall safe, opened it, and removed the box holding the velvet pouches. She carried it to the bed and removed each pouch from the box, setting them, one by one, on the bedspread.

Lily sat on the side of the bed and glanced from the velvet pouches to Danielle. "I wanted to come over here yesterday after you told me what you found. But we had that photo thing at Ian's parents, and by the time we finally got home, the kids were a mess."

Just as Lily finished her explanation, Danielle emptied the contents of the first pouch onto the bedspread. Lily gasped at the sight, and Ian, his eyes wide, stared at the diamond bracelet and murmured, "Wow, that's beautiful."

Danielle continued emptying each pouch onto the bed. Reverently, Lily and Ian picked up each piece, closely inspecting each one before gently setting it back on its designated pouch. "Adam's really giving this all back to Jason Aldridge?" Lily asked as she started slipping each piece back into its pouch.

"Marie is rather proud of him," Danielle said.

Lily glanced back down at the filled pouches and then back to Danielle. "What I'm curious about, Walt told us that when he talked to Shawn's ghost over at Mark's house, Shawn asked if Mark and Peter had found *it*, and then he told Walt no one would find *it* now. Did Shawn think there was just one piece of jewelry hidden in the house?"

"I suppose it's possible. But I assume he might have been referring to all the hidden jewelry as something like a treasure. So when he told Walt no one would find *it* now, he meant the treasure."

"So what now?" Lily asked.

"Put the jewelry in the bank and wait until Jason gets back in town, and then the chief will talk to him," Danielle explained.

"Despite the fact that is a fortune, I feel sorry for Jason Aldridge," Ian said. "It'll be opening some painful old wounds while giving him more unanswered questions. Did Roman lie about everything, or did Evangeline hide the jewelry before she left for some reason, and did Roman assume she had taken it with her? It's not like you can tell him Marie and Eva spoke to his wife's ghost."

"The chief thought the same thing," Danielle said. "It's why he's hoping to find something to prove what happened to Evangeline. And it's what Marie and Eva promised they would try to do."

"How can the chief prove anything?" Lily asked. "There's no body."

"Not that we're aware of," Danielle said.

POLICE CHIEF MACDONALD sat in his office with Brian and Joe, the door closed. The chief had just finished telling Joe what they had found under the floorboards in Adam and Melony's bedroom while Joe and Kelly were at his in-laws' house, having Christmas pictures taken.

"What made them look there?" Joe asked. When he was still in the hospital, Brian had told him they didn't believe the break-in at Adam and Melony's was random, and that they suspected the men had been looking for something specific. Joe knew that after Brian visited the care home, they learned Shawn's last patient had been a former resident of Frederickport. The chief had discovered— though it wasn't clear to Joe exactly how—that Roman's best friend was the previous owner of Adam and Melony's house, and the wife had once owned a considerable fortune in jewelry. But for Joe, it wasn't clear how they had come to all the conclusions they had, and he didn't understand why Adam would decide to move his bed and pull up the carpet to check under his floorboards.

MacDonald stared at Joe for a moment before answering. Finally, he said, "I'm not sure. I guess it was a hunch. And they were right. And from what we've learned, Evangeline Aldridge's jewelry vanished the same day she supposedly left Frederickport. According to her sister-in-law, no one has heard from her since."

"What are you going to do?" Joe asked. "Did Jason ever report his wife or the jewelry missing?"

"No. As for what I am going to do, I already did it. That's why I brought you both in here. I wanted to let you both in on what's going on. And this is not something I'm making public at the moment."

"Did you find her?" Brian asked.

The chief shrugged. "Maybe."

Joe frowned and looked from Brian to the chief. "Find who?"

"Evangeline. According to several witnesses, Roman told Jason that his wife had left him and took a fortune in jewelry with her. And apparently, Roman was distraught. According to Evangeline's sister-in-law, Roman had been making her uncomfortable with unwanted advances."

Joe arched a brow at the chief's words. "Did he kill her?"

"It's possible. I understand he owned a house right on the ocean. And on the day she supposedly left, her husband and sister-in-law were in Portland. So if she didn't leave, and something happened to her, what is one way to dispose of a body when you live on the ocean?"

"You said you found her," Joe reminded him.

The chief nodded. "I said I think we may have. This morning, I did some research. I learned that a woman's body washed up on Lincoln Beach on Christmas Day, the same month Evangeline supposedly ran off. The body has never been identified. Since no one ever filed a missing person for Evangeline, she was never on their radar. Back then, DNA wasn't as sophisticated as it is today, and I have no idea if any of her relatives have DNA on file."

"It's also possible the jewelry you found didn't belong to Evangeline, someone else put it there, and it's a coincidence," Joe said.

"I suppose that's possible." The chief knew it wasn't. The jewelry belonged to Evangeline, yet he couldn't tell Joe how he knew that. "But Brian will be taking pictures of the jewelry when he meets with Evangeline's sister-in-law this afternoon."

Joe looked from the chief to Brian, back to the chief. "Brian's talking to her today?"

The chief nodded. "She's a friend of Heather's. Heather arranged to meet her today, and she'll be taking Brian along. According to Heather, she has photographs of Evangeline's jewelry. And if it is Evangeline's, we're hoping her sister-in-law can help us contact one of her relatives so we can get a DNA sample."

"I SUPPOSE it's possible the body's not hers," Heather told Brian as the two drove to Lucy's Diner, where Heather had arranged to meet Allison. They had considered having her meet them at Pier Café, but Brian remembered Carla was working today, and he didn't want to deal with the gossipy server hovering around the table.

"True. The chief didn't have Evangeline's height, so he couldn't compare it with the information they have on the remains, but the hair color is the same as Evangeline's, according to Marie, and the estimated age of the body aligns with Evangeline."

"Did they have pictures of the corpse? Her face? She was in the ocean for three weeks, but still——"

"Yes, they do. But I'm afraid the surf combined with the rocks along that area of the coast made her unrecognizable."

ALLISON SAT at a booth in Lucy's diner with Brian and Heather. She had met Brian before, but she suspected this wasn't simply a social call. After they ordered the food, she discovered her hunch had been correct.

She held Heather's iPhone in hand, swiping through pictures. After a few minutes, she solemnly handed the phone back to Heather.

"Were they hers?" Heather asked gently, yet she already knew the answer.

Allison nodded. "Does this mean Evangeline's dead?"

"Obviously, Roman lied," Heather said. "So it's a real possibility."

"Does Jason know yet?"

"He's out of town until the end of the week," Brian said. "So, no. We haven't told him what we suspect or what was found, and we were hoping to have more to tell him before we dump this on him. I understand after his wife left him, he was pretty broken up."

"She obviously didn't leave him," Allison snapped. "And where is her jewelry? It's worth a fortune, and it rightfully belongs to Jason, if she really didn't leave and take it with her."

"It's been put in a safe-deposit box at the bank," Brian explained.

Allison took in a deep breath and exhaled. "I'm sorry. I didn't mean to sound so abrupt."

"I understand. You've just learned someone you cared about might be dead——"

Before Brian could finish his sentence, Allison said, "You mean murdered."

Brian nodded, but he understood Roman hadn't intentionally murdered Evangeline, yet he was responsible for her death. However, none of that mattered because Roman's actions after Evangeline fell and hit her head had destroyed several lives. Should the body they found be Evangeline's, Roman would be forever remembered as the man who murdered his best friend's wife.

"And the woman they found, you suspect it might be Evangeline?"

"It's possible, but we need DNA from a relative. We were hoping you might put us in contact with someone who could provide DNA," Brian said.

Allison considered the request for a moment. Finally, she said, her tone solemn, "I should still have my husband's old address book. It should be in my cedar chest. I'll look when I go home. His cousins are in there. I never really knew them. Met a few when we were first married. Several sent condolence cards after my husband died. And none of them ever contacted me after Evangeline disappeared, although, the private investigator I hired, I gave him the address book, and he contacted a few of her cousins. But none had heard from her. I'm pretty sure he gave me the book back."

"It would be very helpful. Thank you," Brian said.

"I'd like to request one thing."

"What's that?" Brian asked.

"If possible, wait until you have the DNA results before you tell Jason. Discovering Angeline's jewelry has been in the house all these years, I don't know how he'll react. It broke him when he thought she had left him. If the body is hers, at least he can get some closure. But if it's not…" Allison didn't finish her sentence but closed her eyes for a moment.

"I understand," Brian said, his voice soft. "However, they also have pictures of the clothing the woman was wearing at the time, so it's possible Jason will be able to identify his wife by that. Of course, the DNA will still be needed. And even if it turns out not to be her, we still must tell him what was found."

Allison nodded and took another deep breath before exhaling slowly and opening her eyes, her emotions now calm. She looked at Heather and smiled. "Wow, this is some wild coincidence."

"What do you mean?" Heather asked.

"How we ran into each other the other day at Pier Café, and I ended up telling you about Evangeline, and it turns out your boyfriend is working on a case involving her."

Heather smiled weakly. "Yeah, that is a wild coincidence."

Allison reached out and put her hand over Heather's. "Although they say there is no such thing as coincidences."

"Umm…what do you mean?"

Allison's smile widened, and she patted Heather's hand. "Because I think Evangeline brought us together and wanted me to tell you about her."

Heather's mouth curled into a genuine smile. "You may be right."

THIRTY-THREE

Before leaving work on Sunday, Joanne sat down with Danielle to go over her work schedule. She planned to help Danielle prepare for her Christmas dinner, and both Christmas Eve and Christmas this year fell on days Joanne had been taking off. They decided Joanne would come in on Thursday for half a day and take off until Monday, when she would come back to work. Meanwhile, Danielle prepared for Christmas.

Since Heather and Brian's meeting with Allison on Monday, most everyone's attention had returned to Christmas. There was nothing any of them could do to help Evangeline; they had to wait for the DNA results. The last Danielle had heard, Allison had turned her late husband's phone book over to the chief, and he planned to use it to contact Evangeline's relatives to get a DNA sample.

By Tuesday, all the gifts Danielle had ordered online had arrived. She spent that afternoon wrapping the Christmas presents in the parlor while Christmas carols played in the background. Max helped her wrap the packages, yet his idea of help was swatting at the gold ribbon or pouncing on an unfurled roll of wrapping paper to hear it crinkle.

Walt stayed in the living room with the twins, with the Christmas tree lights on and a comforting fire crackling in the fireplace. When not attending to Addison or Jack, Walt sat in his easy chair, reading his book while frequently glancing over the top of its cover to make sure his little ones hadn't crawled off the quilt toward the tempting Christmas tree.

On Wednesday evening, Walt took the twins across the street, where he and Ian visited and watched their children—with Marie's help—while Danielle and Lily went Christmas shopping. One thing on their shopping list was ingredients to make Marie's divinity. Marie had agreed to teach those interested how to make her divinity. Danielle offered to hold the class at Marlow House on Friday, when Joanne was not working. They couldn't do it at Adam and Melony's because their kitchen wasn't stocked with the necessary cooking utensils.

When Thursday rolled around, the chief called Danielle to tell her one of Evangeline's cousins had agreed to give a DNA sample.

"How long do you think it'll take?" Danielle asked the chief.

"I'm not sure. We haven't gotten the sample yet. But if we get it in time, it's possible to get it back by Christmas."

"When are you going to say something to Jason Aldridge?"

"That's one reason I'm calling. Is Joanne working today?"

"Yes, Joanne should be here in a little bit. She's only working a half day. She's going over to Chris's this afternoon to get the guestroom ready for Noah. He'll be here tomorrow."

"That's right, I forgot. Chris's brother is coming for Christmas. I've been a little preoccupied since our newest hire proved not much different from our last new employee."

"In your defense, you didn't hire Clay."

"True. Anyway, I was wondering if you can ask Joanne if she knows when Jason is coming back. Evangeline told Marie and Eva he planned to return at the end of the week, but that could be today or this weekend."

"Is it okay if I tell her about finding the jewelry?"

"You haven't yet?" Danielle heard the chuckle in his voice when he asked.

"No. She knows a little about what's going on, but we haven't seen her since Sunday."

"That's fine. But——"

"Ask her not to say anything to anyone," Danielle finished for the chief.

WHEN JOANNE ARRIVED at Marlow House later that morning, she found Danielle in the parlor, hanging Christmas cards on the wooden Christmas card display Walt had recently attached to the wall adjacent to the parlor desk.

"Morning, Danielle," Joanne greeted as she walked into the room. "Where are Walt and the twins?"

Preparing to hang a card on the display, Danielle paused and turned to Joanne and smiled. "Morning. Walt's upstairs, giving the twins a bath."

Joanne frowned. "This time of day?"

Danielle chuckled. "As you know, we've been trying to teach the twins how to feed themselves with a spoon. So, of course, that means a bowl of oatmeal on the highchair tray."

"Oh my, what happened?"

"I was making toast while Walt sat with the twins. He stood up to pour himself a cup of coffee, and when he did, Addison decided to pick up her bowl of oatmeal and wear it as a hat. She found it hilarious and started giggling. Wanting in on the fun, Jack copied his sister. But once he dumped his oatmeal on his own head, I don't think he liked how it felt. He started crying. And then Addison started crying."

Joanne laughed. "Poor Walt."

"Walt and I cleaned up the twins and took them upstairs to have a bath and wash their hair." That was partially a lie. Marie had helped Walt take Addison and Jack upstairs.

"Those two keep us all on our toes."

"They do. Oh, I need to ask you something; just let me hang

these last two cards." Danielle turned back to the rack and started to hang the card she had been holding.

"Have you gotten many Christmas cards this year? I don't get nearly as many cards as I used to."

After hanging the card she had been holding, Danielle turned to Joanne. "No, me neither." Danielle picked up the remaining Christmas card on the desk and showed it to Joanne. "This one is from Madeline."

"Oh, how is she?" Joanne understood Madeline was Danielle's ex-mother-in-law.

Danielle turned from Joanne and hung the card on the display, adjusting it slightly. "She's doing great. She and Finn are spending Christmas in Tahoe with some friends. And she asked me if we'd be up for a visit after the first of the year."

"Wonderful. I like Madeline. And she seemed quite taken with the twins." Madeline had visited several months earlier.

"She always wanted to be a grandmother."

DANIELLE SAT on the parlor sofa with Joanne. She had just filled her in on all that had happened, leaving out any of the parts involving ghosts.

"And the chief believes the body they found in Lincoln City might be hers?"

"We know Roman lied about Evangeline taking the jewelry with her. What else did he lie about? According to her sister-in-law, Roman's attention had been making her feel uncomfortable. And if he disposed of her body in the ocean on the day she disappeared, it could have washed up on Lincoln Beach at the end of the month. The body has never been identified."

"I just want to tell you the dynamic duo are—" Marie announced as she appeared in the parlor but immediately stopped talking when she saw Danielle wasn't alone.

"So what did you want to ask me?" Joanne asked.

"Do you know when Jason is coming back?"

"All I know, he had a couple of doctor appointments, specialists he sees there. I assume he'll be back by the weekend. But I don't know what day he's coming home."

When Joanne left the room, Marie said, "Evangeline talked about watching her body getting washed out to sea, and how she followed Jason back to her house and stayed with her husband. But it's also possible that during that period she returned to find her body and knows what happened to it, and she didn't mention it to us. If I knew where she was staying in Portland, I'd go ask her. But I suppose I'll have to wait until she returns to ask."

***

ADDISON CLUTCHED a chunk of sourdough bread in one hand and wiggled her feet as she sat on her mother's lap at the kitchen table while her brother was in the living room with their father. Earlier that day, Danielle had offered to show Joanne pictures she had taken of the jewelry they found at Jason's old house. Before leaving for Chris's house, Joanne had accepted the offer and now sat at the kitchen table next to Addison and Danielle, swiping through pictures on Danielle's iPad.

"Oh my. These are beautiful," Joanne murmured before swiping to the next one. She paused for a moment and looked at Danielle. "Do you ever regret sending the Missing Thorndike away? Not being able to wear it?"

Danielle shook her head. "No. While beautiful, I don't need something that expensive—something people keep wanting to steal. It got Cheryl killed. It caused way more trouble than it was worth. Anyway, it belongs on exhibit. I'm sure Eva Thorndike would approve."

Joanne smiled. "I'm sure she would." She looked back down at the iPad and swiped to the next picture.

"I'd like to see them," a voice Joanne couldn't hear called out. Danielle turned abruptly in her chair, holding tight onto Addison. She came face-to-face with Shawn Hoffman. Addison waved to Shawn.

"She can see me too?" Shawn asked.

"Well, I'd better get going." Joanne closed the cover of the iPad and stood up.

Danielle turned back to Joanne, the ghost still behind her, and Addison waving a fist of squished sourdough bread at him.

"She can't see me, can she?" Shawn asked as he stared at Joanne, who looked as if she was looking at him—or more accurately, through him.

"Thanks for everything. See you tomorrow," Danielle told Joanne, forcing a smile, before glancing behind her. Shawn was still there, this time waving to Addison and making silly faces at her.

When Joanne left a few minutes later out the kitchen door and was out of earshot, Danielle turned to face the ghost. "Why are you here?"

Shawn shrugged and then nodded to Addison. "Cute kid."

"Thank you. But you didn't answer my question."

"I returned to the house we broke into. I know you know about Roman. I hung out with Adam and Melony for part of the day. Of course, they didn't realize I was there. They talked about me and Peter and Mark. And what they know about Roman and Evangeline. They talked about finding the jewelry. Adam was telling Melony you took pictures of the treasure before you put it in your safe-deposit box. I was wondering, can I see? I'd like to see what I gave my life for."

Danielle pointed to an empty chair at the table, her other hand still holding onto Addison. After he sat down, she positioned the iPad on the table in front of him and began scrolling slowly through the images. She got halfway through the pictures when he abruptly stood and said, "I don't want to see any more."

"Why?"

"Because I can't believe I risked everything for those. I'm dead because of them. Not to mention, I almost got Adam killed. I'm glad Marie's ghost intervened."

"You know about that?"

Shawn nodded. "Yes. Adam and Melony were talking about it.

They're nice people. Would you tell Adam I'm sorry for what I did? I almost got him killed."

"I will. What are you going to do now?"

Shawn dug his hands into the pockets of his hoodie and shrugged. "After Peter killed me, I wanted to haunt him and his brother. I wanted to make their lives miserable. Then I found out they were dead too. Later, I realized that haunting them, if they were still alive, wouldn't have made me feel better. I was so foolish, I threw everything away."

"I'm going to ask you a serious question. Will you answer it truthfully?"

Shawn shrugged again. "What's the question?"

"Let's pretend your fairy godmother shows up—"

"Are there really fairy godmothers?" he asked seriously.

"I don't know. But let's pretend there are. And yours sends you back in time to the hour before you told Peter about the treasure. She waves a magic wand and tells you that this time, when you break into Adam's house, he won't be there because he won't have food poisoning, and no one will shoot you. What would you do?"

Shawn considers Danielle's question for a moment and then says, "I wouldn't tell Peter. I would find Evangeline's husband and tell him about Roman's deathbed confession. That's what I should have done. That's what I wish I had done."

THIRTY-FOUR

"Who all is going to be here for Marie's cooking class?" Lily asked Danielle late Friday morning as she sat in the kitchen of Marlow House, having a cup of hot cocoa and Christmas cookies with Connor and Danielle. Connor sat on the chair next to Lily, his mop of strawberry blond hair in disarray after removing his knit cap he'd worn over to Marlow House. The cap, along with his and Lily's jackets, now hung on the coat rack by the back door.

Danielle, with her long dark hair pulled into two braids, stood at the open pantry, taking a quick inventory, making sure she had the ingredients to make divinity. She turned to Lily. "Adam and Mel, of course, will be here. Adam's the one who is really excited about this. Cooking is not really Mel's thing, but she's coming over anyway and hanging out with Walt and the twins—and with Ian and your two, if Ian decides to come over too. Heather is getting off early today because Chris is taking off early, and she wants to learn how to make divinity."

"Oh, that's right. Noah's coming today. How long is he staying?"

"Through the New Year." Danielle turned back to the pantry, closed its door, and walked to the table and sat down with Lily and Connor.

"I wonder how he enjoys working for his baby brother, and if he misses teaching."

"From what Heather says, Noah loves his job and is doing some great things. I don't quite understand what it is exactly, but it has something to do with setting up after-school programs in low-income communities. Heather called them Enrichment Afterschool Programs, but I'm not really sure what that means."

"Sounds interesting. I wonder if he misses working with the kids. I miss the kids; I loved teaching. But I'm loving my life right now, being able to spend time with my babies, and they grow up so fast. So, anyone else going to be here?"

"Evan and Eddy Jr. They have a half day today; then Christmas break starts. Last night I told the chief they were welcome to come over this afternoon while he's at work. Told them about Marie's cooking class. Both boys wanted to come. I doubt Evan will want to be part of the cooking class, but I suspect Eddy will."

Lily chuckled. "Yeah, Heather will be there. That kid has such a crush on her."

⸻

KELLY AND JOE MORELLI sat across from each other at a booth at Pier Café on Friday afternoon. They had finished ordering lunch, and Carla had left to get their drinks.

"I'm about done Christmas shopping," Kelly announced. "Lily still hasn't told me what she wants me to bring over to her house on Christmas Eve. Mom said Lily's doing Mexican food. I'm wondering if she's placed an order for tamales from Beach Taco yet. We could bring that."

"What about making them yourself?" Joe suggested.

Kelly arched her brow. "Seriously? Have you ever made tamales? I sure haven't."

"Umm, no. But you can get a recipe online."

Kelly laughed. "Tamales aren't something you can just decide to make."

"Why not?"

Kelly shook her head. "Trust me."

"It was just a suggestion."

They sat in silence for a few minutes when Kelly asked, "When is the chief going to tell Jason Aldridge what Adam found in his old house?"

Joe glanced across the café at Carla, who was now walking their way with their drinks.

"Don't say anything around Carla," Joe whispered.

Kelly frowned. "I wasn't going to."

The next minute, Carla showed up with their beverages. After setting an iced tea in front of Joe and a soda in front of Kelly and chatting a moment, Carla walked away.

"Can I talk now?" Kelly snapped.

"I just meant she was walking over here with our drinks, and I didn't want her overhearing anything about what was found. As for the answer to your question, like I told you before, he plans to talk to him when he gets back in town. And we don't know when that's going to be. According to one of his neighbors, she thought he would be back at the end of the week."

"Of all the places Adam could have looked for a treasure, he starts by pulling up the carpet and then the floorboards under his bed." Kelly shook her head. "That's a big house, lots of places to search. He just happened to look there first?"

Joe shrugged. "The chief said something about him having a hunch."

"Oh, BS."

Joe, who had just picked up his glass of iced tea, paused a moment and cocked a brow at his wife. "BS how?"

"Come on, do you honestly believe a thought popped into Adam's head that said, 'Gee, if those guys were looking for a hidden treasure, I bet it's under my bed. Let's move our bed, pull up the carpet, and have a look!'" Kelly snorted and picked up her glass of soda and took a drink.

Joe set his glass back on the table. "Then what do you think happened?"

"Three possibilities. Number one, Adam has a sixth sense that no one knows about that told him where to look. I don't think that's the case, but I suppose it's possible. Two, Adam tore his house apart before he found it. Although I doubt it's number two, and not just because the chief acted like under his bed was the first place Adam looked. I can't see Mel letting him tear apart the house. But we have a third possibility."

"What's that?"

"Chris."

"Chris?"

"Yeah. I did a little Googling after you told me what Adam found. There are things called ground-penetrating radar, wall scanners, and thermal-imaging cameras that could help someone find something hidden without ripping off paneling and flooring. And Chris, with his money and connections, would be able to get his hands on something like that. That's probably what happened. Chris got ahold of a high-tech gadget so Adam could scan his house and see if there was something hidden. That's what it had to be. I just don't know why they're keeping that part a secret."

AFTER LUNCH, Joe headed back to work while Kelly stopped by her brother's house to ask Lily about the tamales. Not wanting to wake Emily Ann in case she was sleeping, Kelly used her key to get in. But once inside, Sadie didn't come to greet her. Kelly walked through the first floor, but no one was home. She walked back outside, locked the door, and walked over to the garage and peeked in the window. Both cars were inside. Kelly glanced across the street and noticed Melony and Adam's car parked in front of Marlow House.

Wherever Ian and Lily had gone, they had walked and taken Sadie. *They have to be at Marlow House*, Kelly thought. Instead of calling Lily's or Ian's cellphones, Kelly walked across the street. Rather than going to the front door, Kelly entered the front gate and made her way to the side door into the kitchen. As she walked past the kitchen window, she glanced inside and saw a room full of people. But it wasn't the people gathering in the kitchen that caught her attention; it was what looked like a bottle of something floating above the kitchen cabinet—floating.

THOSE WANTING to learn Marie's secret for making perfect divinity filled the kitchen: Danielle, Lily, Heather, and Adam. Eddy was also in the kitchen, but he really didn't care about learning how to make divinity.

Marie stood by the kitchen counter, to the right of where Danielle had arranged the divinity ingredients. Danielle, Lily, Adam, and Eddy sat around the kitchen table, facing the counter, while Heather stood behind the table, her back to the kitchen window, as she faced Marie and played interpreter.

At the kitchen counter, Marie levitated a bottle of corn syrup as she discussed each ingredient necessary for the recipe. Eddy turned to Heather, who was busy repeating Marie's words, when he noticed motion from the kitchen window. Eddy abruptly stood, placing his body between the window and counter, and whispered, just loud enough for the people in the room to hear, "Someone's looking in the window."

The bottle of corn syrup returned to the counter as the kitchen door flew open, and Kelly rushed into the house, her eyes wide as she stared at the kitchen counter. She pointed at the corn syrup, but before she could say anything, Danielle started clapping, stood, and said, "That was amazing, Eddy! Walt will be so proud!"

Kelly shook her head as if trying to clear her thoughts. "I'm sorry I just barged in. I was going to knock." She pointed to the bottle of corn syrup on the counter. "But, but…that was floating in the middle of the air."

Danielle turned to Kelly and grinned while everyone else in the room looked confused. "And isn't that wonderful? That's a hard trick. It took Walt ages to get it right. But Eddy, he's a natural."

Kelly looked at Danielle. "Are you saying Eddy made that fly?"

"Well, it didn't actually fly," Danielle scoffed. "Eddy just made it look that way."

Kelly looked at Eddy. "Wow. That was pretty cool."

Eddy grinned at Kelly. "Thanks."

"I'm sorry." Kelly looked embarrassed. "I didn't mean to barge in without knocking. But I needed to talk to Lily, and I thought she might be here. But when I walked by the kitchen, I saw…"

"No problem," Danielle told her. "Don't worry about it."

Evan walked into the kitchen and stopped suddenly when he saw Kelly. He glanced around before asking, "You haven't started the divinity yet?"

"Divinity?" Kelly asked.

"Yeah, Heather knows how to make divinity," Lily lied. "She was going to teach us, and then Eddy showed us his new magic trick Walt taught him."

"Divinity?" Kelly walked over to the counter and looked over the ingredients. She turned to Heather. "You're using corn syrup? That stuff is horrible for you."

"My recipe calls for corn syrup." Marie sounded insulted. And while Kelly couldn't hear her words, she continued, "It won't kill you. A full life is about enjoying things in healthy moderation."

Heather leaned over to Danielle, who was still standing, and whispered, "Do you think our cinnamon roll consumption qualifies as healthy moderation?" Danielle suppressed a giggle while Kelly stood across the room, waiting for a response to her criticism of corn syrup.

THIRTY-FIVE

Kelly didn't stick around to learn how to make divinity. When it became clear no one was taking her concern about corn syrup seriously, she said her goodbyes, claiming she had Christmas shopping to do. She told Lily she would talk to her later and never mentioned the tamales. Kelly had no desire to sit around and listen to Heather teach a recipe that she would never make. Plus, no one invited her to stay. She had no idea how relieved those gathered in that kitchen were at her departure.

By the time the chief arrived to pick up Evan and Eddy, the cooking class was over, and all the living guests except Adam and Melony had gone home. Walt greeted MacDonald at the front door and then brought him to the living room, where everyone congregated. The twins were upstairs with Marie, napping. The first thing out of Eddy's mouth, upon seeing his father, was to tell him about the floating corn syrup bottle and what Danielle had said to Kelly.

"What happens if Kelly asks you to do the trick sometime?" Edward teased as he took a seat on an empty chair.

Eddy's eyes widened. "Dang, I didn't think of that."

"I bet Danielle will come up with something to tell her if she asks." The chief winked at Danielle. Before Danielle could reply, her phone rang. She picked it up from the end table, looked at it, stood, and walked into the hallway to answer the call.

"So, where is the divinity?" MacDonald asked. "Don't I get a sample?"

"It has to sit for twenty-four hours," Adam told him.

The next moment Danielle returned from taking her call and announced, "That was Joanne. Jason Aldridge is home. He pulled up in his driveway about ten minutes ago."

The chief groaned and leaned back in the chair.

"I see you aren't looking forward to talking to him," Walt said. "I can understand, considering the man is about to learn the woman he loved didn't leave him, and she's probably dead."

"He's also about to learn he's a very rich man," Adam added.

"Talking to him per se has never been the issue. It's what I have to say that bothers me. It's not about having to tell him his wife is dead. Unfortunately, it won't be the first time I've had to have that conversation with someone."

"What is it, Eddy?" Melony asked.

"When Joe came back from lunch, he asked me if Chris had been involved in finding the treasure."

"Involved how?" Danielle asked.

The chief recounted the conversation he'd had with Joe, involving a conversation Joe had had with Kelly during lunch that day, and then Joe had asked if there was something the chief wasn't telling him.

"I can understand Kelly's train of thought," Melony said. "In fact, I've been thinking about that myself. Not that anyone can do anything—it's just something that's going to make people think something about the story is off."

"Sounds like you need to come up with something else to tell him," Walt suggested. Walt and MacDonald looked at Danielle as if they expected her to say something.

After a few moments of the two staring at her in silence, she frowned at them. "What?"

"Come on, Danielle. You're good at this. When Kelly walked

into your house after seeing things floating in your kitchen, you immediately came up with a story," the chief reminded her.

"Things were not floating in my kitchen. It was one thing. And it was more hovering than floating."

"Come on, Danielle, try," Walt urged. "There must be something the chief can say that will make the story more plausible."

"What could possibly be said? Everyone knows this entire thing was a hunch from the beginning. We didn't even know what the treasure was when we suspected there was something in Adam's house," Danielle argued. "Why would he know where to look?"

They all considered Danielle's words in silence. Finally, Adam stood. "I know."

Everyone looked at Adam, and Melony asked, "What?"

"What about this scenario…" Adam sat back down in his chair, leaned back and crossed his legs casually, folding his hands on his lap. "The police thought the men might have been looking for something specific in my house, that it wasn't a random burglary, but what? I kept going over this in my mind, and then I remembered something I had forgotten. You see, after the men tied me up and Mark's brother announced he was going to kill me, I was in survival mode. But later, much later, I remembered something the brothers were talking about when I was being tied up. They said something about having to rip up the carpet in the bedroom. So when I remembered this, I wondered, is that where something was hidden? Most of the flooring in this house is hardwood, but our bedroom is carpeted. So I impulsively ripped up the carpet. We all know how impulsive I can be."

"Wow, that's good," Danielle said.

"Not bad, Adam," Walt agreed.

"Also, when talking to Joe the next time, tell him when you picked up Eddy and Evan tonight, Adam was here and you asked him if he used any special equipment to find the treasure, and that's when Adam told you what had inspired his hunch to look under the carpet," Danielle told the chief.

MacDonald nodded. "I feel much better about this."

"Are you going over there now?" Melony asked.

MacDonald shook his head. "No. He just drove in from Portland. I imagine he's tired. And frankly, I'm exhausted myself. I'd rather get a good night's sleep before I talk to him. Plus, I was planning to have Colleen call him and arrange for him to come into the office. It's too late in the day to do that now. However, there is no guarantee he'll be able to come in tomorrow."

"But, Dad, tomorrow's Saturday, and you promised we'd get a tree," Evan said.

"Evan, why don't you and Eddy let your dad bring you over here tomorrow morning. Heather, Lily, Connor and I are making graham-cracker gingerbread houses. You boys can join us. And when your dad gets back, maybe you guys can get your tree then," Danielle offered.

"I'm okay with that," Eddy said. Yet they all suspected he didn't want to stay because of the gingerbread houses.

WHEN EVAN and Eddy arrived on Saturday, Danielle greeted them each with their own Christmas apron. Eddy's had a picture of Grinch, while a Christmas elf adorned Evan's. They soon learned the gingerbread-decorating party had expanded beyond the original attendance list Danielle had shared. Chris's brother, Noah, had arrived the night before, and both brothers had stopped by Marlow House that morning to say hello. Not long after they arrived, Danielle invited them to stay for the gingerbread-decorating party.

Instead of staying in the kitchen, they moved everything out to the dining room, added an extra leaf to the table, and covered the table with a vinyl Christmas-themed tablecloth. The twins each sat in their highchairs, munching on pieces of graham crackers. Connor sat at the table between his mother and father, with Ian holding Emily Ann. Marie was there too, ready to help with any of the little ones.

To Eddy's disappointment, Brian had Saturday off and was there when he and Evan arrived. Heather, who had made an extra effort to locate an array of novelty candy to decorate the houses, arranged the candy in bowls along the center of the table.

The houses were made of graham crackers instead of gingerbread, held together with hot glue instead of stiff frosting. After Chris and Noah decided to stay, Walt took them to the kitchen to assemble a few extra houses, using graham crackers and Danielle's hot glue gun.

By noon, they were all sitting around the table—Walt, Danielle, Ian, Emily Ann, Lily, Connor Evan, Eddy, Heather, Brian, Noah, and Chris. Everyone except the three youngest had Christmas aprons Danielle had given them, each one unique. Instead of a Christmas apron, the twins and Emily Ann wore Christmas bibs.

"How come you don't use real gingerbread?" Eddy asked as he used frosting to attach candy to his house.

"In my family, we used to make a lot of different kinds of Christmas cookies each year," Danielle began.

"Like you still do," Lily teased.

Danielle flashed Lily a smile and then continued, "We just didn't want to spend the time making gingerbread that we wouldn't eat."

"Hey, I'd eat a real gingerbread house," Evan said. "But not with hot glue."

"Yeah, you sound like my cousin, Sean." Danielle chuckled. "We made them out of graham crackers instead of gingerbread. It was fast and cheap. Holding them together with hot glue was something that a friend suggested. Made it sturdier. Anyway, it became one of our Christmas traditions, like my Christmas apron and our cookies." Unlike everyone else at the table, Danielle's apron was one she had worn when her parents were still alive.

"I think everyone should share what special Christmas traditions you had as a kid," Heather suggested as she carefully applied miniature marshmallow snow to the roof of her graham-cracker house.

"I'll go first," Noah offered. "We didn't have a lot of money, but every Christmas Mom would make fruitcake from a recipe passed down from her grandmother. Fruitcake gets a lot of shade, but Mom's was good, and I looked forward to it every year. I've never tried making it, but I have her recipe"

Chris glanced at his brother. "I wish I could remember that. You have the recipe? We need to make that again. Keep the family tradition going."

Noah smiled at Chris. "We could do that, but we'll have to wait until next year because it takes a couple of months to make."

"A couple of months? No way!" Eddy said.

"My grandmother used to make homemade eggnog every Christmas," Walt said as he broke a graham-cracker piece in half to hand to the twins.

"Do you have your grandmother's recipe? If not, I could find one," Danielle said. "I could use my sous vide machine to pasteurize the eggs first so I don't kill everyone from salmonella."

"Dani, you crack me up," Lily said with a snort.

"And you don't need to pasteurize the eggs. I imagine Walt's recipe includes brandy, and that stuff will kill all the bacteria," Ian teased.

"I have a question," Evan asked loudly.

"What?" Danielle asked.

"Aren't Christmas trees and hanging stockings Christmas traditions?"

"Certainly," Danielle said.

"Okay, but family Christmas traditions seem different. Something that not everyone does. Like our family never made divinity or eggnog. My aunt Sissy once bought us Christmas sweaters, but this is my first Christmas apron."

"A lot of families share similar Christmas traditions," Danielle explained. "While others are more unique to a particular family."

"I don't think we have any. None that are special to us," Evan said.

"Yeah. We did," Eddy said. "We used to hang Mom's Christmas picture up every year, and then she'd tell stories about the picture. Dad would make popcorn, and she'd make up a new story every Christmas Eve."

"We don't do that now," Evan reminded him.

Danielle set the candy she had been affixing to her mock gingerbread house down on the table and looked at Evan. "Christmas traditions can change over time in each family. When my grandmother was little, their tradition was to put up their tree on Christmas Eve. I like to put up a tree earlier because I want to enjoy the decorations longer. A lot of families put up their decorations right after Thanksgiving. Some traditions we bring from our childhood; others we create when we start our own family."

"Like us, we do a family Christmas diary every year. It's something Ian started. He got the idea from a blog post," Lily said.

Danielle glanced around at all the people at the table and then looked back at Evan. "Nothing in this world stays the same, but traditions link us to our past and spark memories. Chris and Noah lost both parents and were separated when Chris was very young, so Chris doesn't remember those family traditions of his birth family. But he has the opportunity now to embrace the tradition Noah just shared. I lost my childhood family years ago, but in memory of them, I share those traditions with my family now. And together, Walt and I create new traditions that someday, Addison and Jack may carry on."

"And sometimes children choose not to carry on the Christmas traditions of their childhood and substitute them with their own," Lily interjected.

Danielle looked at Lily. "By that smile, you've obviously thought of something specific. What is it?"

"I remember the year one of my cousins got married. She hosted Christmas that year, and when my aunt found out her daughter intended to serve a crown roast instead of turkey for Christmas dinner, she called Mom practically in tears. The family had always had turkey for Christmas dinner. My aunt told Mom she didn't know what her daughter was thinking."

"What did your mom tell her?" Heather asked.

"She told her she was probably thinking, *I just had turkey for Thanksgiving. I don't want it again*," Lily said with a giggle. "And then Mom warned her not to say anything to her daughter."

"Like I said, nothing in this world stays the same," Danielle said with a wistful smile.

THIRTY-SIX

When Colleen from the Frederickport Police Department contacted Jason Aldridge on Saturday morning, she told him there was an open case and he might be an unwitting witness. She asked him to come into the police station for a witness interview. Jason, who was aware of the recent case, remembered how the police had knocked on his door after the escaped prisoner's car had been abandoned in his neighborhood. He never considered the police wanted to ask him questions because he had once owned the house they had broken into, but assumed the interview had something to do with the abandoned car and what he had seen during that time.

Jason arrived at the police station precisely one minute before his appointment with Police Chief MacDonald. Colleen showed him to the chief's office. When they entered the office, MacDonald immediately stood from behind his desk, walked around said desk to greet Jason, thanked him for coming, and motioned to one of the chairs for him to sit. Colleen left the office, closing the door behind her. The chief remained standing, now leaning against the edge of his desk and looking at Jason, who had just sat down.

"I WAS TOLD you wanted to talk to me about an open case. I'm assuming it's about those men who broke into Adam Nichols's house, and the car they abandoned in my neighborhood. But I never saw anything. I was in the house for most of that day, watching television. I'm afraid I don't have anything that might help."

"It is about the break-in, but it doesn't have anything to do with the car that was abandoned." MacDonald stood up straighter, no longer leaning on the desk. He turned around briefly and picked up a large envelope from atop his desk. He turned back around and handed the envelope to Jason. "I'd like you to look at these."

Jason took the envelope and started opening it. MacDonald moved around his desk and sat down behind it. Folding his hands on his desktop, MacDonald watched as Jason slipped an eight-by-ten-inch photograph from the envelope. Jason stared at the picture with a frown, saying nothing, frozen in place. Several moments later he started pulling the rest of the photographs from the envelope, one by one, giving each a quick glance before removing the next one. When all ten photographs were removed from the envelope, he stared at them, shaking his head, and then looked up at the chief.

"Where did you get these?" Jason demanded, his hands trembling as he held onto the stack of photographs.

"Do you recognize the jewelry?"

"Yes. They belong to my wife…my ex-wife, Evangeline. Why do you have these pictures?"

"Adam Nichols found that jewelry under the floorboards in the master bedroom of the house you sold him. We suspect it's what those men were after."

Jason shook his head vehemently and stood. Some of the photographs almost fell onto the floor, but he caught them. He took a step toward the desk and tossed the photographs and envelope onto the desktop, as if he couldn't get rid of them fast enough. "No. That's impossible. Evangeline took them with her twenty years ago when she left."

"No, she didn't. We believe Roman hid them in your house."

Jason froze and stared at the chief. After a moment of silence, he asked in a whisper, "What do you know about Roman?"

The chief nodded at the chair Jason had been sitting in. "Please sit down; let me explain."

Jason took a step backwards, his hands reaching for the arms of the chair he had been sitting in. His eyes still on the chief, Jason almost stumbled when he sat back down on the chair, his hands still gripping its arms.

"Because of what the robbers said to Adam during the break-in, we were fairly certain they were looking for something specific. Something hidden in the house. After one of the men was killed, a man by the name of Shawn Hoffman, we discovered he had been working at an assisted-living facility until about two weeks before the break in. On Shawn's last day on the job, he spent most of it with a dying patient, one who passed away during Shawn's watch. That man was Roman Sellars."

Jason frowned. "Roman is dead?"

The chief nodded. "Adam was in shock after the break-in, and it took him a few days to remember everything that had happened. One of the things he eventually remembered was something one of the men said when he was being tied up. About needing to pull the carpet up in one of the bedrooms. There is only one bedroom in that house with carpet, and last Sunday Adam found the jewelry under the floorboard in that bedroom. The woman who dates one of our officers on the case is friends with your wife's sister-in-law. Allison recently told her about your wife, and she had also mentioned a Roman. Roman is not that common a first name, and one thing led to another, and here we are."

"I don't understand. Where is Evangeline?"

"I have since interviewed Allison. She told me she was there when Roman told you your wife had left and claimed to have seen her take the jewelry. Our theory is that Roman is the one who took your wife's jewelry from the safe and hid it under the floorboards. We believe he gave a deathbed confession to Shawn, telling him about the hidden jewelry."

Jason frowned. "Why did he lie? Where is Evangeline?"

"I'm sorry to tell you this, but we believe she's dead. Allison never heard from Evangeline in all those years, aside from one typed letter. We've contacted Evangeline's other family members—cousins—and none of them have heard from her since her brother's death."

"No…no. She can't be dead."

MacDonald told him about the unidentified body that had washed up at Lincoln Beach. He told him about the pending DNA test, and how Allison had told Heather about Evangeline's discomfort with Roman's attention. MacDonald knew what had really happened that day, only because of what they had learned from Evangeline's ghost, but he couldn't come out and say that. Instead, the chief framed it as a theory, telling Jason they believed it was possible Roman might have used Jason's trip to Portland with Allison as an opportunity to seduce his wife, but she resisted, and something happened—perhaps she slipped and hit her head. Roman panicked, disposed of her body in the ocean, and to make everyone believe she had left of her own volition, he hid her jewelry.

Somewhere in the middle of the emotional conversation, MacDonald moved from behind his desk to sit in the chair next to Jason. When the full reality of all that MacDonald had told him fully registered, Jason broke into sobs, as if he had lost his wife all over again.

MacDonald recognized that pain. The pain of losing the love of your life. He couldn't imagine if Cindy had simply disappeared from his life, with him left to believe she had abandoned him without a word. Only to discover two decades later that she had never left, she had never stopped loving him. He would be forced to grieve all over again, but this time, weighed down by the guilt, the guilt of losing faith in her because of one man's lie.

MACDONALD OFFERED to drive Jason home after he regained his composure. Jason thanked him for the offer but declined.

MacDonald then insisted on walking him out to his car and following him home, to make sure he got there safely. Jason didn't argue.

Jason hadn't seemed in a hurry to take possession of the jewelry, and since it was the weekend and the bank closed early on Saturday, there was nothing they could do this weekend. When Allison had given the chief her husband's phone book, she had also given him the documents she found in his papers, regarding the family jewelry his sister had inherited, along with a copy of his sister's will, which clearly stated the jewelry was to go to Jason. With the documents and what he learned from Evangeline, MacDonald had no doubt Jason was the rightful owner of the jewelry.

By the time MacDonald picked Evan and Eddy up at Marlow House, he was drained emotionally yet prepared to keep his promise to Evan to get the Christmas tree. Upon arriving at Marlow House, he told everyone how the meeting had gone and went on to say he didn't know how he would handle all this if he was in Jason's place, especially because he understood what it was like to lose a wife whom you loved with all your heart.

Marie, who had been in the living room with the others, listening to MacDonald recount the interview with Jason, noticed Edward's eyes fill with tears as he mentioned his own wife, and how he kept the tears at bay while forcing a smile and telling his sons they could buy a Christmas tree today.

"Evan," Marie said gently, only the mediums hearing her words.

Evan looked at Marie just as she placed a finger over her own lips to signify to Evan not to say anything as she spoke. "It's clear your father has had an emotional day. He looks exhausted. Why don't you suggest you all just go home tonight? Order pizza, make some popcorn, watch a movie together, and you can all get a tree in the morning when he is more in the mood. You'll all enjoy it more."

AS MACDONALD DROVE HOME with Evan and Eddy late Saturday afternoon, he was relieved they didn't have to stop at a

Christmas tree lot, grateful for Evan's unexpected suggestion to buy their Christmas tree tomorrow. Eddy didn't have a problem with waiting one day, and he liked the idea of ordering pizza for dinner. Edward also liked that idea because it was one thing they could order and he didn't have to pick it up.

Evan sat in the backseat, his mock gingerbread house sitting on a box lid on his lap as he chatted away about the family Christmas traditions everyone had shared while working on the gingerbread houses. Eddy, who sat in the passenger seat, his mock gingerbread house also on his lap, it too sitting on a box lid, asked his father why they no longer hung up the Christmas picture. MacDonald had no real answer for them.

AFTER THEY RETURNED HOME, Evan and Eddy set their graham-cracker gingerbread houses on a table in the living room, and Eddy said the room needed more decorations like Marlow House. MacDonald had brought down one box of Christmas decorations on Thanksgiving weekend, yet had left the tree decorations in the attic, waiting for a tree. MacDonald glanced around the living room, noting the sparse Christmas decorations despite the fact all the decorations that had been in that lone box had been put out.

The boys headed to the kitchen to get something to drink and argue about what they wanted on the pizza, and MacDonald went to the attic, neither boy noticing his departure.

Once in the attic, MacDonald walked to where he kept the Christmas decorations. In one corner, behind a box of Christmas tree lights, he spied the slim oblong package holding his wife's Christmas picture—the signed Wysocki lithograph he had bought for her those many years ago. She had loved that picture.

He gently lifted the package holding the framed lithograph from behind the box of lights and then slipped the framed picture from the package and looked at it. He smiled at the nostalgic Christmas scene as memories flooded back. Simple memories. Treasured memories. Christmas memories.

EDDY AND EVAN were still in the kitchen, now eating some of the Christmas cookies Danielle had given them after one of their recent visits to Marlow House. A snack before dinner. Eddy was about to dunk his cookie in a glass of milk when he heard pounding in the living room. He quickly dunked his cookie, shoved it in his mouth, got up from the kitchen table, and started to the living room, Evan following behind him.

When the boys got to the living room, they saw their father standing before a framed picture hanging on the wall. It hadn't been there five minutes earlier. Hearing his sons enter the room, Edward turned to his boys and grinned. "What do you think?"

Both boys looked at what their father had just hung up and smiled. Eddy Junior said, "It's Mom's Christmas picture."

Hammer in hand, Edward said, "I thought we needed to put it up again."

"Are we going to hang it every Christmas now?" Evan asked.

Edward glanced briefly at the picture and then looked back at Evan. "We're going to do what your mom wanted. I'm going to leave it up year-round. And be prepared; on Christmas Eve, each of us needs to come up with a story about the picture. Let's see who comes up with the best one."

"Just like Mom used to do," Eddy said.

The chief looked wistfully at the picture. "Your mom's not here to make up the story like she used to do every Christmas Eve. We need to do it for her."

"It's like Danielle said, sometimes Christmas traditions change over time. She said nothing stays the same," Evan said.

MacDonald nodded and with a sigh said, "She's right."

THIRTY-SEVEN

Danielle had called Joanne on Saturday evening to tell her the chief had talked to her friend, and he now knew about what had been found at his old house. "I just thought you would like to know," Danielle had told her.

Joanne resisted the temptation to go over to Jason's and check on him, but she couldn't help worrying about him. Instead, she spent the evening baking his favorite cookies. The next morning, Joanne filled a clean tin with cookies and took them over to Jason's house.

JOANNE STOOD on Jason's front porch, the tin of cookies in her hands, as she anxiously waited for him to answer the door. He didn't answer on the first ring. But he had parked his car in the driveway when he came home from the police station yesterday and had not bothered to move it into his garage, so he couldn't pretend he wasn't home, and it wasn't like Jason had friends who picked him up to go places. She rang the bell a second time. Joanne was about to ring a third time when the door slowly opened. Jason stood in his front doorway, his eyes red-rimmed and expression blank while his right hand held the outer edge of the front door.

"Good morning, Jason," Joanne said tentatively.

Jason said nothing; he gave a nod and just stood there. They stared at each other for what seemed like eternity but was probably only seconds, neither saying anything. Finally, Joanne said, "Can I come in? I brought you some cookies I made last night."

The door opened wider. Jason gave a nod, and then he turned and walked away, leaving the door open for Joanne. She stepped into his house, closing the door behind her. She followed Jason to the living room and set the tin of cookies on the coffee table. Jason sat down on his recliner, and she took a seat on the sofa, directly across from him.

Joanne sat straight, her hands folded primly on her lap as she studied his face. But he wasn't looking at her. "I didn't come over to bring you cookies. They're a ruse. I came over to check on you. I'm worried about you, Jason. Danielle called me last night and told me what happened. She thought I would want to know because we're friends." He already knew both Danielle and Adam were Joanne's friends, so it wasn't a surprise to discover she was aware of what he had learned yesterday. Jason's head turned slightly, and he looked at Joanne. He said nothing; he just looked at her.

"I can't imagine what you're going through. What you're thinking…feeling. But I want you to know I'm your friend. I'm here for you. And if you need anything, tell me. Anything. Even if it's just to tell me to leave you alone and go home."

Jason stared at her for a moment longer, then said, "I don't have her picture."

"Excuse me?"

"The month after Evangeline left, I burned everything of hers, including all the photographs I had of her. But she didn't leave me. She never left me. I haven't seen her face since the morning she said goodbye. I want to see her face again." His tears began to fall, and moments later Joanne was by his side, comforting him as she knelt by his chair, wrapping her arms around his shoulders as sobs racked his body and he buried his face in her shoulder.

DANIELLE AND WALT sat on one side of a booth at Pier Café, while Heather sat across from them. Addison and Jack each sat in highchairs at the end of the booth. Heather had just opened a packet of crackers and was now handing each of the twins one. "You know, my Christmas gift to watch Addison and Jack was so you two could go out and have adult time—I sorta figured I would stay at Marlow House and watch them for you there." Earlier that day, Heather had arrived at Marlow House to watch the twins so Walt and Danielle could go out for lunch, but they had talked her into joining them and bringing the twins along.

"I understand. But it's such a beautiful day today. No rain. Sunshine. Not a typical December in Frederickport. We wanted to get the twins out, and you, too." Danielle flashed Heather a grin.

"Well, I appreciate the invite. And Addison and Jack always seem to put a smile on Carla's face." Carla had already taken their order and brought their drinks, but when first showing up at the booth, she had gushed over the twins for five minutes before taking out her order pad.

The discussion moved from Carla to Chief MacDonald's meeting with Jason Aldridge when an older couple and an elderly woman took the booth next to them. Heather and Danielle continued to talk, paying no attention to the people at the next booth while Walt stared at the younger of the two women. She looked familiar. Carla walked up to the table, carrying a water pitcher and a coffeepot. She asked if they wanted coffee and then moved her hand and the coffeepot through the older woman— through her body—before filling a cup with coffee. As Carla walked away a few minutes later, Walt remembered.

"Melissa?" Walt called out.

Melissa, the woman he had met at the care home, smiled at Walt. "I thought that was you. I was about to say hello, but I didn't want to intrude. These must be the twins you told me about; they're adorable."

Walt smiled. "Melissa, I would like you to meet my wife,

Danielle, and our good friend Heather Donovan. I met Melissa in Oregon City, at the care home I visited with Edward. I believe I mentioned her, Danielle."

"And I'd like you to meet my husband, Dave. Dave, I met Walt at the care home when I was visiting Mom."

Brief greetings were exchanged, and when no one introduced the elderly woman, Heather started to say something, but Walt cut her off and asked Melissa, "How is your mother?"

Melissa smiled sadly. "Mom passed away two nights ago. Last night, after dealing with everything at home, we decided to come here for Christmas."

"You can see me, can't you?" the elderly woman asked. Who she was asking, it wasn't clear.

"Just the two of you?" Walt asked.

Melissa nodded. "Yes. But that's okay."

"No, it's not," the older woman said. "Melissa and Dave should not be alone this Christmas; it isn't right. They need people around them. Melissa has always been an amazing daughter…an amazing mother. I understand why my grandchildren can't come this year; it's not their fault. But Melissa and Dave shouldn't be alone. The house here isn't even decorated for Christmas. No Christmas tree, and they're talking about having turkey sandwiches for Christmas. That's no way to celebrate Christmas."

"Melissa, we'd love for you and your husband to join us for Christmas," Danielle blurted. Melissa looked startled and a little embarrassed by the offer and started to graciously decline, but Danielle cut her off. "I don't know if Walt mentioned, but we have a bed-and-breakfast called Marlow House. Currently, it's closed—because of the twins. But I love to entertain, and we always have a large group at Christmas—family and friends—and there is always room at the table for new friends. We'd love to have you."

Melissa's eyes widened as she looked from Danielle to Walt, back to Danielle. "Oh, my gawd, Marlow House?" She looked at Walt and shook her head. "I feel like such an idiot. You are Walt Marlow, that Walt Marlow. I am a huge fan."

Walt grinned. "I don't think I mentioned my last name when we met."

Melissa looked at Danielle with a bright expression. "I am very familiar with Marlow House—not that I've ever been inside. Mom and Dad used to live in Frederickport. In fact, we're staying in their old house. It's become a vacation home for our family. I remember when my parents lived here, Marlow House was the most famous house in town—and a little mysterious. When I heard it wasn't open as a BnB anymore, I was disappointed. I always wanted to come and stay some weekend but never got the chance."

"She never got the chance because she was always taking care of me," said the elderly woman—who Walt, Danielle, and Heather now realized was a ghost.

"What was your mother's name?" Heather asked.

"Margaret," Melissa said.

"I'm sorry about your mom," Heather said, looking at Margaret. "But you should accept Danielle's offer. I'll be there. Amazing food and good company. Well, maybe my company is not the best, but everyone else coming is very cool." Heather grinned mischievously.

Margaret looked at Heather and smiled. "Thank you."

Heather gave Margaret a nod, and if Melissa wondered why it looked as if Heather had nodded at the empty seat next to her, she said nothing.

Melissa leaned over, whispered something to her husband; he nodded, and then she looked back to Danielle. "You know what? I would love to accept your offer," Melissa said, her smile beaming.

THE FOOD at Melissa's table arrived not long after Carla brought the food to Danielle's table. After Danielle's table finished eating, they ordered dessert. Melissa and Dave, who weren't ordering dessert, finished their lunch and stood up. Melissa thanked Danielle again for the dinner invitation and asked if she could bring anything.

After Melissa and Dave said their goodbyes, and as Danielle's table waited for dessert, the twins started getting restless. Before the dessert arrived, they removed the twins from the highchairs, moving Jack to stand on the bench seat between Walt and Danielle, while Addison sat on Heather's lap.

Carla had just dropped off three plates of apple pie a la mode and left their table when Joanne walked into the diner. She spied Danielle's table and stopped to say hi, but ended up staying and sitting next to Heather and Addison.

Addison moved from Heather to Joanne's lap as Heather ate her dessert. Carla returned to the table and took Joanne's order. After Carla left the table, Joanne told them about her visit with Jason that morning.

"I feel so sorry for him," Heather said.

Joanne let out a weary sigh. "I just wish I could help him."

"It might help if he had a picture of me," a woman's voice said. Everyone but Joanne looked up to see a beautiful woman standing by the booth. She wore a red floor-length dress trimmed in white fur.

"Evangeline?" Heather asked the woman.

Joanne, who could neither see nor hear the woman standing next to her, looked at Heather and said, "Yes, her name was Evangeline."

"Jason needs closure. A picture of me might help him say goodbye. And he needs to mend fences. Allison could help. They need each other. They are family."

"You mentioned he was distraught because there were no pictures of his wife?" Danielle asked Joanne.

Joanne shifted Addison on her lap, ignoring the fact the small child was reaching toward the aisle—and the pretty woman Joanne couldn't see.

"Yes. He kept saying he hadn't seen her face in twenty years; he just wanted to see it again, one more time." Joanne shook her head sadly. "And he mentioned how horrible he felt that he'd pushed Allison away all those years, blamed her for everything when she'd lost not just her sister-in-law, but her best friend."

"Joanne, I have an idea, something that might help," Heather said.

Joanne looked at Heather. "What?"

"I'm friends with Allison. Let me call her, and then I'll take you over there. I'm sure she has some photographs of Evangeline."

THIRTY-EIGHT

After leaving Pier Café on Sunday, Heather called Allison and discovered she was out of town for a few days but would be back on Tuesday and would be available then. While Heather and Joanne met with Allison late Tuesday afternoon, Walt and Danielle did a final grocery run for Christmas dinner, taking the twins with them and using two grocery carts.

As everyone prepared for Christmas, buying last-minute gifts, wrapping packages, preparing for holiday gatherings, the Frederickport Police Department waited for the DNA results. They arrived early on December 24, and while the chief had Christmas Eve and Christmas Day off, he went down to the station to pick up the results and then stopped by Jason Aldridge's house.

When leaving the police station for Jason's house, MacDonald had his office call Jason and inform him he would stop by in a few minutes with the DNA results.

The front door opened as the chief walked up Jason's front walkway, an envelope in his hand. Jason gave a nod of greeting and opened the door wider. A moment later, the two men stood just inside Jason's house, the door still open.

"What does it say? Was it her?"

MacDonald handed Jason the envelope he held. It contained the DNA results. "Yes, we're confident it's her. The woman found on Lincoln Beach was a first cousin to the DNA sample Evangeline's cousin gave us." No one was really surprised, considering the first time MacDonald met with Jason, he had asked identifying questions and learned Evangeline had been the same height as the body they had found, plus she had the same hair color, eye color, and according to Jason, the hair length matched. As for the pictures of the woman's clothing, Jason had said they might have been his wife's, but he wasn't sure.

"I'm so sorry," MacDonald whispered.

"Hello?" a voice called out. Both men looked toward the open doorway and found Joanne standing on the front porch, a small package in her hand.

"It was her, Joanne," Jason called out. He looked back to the envelope, a blank expression on his face, looking like a man who no longer understood his world.

Joanne walked into the house. The three exchanged a few words, and minutes later the chief said his goodbyes, leaving Jason alone with Joanne. She led him into the living room.

Once in the living room, Jason tossed the unopened envelope onto the coffee table and sat down in his recliner.

"I brought you a present," Joanne said. She handed him not a package wrapped in holiday paper, but a medium-sized paper bag with something inside.

Jason shook his head and tried to push it away, silently saying the last thing he cared about was a Christmas gift. But Joanne gently pressed the package back into his hands and said, "Please, just open it."

Reluctantly, Jason opened the sack and pulled out an eight-by-ten framed photograph. Confused at first, he took a closer look and then froze. It was of his late wife. She wore the red Christmas dress he had always loved on her, her beautiful face smiling for the camera. He stared at it for a moment and then stammered, "I don't understand…how did you…where did it—"

"Allison gave it to me," Joanne answered before he had time to finish his question. "I saw her yesterday. She wanted you to have this."

LILY AND IAN scheduled their Christmas Eve celebration from 4 p.m. until 9 p.m. They invited guests to stop by anytime during those hours. They could stay for just a few minutes or the entire time. Slow cookers were set up on the kitchen counter, keeping warm shredded meats, beans, rice, and dip. Flour and corn tortillas, chips, salsa, guacamole, queso, sour cream, shredded cheese, enchiladas, tamales, chili relleno casserole, diced vegetables, paper plates and napkins were arranged on the breakfast bar and kitchen table, which Ian periodically rotated, making sure nothing that needed refrigeration was out too long. A small bar was set up at the end of the counter with plastic cups.

Throughout the house were plates of homemade cookies and bowls of Christmas candy. During the evening, a few guests—those not familiar with Sadie—expressed concern that the dog might snag some of the chocolate cookies when no one was looking. But Ian and Lily didn't worry. Walt had long ago explained to Sadie why she couldn't have any of those foods.

Instead of bringing Hunny with him, Chris left the pit bull at Marlow House with Max. Not that Hunny wouldn't behave, but Chris understood she sometimes made strangers nervous, plus Max enjoyed the dog's company.

HEATHER HAD ARRIVED with a tin of divinity. As she and Brian walked into the living room, she set the open tin on one of the end tables and then followed Brian over to say hello to Joe. She stood with the two men for a minute, absently glancing around the room to see who else had arrived, not paying attention to the conversation between the two men, when Marie suddenly appeared.

"Heather, you look quite festive!" Marie exclaimed. "You look like an adorable elf." Some women might have been insulted at that observation, but that was actually the look Heather had been going for. She wore a calf-length formfitting dress made from an evergreen velour, with red boots, and her long black hair was pulled back and adorned with holly.

Heather flashed Marie a smile, and then the two looked across the room and noticed Kelly had just stopped by the table with the divinity and seemed to look at it, a frown on her face.

"I wouldn't put it past that girl to dump my divinity in the trash," Marie snapped, "but if she does, she'll be sorry."

They watched as Kelly eyed the candy and then hesitantly reached down and picked up a piece. She brought it to her nose, gave it a sniff, and then took a bite. Her eyes widened, clearly surprised by its taste, and then she popped the entire piece in her mouth. Kelly grabbed a second piece and then walked toward her husband.

"Have you guys tried this?" Kelly asked as she showed Joe, Brian, and Heather the piece of candy. "I don't know who made it, but this is delicious." Kelly quickly devoured the second piece without offering any to Joe.

"Imagine that," Marie murmured. Heather giggled.

Kelly frowned at Heather. "What's funny?"

"It's the divinity. You know, made from deadly corn syrup." For a brief moment, Kelly looked horrified as she looked back at her fingers, still sticky from the candy she had been holding.

Heather patted Kelly's shoulder and said, "Don't worry. I doubt that has enough corn syrup to kill you."

OTHER GUESTS STARTED ARRIVING SPORADICALLY, yet those, like Carla and her date, only stayed for about twenty minutes before leaving to go to another Christmas gathering. The chief arrived with his sons not long after Melony and Adam.

"Is it true you won't be joining us for dinner tomorrow?"

Melony asked MacDonald as the two stood at the kitchen counter, each filling a paper plate with food.

"We're spending it with Sissy." Melony understood that was Edward's sister. "Lily invited her and Bruce tonight. They might stop by later to say hi, but I'm not sure. I know they're going to a Christmas party at their friend's house."

LILY SAT ON THE SOFA, nursing Emily Ann, a receiving blanket draped lightly over the baby's head, concealing Lily's breast. Danielle walked into the living room, Addison in her arms, and sat next to Lily. Addison reached out to touch Emily Ann, but Danielle gently pushed her hand away. "Everything looks delicious, Lily. Where did you get the tamales? Beach Taco?"

"No, I bought them from Rosa Garcia."

Danielle nodded in recognition. That was the woman who sold homemade tamales to locals. "I wondered if that's where you got them. I just split one with Walt, and it was probably the best tamale I've ever had."

"Yeah, Ian likes the ones she makes. Kelly offered to order some from Beach Taco, but I told her we'd already taken care of it."

"Oh, I need to tell you Joanne probably isn't making it tonight. She wanted me to let you know and tell you she'd see you tomorrow night."

"Why isn't she coming?"

"Sounds like she's spending Christmas Eve with Jason Aldridge."

EVAN SAT in Connor's bedroom, talking with Walt, while Connor sat nearby on the floor with Jack, both playing with a new toy Connor's grandmother had brought him. The chief walked into the room holding a beer and looked at Evan. "So this is where you are." He glanced down to Connor, who was just handing Jack a toy, which Jack immediately shoved in his mouth. "Helping with the little ones?"

"Walt's helping me with my story," Evan announced.

MacDonald arched his brow. "Isn't that cheating? Going to a professional author to help write your story."

Evan grinned. He didn't look a bit guilty.

"Evan was telling me about your new family tradition," Walt said. "Was that the picture you told me about at Mark's house?"

MacDonald walked further into the room and sat down on the floor next to Walt's chair. He took a sip of beer and then said, "Yes. Every Christmas Eve, Cindy would make up a new story about the picture. One year she said all the people in the picture were gathering to have a Christmas party in the church. Another year, they were all gathering to take a trip to the North Pole to see Santa. But after she died…well…I left it in the attic." MacDonald took another drink of beer.

"Because she wasn't there to tell her story on Christmas Eve?" Walt asked gently.

MacDonald nodded. "But this year, I decided to hang it up again. And I won't be taking it down. I like the picture; it makes me feel happy. Reminds me of Cindy and the Christmases we shared— especially the most recent." Walt understood MacDonald was talking about the dream hop he and his boys had had two Christmases prior, when Cindy's spirit had visited her family. "And when we go home tonight, after leaving here, I'm making popcorn, and we're going to see which one of us can come up with the best story." He looked at his son and added with mock seriousness, "And you have to make up the story yourself. No fair cheating!"

CHRISTMAS EVE WAS ABOUT to fade into memory. Most of the guests had gone home already. Kelly and June helped Ian put away the food in the kitchen while Lily got Connor and the baby to bed, Joe took out the trash, and Ian's father, John, gathered any stray glasses or dishes left out by guests.

"I'm going to miss you tomorrow," June told Kelly.

"Mom, we'll see you in the morning," Kelly promised. They planned to open gifts at Ian and Lily's before going to Joe's parents' house on Christmas Day.

After she finished in the kitchen, Kelly walked through the living room and stopped by the table with the divinity. Looking down at the tin, she saw there were two pieces left.

Joe walked into the room. "Any more trash in here?"

"I don't think so." Kelly remained standing by the table. Joe glanced around the room and then turned and headed back to the dining room. Once he was gone, Kelly snatched a piece of the candy and took a bite. She smiled, savoring the taste, and then finished the piece and looked back to the doorway. She was still alone—or so she assumed. Kelly grabbed the last piece of divinity and ate it.

But she wasn't alone. Marie had been standing next to her the entire time, watching. Kelly picked up the now empty tin and looked at it with longing. "Why do things that are bad for you taste so darn good?"

THIRTY-NINE

When Walt and Danielle brought Addison and Jack downstairs on Christmas morning, each baby still wearing their comfy footed Christmas pajamas, they found a cozy fire flickering in the living room hearth. They could smell the scent of freshly brewed coffee from the kitchen, and the two highchairs had been moved into the living room near the sofa, ready for Addison and Jack to have breakfast. It was all Marie's Christmas gift to the family.

Max greeted them first; he sat on the back of the sofa, his black tail twitching as he let out several loud meows. Before the twins' arrival, Max had typically greeted Danielle by weaving in and out between her feet while purring, yet Walt had explained to Max, he could no longer do that with Danielle when she carried one of the babies; she might trip.

Danielle was just saying hello to Max when Marie called out, "Merry Christmas! I'm going to bring you coffee and each a slice of that quiche Danielle made yesterday, then feed the twins while you two enjoy your coffee and quiche."

"Marie, that's sweet, but I figured you'd be at Adam and

Melony's this morning." Danielle handed Addison to Marie after the baby reached out to the grandmotherly ghost.

"Oh, pshaw, those two have long since grown past the age when they get up early on Christmas morning. I'll go over there after they wake up."

THEY HAD FINISHED THEIR BREAKFAST, Marie had returned the highchairs to the kitchen, and Walt and Danielle sat on the floor by the Christmas tree, each with a baby sitting between their legs and a Christmas stocking.

"You actually wrapped each one of their stocking gifts?" Marie asked as she watched Jack pull another wrapped gift from his stocking before tearing off the wrapping paper and throwing the torn pieces of the paper, along with the gift, on the floor before removing another package from the stocking.

Danielle smiled. "Walt asked me the same thing. But growing up, Mom always wrapped every single one of my stocking gifts. Opening my stocking was probably my favorite thing on Christmas morning."

"I got an orange and some walnuts in mine," Walt snarked.

Marie, who had been holding Danielle's iPhone and taking pictures of the twins opening their stockings, paused when the phone rang. She looked at the cellphone. "Oh my, I might be able to use the camera, but I doubt I can answer this thing." The next moment the cellphone floated from Marie to Danielle.

After Danielle grabbed the cellphone in midair, she answered it and then said, "Okay, I'll tell her. See you this afternoon." Danielle set the phone on the floor next to her and looked at Marie. "That was Adam. He wants me to tell you he and Melony are up now."

"That means it's time for me to go. I enjoyed spending the morning with you. I'll see you later. Merry Christmas." The next moment, Marie vanished. Addison immediately put out her hand, as if to call Marie back, but was then distracted when her father reached over and pulled a gift from her stocking and handed it to her.

Danielle stared at where Marie had been a moment earlier while Walt said, "That's sweet; she's spending Christmas morning with Adam and Mel."

"Yeah," Danielle said, her tone flat, her expression blank as she continued to stare where Marie had been.

Walt frowned at Danielle. "Does that upset you? She still sees you as family."

Danielle shook her head briefly as if waking up from a thought and flashed a grin at Walt. "No, I wasn't thinking about that."

"What were you thinking about?"

"Oh, just about how Addison and Jack are growing up in a world where people just disappear. Not to mention things floating across the room."

"Aside from the things floating across the room, we've already determined most children can see ghosts—at least when they're young. So it's conceivable that at this very minute there are other families in Frederickport who are at this very moment opening their Christmas presents and have no idea that some grandparent or other family member who has passed is watching—joining them for Christmas."

"Yet the little ones can see them come and go." Danielle chuckled. "So in that respect, I guess Addison and Jack's experience is not that unique. It's just the other parents are unaware of what their children are seeing."

JOANNE WAS the first to arrive at Marlow House that afternoon. The extra table had already been put in the dining room, and both tables were set, ready for Christmas dinner. Walt and Danielle had done it while the twins took a morning nap, and Walt had used his telekinetic gift to streamline the task.

Danielle was in the kitchen with Joanne, going through her dinner to-do list, making sure they were on track. She sat in the kitchen, drinking a cup of eggnog while checking items off the list. It wasn't homemade eggnog like Walt's grandmother had made, but from a carton she'd picked up at the grocery store on Tuesday.

Joanne sat at the table across from her, peeling potatoes. She looked up at Danielle. "I'd really like to thank you again for letting me invite Jason."

"We're happy to have him. How is he doing? What did he say about the picture?"

Joanne shrugged as she continued to peel potatoes. "Honestly, he didn't say much. He just kept looking at it, like seeing an old friend he hadn't seen in years. But in his case, the love of his life."

"That poor guy."

"But I think it helped him. We sat there for a while, him not saying anything, and then he just started talking. We talked for hours. I couldn't leave him and go to Lily's. He needed someone there to listen."

"Lily understood. So when is he going to be here?"

"I told him when we were eating and suggested he might want to get here about an hour before that."

WITHIN A COUPLE of hours of Christmas dinner, guests started arriving at Marlow House. They found the doors to the parlor, living room, library, and dining room open and inviting, with a cozy fire flickering in each of the fireplaces on the first floor. The scent of pine drifted throughout the house from the candles arranged on the fireplace mantels. The rooms—along with the enormous entry hall —had been decorated for the season, which included antique ornaments, snow globes, garland, potted poinsettia plants, candles, and a nativity scene set up in the library. Each room had a bowl of Christmas candies and treats, with appetizers arranged on a table in the living room, next to the home bar.

When Melissa and Dave arrived, Walt, with Eva by his side, answered the door. The ghost of Melissa's mother stood next to Melissa and Dave. Walt greeted the couple while Eva greeted Melissa's mother, Margaret, who seemed quite excited to meet another spirit, especially one so famous.

Walt gave them a tour of the first floor, the last room being the library, where they found Ian's mother, June, sitting alone, studying the nativity scene. After introductions, Melissa, who was about June's age, stayed in the library and talked to June while Dave went with Walt to the living room to get a cocktail.

"I'm so sorry to hear about your mother," June told Melissa after Melissa explained how she met Walt, and how he had invited her for Christmas dinner. "Walt and Danielle are very gracious hosts," June told her. "And Danielle is a wonderful cook. My son and daughter-in-law live across the street and are very close friends of the Marlows. I just wish my daughter could be here tonight."

"Your daughter?" Melissa asked.

June went on to tell her all about Kelly and Joe and why they weren't coming tonight. When she finished, Melissa smiled compassionately and said, "I understand how you feel." She then told her about her own two children and grandchildren and why she wasn't spending Christmas with them this year.

When Melissa finished, she noticed June seemed to tear up. Momentarily placing her hand on June's, Melissa asked, "Are you okay?"

June blinked away the tears and smiled sheepishly. "I feel…a little ashamed of myself. You just lost your mother and can't spend Christmas with your children and grandchildren, and here I am whining about not spending the entire day with my daughter, when I have been surrounded by my family all week."

"It doesn't mean your feelings aren't valid," Melissa said.

"Perhaps, but I'm suddenly reminded of what my grandmother used to tell me—count your blessings. I need to remember that more often."

Melissa smiled. "I'll admit, I've been having something of a pity party for myself lately."

"You just lost your mother; it's understandable."

Melissa shrugged. "I know. But I think I need to come to terms with the reality of life."

"How so?"

"Nothing stays the same. This morning as Dave and I sat in my parents' old house, drinking our coffee alone on Christmas morning, no Christmas decorations around—we didn't even put up a Christmas tree at our house this year—I thought back to all my Christmases of my youth, of my children's youth. All those precious memories. As we get older, we need to accept the fact that the Christmases we experienced in our youth are over. We need to adapt."

June frowned. "Adapt how?"

"When my children were young, we always spent Christmas with my sister's family, my parents, my in-laws, my sister's in-laws, and my aunt and uncle. Not long after I married, my aunt and uncle had a falling-out with their only son. They had been close when he was little, but basically, they didn't care for their daughter-in-law. After I got married, they started spending Christmas with us. I doubt they ever fully enjoyed those Christmases, because they spent so much time bemoaning the state of the relationship they had with their son—which, to be honest, was in good part their own fault. But my point being, while I can't be with my children or grandchildren this year, I'm spending it with the husband I love, I'm in this beautiful house, meeting new friends, and by the wonderful smells coming from the kitchen, I suspect I am going to have a delicious dinner. So I suppose I need to embrace a different type of Christmas that might not include my children."

WHEN BRIAN AND HEATHER ARRIVED, they brought a guest, Heather's friend Allison. Heather had already asked Danielle if she could bring her, so Danielle wasn't surprised. Allison thanked Danielle for the invitation, and Heather went on to introduce Allison to those she didn't know, leaving Brian in the living room, talking to John and Dave.

Chris, Noah, Melony and Adam mingled in the entry hall, each drinking a cocktail and standing next to the center hall table where

Danielle had placed an assortment of sweets and nuts, when Heather walked up with Allison and introduced her to Noah, the only person in the small group she didn't know.

Unbeknownst to the non-mediums, Marie, Eva, and Margaret stood by the door to the parlor, chatting, discussing whatever it was ghosts talked about at Christmastime. Walt stepped out of the hall bathroom just as the doorbell rang. He went to answer it, giving the three spirits a nod as he passed.

After opening the door, he found Jason standing on the front porch, a wine bottle in hand and his wife's ghost by his side. "Welcome to our home. I'm Walt Marlow. I assume you're Joanne's friend Jason."

"Yes, and thank you for inviting me, Mr. Marlow."

"Please call me Walt." Walt and Jason shook hands, and Jason handed Walt the bottle of wine as he stepped into the house, Evangeline by his side.

Allison, who was still visiting with Heather and the others in the entry hall, stopped talking when she saw who had just entered the house. What she didn't see was her sister-in-law's ghost, or how Evangeline joined Eva and Marie, who then introduced Evangeline to Margaret.

Without thought, Allison stepped away from the others and walked slowly toward Jason.

FORTY

Jason didn't notice Allison at first. He was busy chatting with Walt as they walked in her direction, but he stopped abruptly when he spied her, his eyes wide. Walt stopped too, as did Allison. Allison's and Jason's gazes locked. They stood about ten feet from each other. After a moment, Allison took a step towards Jason and Walt, and then another and another until she was about five feet from them.

"Allison." Jason's voice was barely a whisper.

Walt said something to Jason the others couldn't hear before stepping away from the pair and walking toward Heather and those gathered around the center hall table.

Allison smiled at her brother-in-law. "Hello, Jason."

"Allison...I...I have to apologize."

Allison shook her head. "No, no, you don't, Jason. I understand why you thought what you did. You didn't know. None of us did. And I am so sorry about Evangeline. I've missed her too." Without another word, the two old friends embraced.

Across the entry hall, those standing by the center hall table silently watched. After a moment, the embrace ended. Allison said something they couldn't hear as she motioned to the parlor.

"This has been one crazy Christmas," Adam said after Jason and Allison stepped into the parlor and out of their sight.

"It's never boring at Marlow House," Noah said before taking a sip of his drink.

Adam glanced around the entry hall. "Have you guys seen my grandma?"

Heather pointed toward the doorway leading to the parlor. "Marie is standing over there with Eva, Margaret, and Evangeline."

"Evangeline, as in the ghost of Jason's wife?" Melony asked.

Heather nodded.

"Who's Margaret?" Adam asked.

"Melissa's mom," Heather explained.

"Who is Melissa?" Adam asked.

"I don't think you've met her yet. The last time I saw her, she was visiting with June in the library. You might have met her husband, Dave. He's in the living room, talking to John and Brian. I met her at the care home Shawn Hoffman worked at when I went there with Edward. She and her husband have a house here, and when I found out they were spending Christmas alone, Danielle and I invited them to join us," Walt explained.

"Oh, so she brought her mother's ghost with her?" Adam snickered. "This is crazy."

"I doubt she brought her, exactly. Spirits sort of go where they want, and I don't think Melissa is a medium," Heather said.

"So there are four spirits here right now?" Melony asked. "Not just Eva and Marie."

Heather shrugged. "Four ghosts; I have no idea how many spirits there may be, since it's Christmas."

"What do you mean?" Adam asked.

Chris looked at Adam and smiled. "Remember what we told you; spirits who choose not to move on are what we call ghosts or spirits. But spirits who move on, we just call them spirits, not ghosts. And while they have moved on, it doesn't mean they can't still be around us. It just means we can't see them. At least, not unless you're a medium like Fin Walsh. And while he can see and communicate with them, he can't do it in the same way we can with ghosts."

"It's entirely possible all of our parents are with us right now," Heather said. "Well, not Adam's parents; he's the only one whose parents are still alive."

Adam let out a snort. "Says a lot about the relationship I have with my parents. Everyone else here has probably spent more recent Christmases with their parents than I have, and your parents are all dead."

CHRISTMAS DINNER at Marlow House proved festive, chaotic, and full of joy. Emily Ann had fallen asleep ten minutes before Joanne and Danielle called everyone into the dining room. They put the baby down to sleep in one of the portable cribs that had been moved from the living room to the downstairs bedroom before the guests had arrived that afternoon. Sadie slept in the doorway of the bedroom, prepared to get Lily or Ian if the baby woke up.

At the dinner table, Addison and Jack didn't stay in their highchairs after finishing their Christmas dinner, but found themselves passed around the dining room table, happily receiving snuggles, and lingering on some laps longer than others. They would have removed Connor from his highchair, but after he finished his dinner and his father took away his almost empty plate, the toddler folded his arms, rested them on his highchair tray, laid his head down, and promptly fell asleep while waiting for Ian to bring him dessert. Connor had had a full day and was now simply over it.

LILY AND IAN left first with Sadie and their children; they needed to get Connor to bed. June and John left next, but not before June and Melissa exchanged phone numbers. Within thirty minutes, all who remained at Marlow House with Walt and Danielle and the twins were Chris, Noah, Heather, Brian, Melony and Adam.

Walt and Danielle headed upstairs to put the twins down for the night. Like Connor, they were more than ready for sleep. Downstairs, their friends finished tidying up the house. They collected the stray glasses and plates throughout the house; Heather put any uneaten cookies and treats from those plates into a storage food container, and Chris and Noah took out the trash.

When Walt and Danielle returned downstairs, they peeked in the kitchen and dining room before going to the living room and saw the rooms were all tidy and everything put away. They found their friends lounging in the living room and talking.

Danielle looked around the room and noticed there were no empty glasses or dishes sitting around. "Wow, thanks, guys."

"Considering that delicious dinner, it was the least we could do," Brian said.

"Joanne had already put most of the leftovers away and loaded the dishwasher," Melony said.

"Is Grandma upstairs with the babies?" Adam asked.

Danielle sat down in the rocking chair next to the Christmas tree. "No. I haven't seen her since dinner."

"I haven't seen any of them," Heather noted.

Walt sat down on the floor next to Danielle.

"I have to say, this was a better Christmas than the first one I had at Marlow House," Noah said with a chuckle.

"No kidding. Nice not to have the guests plotting to kill me," Danielle snarked.

"Or trying to frame me for murder." Heather looked at Melony and Adam. "Remind me to tell you about that Christmas."

"I know about that Christmas," Adam said.

The mediums all laughed, and Chris looked at Adam. "Actually, Adam, there is a lot that happened, let's say behind the scenes, you didn't know. But we can tell you and Mel all about that later."

"I wonder if Eva, Marie and their new friends took off to some Christmas party at the cemetery," Heather asked.

Melony's eyes widened. "Ghosts have Christmas parties at the cemetery?"

Heather shrugged. "I suppose it's possible."

"I'm glad you invited Allison," Danielle told Heather. "It was nice seeing Allison and Jason together tonight. Maybe they haven't talked in twenty years, but they sure seemed like old friends, taking up where they left off."

"I have a prediction," Adam said.

"What's that?" Melony asked.

"Jason and Allison are going to hook up."

"And you would be wrong," Evangeline said as she and the other three ghosts appeared in the room.

Melony, who like Adam and Brian, had not heard Evangeline's words, started to say something about Adam's prediction when Danielle cut her off by saying, "You're back. Where have you been?"

"Is Grandma here?" Adam asked. The next moment, after feeling a gentle tug on his right earlobe, Adam smiled.

"I suppose you could say Evangeline and Margaret wanted to see their loved ones one more time," Eva said, answering Danielle's question.

"What do you mean?" Danielle asked as the non-mediums stayed quiet, aware Danielle was speaking to one of the ghosts.

"I no longer have a reason to stay. It's time for me to move on," Evangeline explained. "Jason knows I didn't leave him."

"Evangeline and I have decided to move on together," Margaret announced. "I feel comfortable leaving Melissa. She's proven resilient, and seeing her tonight, her and Dave meeting new friends, getting out, I'm confident she'll be fine."

"You're both leaving." Danielle murmured.

"Who's leaving?" Melony asked.

"Evangeline and Margaret," Heather said. "They're moving on."

"Thank you for everything," Evangeline told the mediums and then looked at Eva and Marie. "And thank you."

Margaret looked at Walt and Danielle. "Thank you for inviting Melissa and Dave for Christmas. It meant a lot to them, and to me."

Melissa and Evangeline turned to Marie and Eva. "When are you coming?" Evangeline asked.

"It's not my time yet," Eva said in a quiet voice.

"And I'm just too busy to go right now. I have things to do," Marie said with a grin.

Evangeline and Margaret smiled at their two fellow ghosts, gave a final nod, and then slowly faded away until they were no longer there.

"Wow, they're gone," Heather said.

"Who's gone?" Melony asked.

"Margaret and Evangeline. They've moved on to the other side," Chris explained.

Heather turned to Adam. "Oh, you couldn't hear it, but right after you gave your prediction for Allison and Jason getting together, Evangeline said you were wrong."

"Just because she's dead doesn't mean she wants her husband to hook up with her sister-in-law," Adam said.

Eva laughed and said, "You'll have to tell Adam he's wrong again."

"What do you mean?" Heather asked.

"According to what Evangeline told us, Jason is already in love with someone, but he's been unable to give her his heart because if Evangeline could betray him so, how could he trust his heart to another woman?"

"And it seems the woman he has already fallen for has been in love with him for a very long time," Marie added.

"Do we know her?" Chris asked.

Marie looked at Danielle. "Dear, if this all works out like I suspect it might, you may want to start looking for a new house-keeper in the near future, because it looks like your current one may be swept away by the man she has been in love with for years, who, it seems, has come into a considerable fortune."

THE GHOST AND FAMILY SECRETS

RETURN TO MARLOW HOUSE IN

The Ghost and Family Secrets

HAUNTING DANIELLE, BOOK 38

Hiring a new housekeeper for a notorious haunted house can come with unexpected challenges, especially when family secrets are at risk. But it's not just the Marlow family secrets the mediums of Beach Drive need to be worried about.

It seems everyone has a family secret, as Danielle and her friends are about to discover.

BOOKS BY ANNA J. MCINTYRE

COULSON FAMILY SAGA

Coulson's Wife

Coulson's Crucible

Coulson's Lessons

Coulson's Secret

Coulson's Reckoning

Now available in Audiobook Format

UNLOCKED HEARTS

Sundered Hearts

After Sundown

While Snowbound

Sugar Rush

NON-FICTION BY

BOBBI ANN JOHNSON HOLMES

Havasu Palms, A Hostile Takeover

Where the Road Ends, Recipes & Remembrances

Motherhood, a book of poetry

The Story of the Christmas Village